HIDDEN WORLD

MARK FULCHER
ANNET LIBEAU

ISBN 978-0-9852095-5-1
Published by Sun Day Consulting, Inc.

1

The stay-alert drug was starting to wear off, and Kryger's brain was so befuddled by lack of sleep that he couldn't trust his reactions. He took the sensible precaution of switching to automatic to let the heavy fighter land itself and follow the signal to its assigned hangar. He was on the verge of drifting off to sleep when the doors trundled open as they recognized the signal from the craft. The doors shut automatically when the craft stopped well inside the hangar and the lights turned on.

He felt inclined to simply deactivate the fighter and sink into much-needed rest without even loosening the straps but sensed bad news when he saw Major Amanzi, a trusted old friend, approaching with a runabout. But even with his mind so obtuse, he made sure the fighter was properly shut down before he popped the door open and pressed the button to unfold the flimsy-looking ladder to the floor, then used it to descend carefully lest he trip and fall on his face. He usually dispensed with this luxury to save time, but he could barely concentrate on putting one foot in front of the other.

"Hi, Dub. What's up?" he asked, trying to sound interested. Dub Amanzi was a wing commander. About eight months ago he had miscalculated his distance from a Bikan light cruiser and veered off too late after bombing it. Both he and his fighter had been badly damaged in the explosion, and he had still been piloting a wheelchair around base when the fleet left Nevus four weeks ago. "Did you decide to spare me the walk, or were you just tired of your usual transport?"

Dub saw and felt the utter exhaustion radiating from his friend but smiled to hide his concern. "No, I regret that it's got nothing to do with anything as mundane as altruism. I'm able to walk a short distance by myself off and on, and I was told, not asked, by the old dodderers to come and collect you because they want to see you without delay. How's the fighting going?" The "old dodderers" was their irreverent nickname for the war council, who lacked combat experience and sometimes issued strange orders to young pilots who couldn't comprehend the logic of it.

"When the admiral ordered me back to base about three hours ago in the midst of a dogfight, the Bikans and their allies were trying to withdraw discreetly. They gave us bloody hell for a fortnight. Most of the pilots didn't get any sleep because our old enemies fought with uncharacteristic cunning and determination. I thought I was being dismissed because I was making foolish, unintentional, and dangerous mistakes.

"Perhaps the Bikans have new allies with some brains and fighting skills because we lost quite a few craft along with their crews, but that's classified information, so don't blabber it out in your sleep." He knew that Dub wasn't the talkative kind and that he could be trusted with such information. "What's so urgent about the council wanting to see me?"

"They didn't tell me, old friend, but they seemed quite impatient about your arrival. I was told to bring you directly to them with no stops on the way."

Kryger had a sudden foreboding. "Oh damn! That means a Bug problem popped up that is so urgent, I was ordered to quit in the middle of a serious skirmish. And I thought I was being favored. I innocently planned to sleep nonstop for at least a week in a decent bed. At least the other guys might get a bit of rest within the next few hours, for as you know, those crazy Bikans usually make sudden exits once they decide that it's time to push off."

During the twenty-minute trip to the council building in a city named Landing, Kryger involuntarily relaxed and fell asleep. Dub was watching him out of the corner of an eye and called his name when his head fell forward. Kryger suddenly became alert, then realized where he was, relaxed, and smiled sheepishly at his friend.

"You may have noticed that I wasn't bragging. I'm a walking disaster looking for a place to happen, and I have a nasty premonition that the uncaring council is going to provide the place."

"My sympathy, old friend; I know how you feel because that's how I ended up in a wheelchair after only three days on the stay-alert drug. But here we are." Dub set the hover-car down below the twelve steps in front of the building. "We can only hope you're allowed a few hours' sleep before they send you off to wherever, but knowing those insensitive old codgers, I doubt it. I was politely requested, mind you, to wait after delivering you, and that alone is ominous enough."

"I don't think I can make it up those steps. There's space enough on top and never much traffic, so will you hover up, please? Tell any busybody who wants you to move to take it up with the council and me. That should shut them up."

"Okay, I'll also offer to give them my wheelchair to suffer in. That should be enough to deter any sensible human being." Dub settled the car down to one side of the wide stairway, well away from the occasional pedestrians.

"Thank you. I appreciate it." Only iron discipline made Kryger get out of the car and kept him upright. He found it difficult to focus on the simple task of walking into the building, but the effort it took wasn't obvious to the few onlookers.

At reception he was sorely tempted to give the guard a rude gesture when he was waved through with the unnecessary comment that he was expected. Another guard wordlessly opened the door to the council chamber and gave Kryger a friendly smile, which he returned as he nodded his thanks. Hoping that the air conditioning inside the council chamber would make him feel better, he unzipped the front of his flight suit and entered slowly, unable to control the fatigue that showed in his walk, voice, and face.

He warily greeted the stern-faced old men seated in a semicircle and sensed their distaste as they smelled the odor emanating from his body, which hadn't been outside the flight suit for a fortnight. He didn't care; they could have been more considerate since he wasn't a robot.

"Ah, young Kryger, thank you for coming so expeditiously," Guar, the chair and spokesman, greeted him politely while taking short shallow breaths. His face was serious and didn't display distaste after the initial shocked reaction. "I'll get to the point immediately. A matter of extreme urgency came up, and you're the only one who can handle it."

Oh damn! I'm really sick of bloody Bugs, Kryger thought despairingly.

"About ten days ago, we received intelligence that a fair world, a little over three hundred light-years away, was rapidly being devastated. Observation by mechanical means confirmed that something out of the ordinary was happening, but the pilot couldn't venture too close because he wasn't immune to Bug control. That's why we need you to go in for a closer look and maybe do something about it."

"Sir, with respect," Kryger interjected when Guar paused, apparently to clear his throat, "I've been on stay-alert drugs for thirteen days, which is four times the recommended duration. I can hardly stay upright, and I can't think straight. Can't it stand over for one day so that I can have a much-needed rest? It's only a three-hour journey, but I can't engage a Bug in this condition and come off best, sir."

"I'm sorry, boy," another councilor replied. "Councilor Guar was going to add that an urgent call for assistance from that vicinity was intercepted about five hours ago. Apparently a meteor prospector's ship, from a race recently rescued from the Hullenii Bugs, was disabled by a meteor and is losing air quite rapidly. The call for help said that he can perhaps survive for eleven hours on his reserve oxygen. You must try to get to him in time and then, if possible, at least quick-scan the planet in question on your way back.

"We won't ask you to confront the creatures this time; just get close enough to check what's going on because, except for Quarr, you're the only one who can resist a Bug's mind power. You can pick up the guy in distress because your ship can accommodate two persons and is being rearmed right now in case you need to fight to get away. You have time for a…ah…quick shower and a meal. The coordinates and a fresh flight suit will be waiting for you."

A shiver of apprehension ran down Kryger's back. He had one of those rare forebodings of disaster waiting, but he couldn't refuse a "request" from the council or an urgent call for help from a lone spaceman in trouble, genuine or not.

"Very well, Councilors, but I smell a nasty, sophisticated Bug trap. I don't think I can face even one of them in my present state." They just looked at him as if he were out of his mind. He shrugged and turned to go but then thought he might as well upset the old fossils—if it could be done. He turned his head halfway around. "This reminds me of an old story, Councilors. Old Benny was on his deathbed, and his wife called the children to come and pay their last respects. They gathered in the lounge, and the teary old mother went in first to prepare the dying man. 'Benny,' she said with a sob in her voice, 'the children are here to say goodbye.'"

"The dying man croaked, 'What? Where are they going?'"

With that repartee, he more stumbled than walked to the door. They were always so serious that he thought they had no sense of humor, but he heard a few suppressed titters, and as the guard closed the door, uncontrolled laughter burst out before it was completely shut. He remained serious-faced and just shrugged when the guard gave him an inquiring look.

He felt somewhat refreshed after the much needed shower and a light meal. Dub took him back to the hangar and made sympathetic noises when told about the emergency call for help in Bug territory, but Kryger refrained from mentioning his reservations. It was just a little too much of a coincidence that the call had come from the vicinity of the troubled planet, but a "polite request" from the council was an implied order he had to obey, no matter whether he could keep his eyes open. The only consolation was that he should have at least two hours' sleep on the way, and when he arrived he would be as wary as an antelope getting a slight whiff of a stalking predator. It was just too dangerous to take even one more stay-alert capsule and expect to resist the dreadful mental powers of a Bug, which was usually linked to seven others that would instantly combine their mental power when Kryger was recognized.

After he'd completed the usual roundabout route to confuse possible chance observers, he entered the destination coordinates into the computer, and to make sure he'd wake up in time to take control of the ship, he switched the ten-minute-prior-to-emergence-into-normal-space warning buzzer to maximum. The irritating din would wake him up with sufficient time to stretch some of the sleep and fatigue from his overtired body. He fell asleep even as he pushed the button to enter subspace.

Kryger jumped when the too-shrill warning shocked him awake, but he didn't attain any height because of the restraining straps. His brain was foggy, but he removed the straps, drank water from a squeeze-bulb, and started to exercise in the confined cockpit to get his blood circulating. After four minutes of trying to push the cockpit sides away from him, he felt alive enough to switch the final reminder off because he didn't require the one-minute-and-ten-second warning that the craft was about to pop out of subspace. The drastic deceleration from 100 light-years per hour, or 1.4 light-years per minute, was quite severe by then, and other reminders would be superfluous.

He checked the time. He had slept for two hours and about fifteen minutes, which wasn't nearly long enough, but at least he felt a little more alive. Although he didn't want to, because it could easily delude him into making stupid mistakes, he took a mouthful of wake-up juice to ensure he at least would feel fully alert at pop-out.

He missed Quarr's unique talent for scanning normal space around the exit point while still a couple of light-years away in subspace, and since his brain was not as sharp as it should be to ably cope with such a situation, he was grateful that there wasn't a surprise party waiting to welcome him when the fighting craft emerged into normal space.

Not surprisingly, the call for help came just as he changed direction to head for the planet about five million kilometers away. "Help! Anyone…Please help me! My freighter is gutted, and I only have enough oxygen left for about three hours. If you can reach me in that time, my coordinates are…" and the numbers came in calmly and clearly with no hint of panic, which warned Kryger, and fatigue miraculously departed as his survival instincts kicked in.

The measured tones were in sharp contrast to the urgency of the message. It sounded just like a recording done under ideal conditions because nobody could stay *that* calm in such a situation, he thought with growing alarm, but even though he was sure he'd been sent into a trap of some sort, he was obliged to investigate on the off chance that it just might be a genuine distress call. Maybe the recorder deliberately transmitted the message so calmly as a warning to the intended victim or victims. He wondered if the ability to instantly jump a million or two kilometers through subspace was known to or suspected by those involved in this elaborate but flawed trap.

When Kryger sensed monkey business like this, his brain sharpened because his life depended on correctly interpreting such situations, but he entered the numbers into the computer as they came while he vainly tried to find signs of life in the vast area of space around him. When finished, the computer indicated that the target area was in the middle of the scattered clusters of meteors on the other side of the planet, and his instruments detected the presence of a metallic object, but his wary mind-scan of that area found no sign of Bug or warm-blooded life.

He pushed the button for the short subspace jump to the given coordinates. Otherwise it would take him three to four hours to reach the place, which would be way too late. He wondered briefly if he was being overly suspicious but decided it was prudent to err on the safe side because of the subtle warning in the message. He emerged about a hundred kilometers short of his objective because the sophisticated detectors wouldn't allow the craft to emerge too close to a heavy object. The fighter was at an angle that would completely miss the cluster of meteors if Kryger didn't apply reverse thrust to slow it to a veritable crawl, which he felt would make him a sitting duck. He made sure the shields were on full power.

Kryger mentally started to search the meteor cluster and was reaching for the throttle to slow down when the instruments shrilled a warning that large objects were rapidly closing in around the craft. At the same time, he sensed a multitude of gleeful chuckles, and he received a direct, harsh, derisively jovial greeting: *Aha! Welcome, cat-face! We can hardly believe our luck! We prepared a trap to lure a human ship with shield technology, but you showed up instead and fell for our painstakingly made recordings. You won't escape this time as we have twenty ships which are responsive to the thoughts of one of us, and we can outmaneuver you no matter what you do. You've escaped our vengeance for much too long, cat-face, and now you will die slowly, but only after we know the location of your planet. We've wondered what you would taste like, and we'll start with one toe at a time and taste our way up until you die of pain and blood loss. But you can be sure that you'll give us what we want long before you die!*

Kryger went cold and shivered. He mentally cursed the insensitive council who had likely sent him to this ignominious death when they could very well see he was almost comatose. But he wasn't dead yet, and there was no giving up anywhere in his powerful two-meter body. He would fight until his last breath, and he had some nasty, unconventional surprises to confound them with.

The ship with the exultant Hullenii speaker on board was rising from behind the cluster of space debris directly in front of him where the alleged miner-in-trouble should have been. He wondered fleetingly how they had managed to conceal their thought emanations, but hardly a moment later, he sent the strongest mind-bolt he could muster into the ship without focusing on the jubilant speaker Bug and then stabbed the button for the short random subspace jump to get him out of the area. In the battle to save the planet Okryon from total destruction, he'd thought of this quick getaway method, which had been subsequently programmed into all ships, and it had saved many lives when ships or fighters were disabled and unable to get away. He emerged half a million kilometers away and faint with exhaustion after the energy expended on the mind-bolt, then checked his instruments just in time to see a rapidly fading explosion in the vicinity of the meteorite cluster. He wondered briefly if the Bugs were bombing the position where he had been a moment ago.

He couldn't know that the energy bolt, not aimed at a specific Bug-mind in the ship but sent just to stun, had killed all eight overconfident Hullenii on the ship, and that the explosion occurred when the uncontrolled ship collided with a gigantic boulder.

There was no known method in which he could be attacked in subspace. Kryger was too spent to fight and therefore quickly punched the coordinates of a recently discovered solar system with a livable planet more than one thousand and five hundred light-years away into the computer. He felt dizzy.

The Hullenii had an inborn compulsion to pass new information to one another. Although information was instantly filed in their vast retentive brains, they didn't have the ability to access the incredibly diverse and valuable scientific data accumulated over very long lifetimes. Perhaps, Kryger thought, one of them had found a humanoid bright enough to cross-reference information and program its computer-like brain to access it. Of course, the method would have automatically been passed on to the whole caboodle, which would have enabled them to have these new ships built, and he'd have to assume they could track him in subspace and would follow since they couldn't miss the chance to do him in.

Of course, he couldn't know the consternation his spur-of-the-moment decision would cause.

2

A century or two ago, a Bug overpowered and eventually destroyed a humanoid race who hooked their fighting ships' controls electronically to the pilot's brain before they went into battle. The Bugs must have liked the idea because their vast brains would superbly control and maneuver a big ship like an agile fighting craft.

The Hullenii's vast minds were faster than any electronic computer. Their brains were, in fact, similar to the organic computers used by Kryger's people, and their ships were designed to be controlled by one of them hooked up with the electronic controls of the ship. That particular Bug became the ship's controlling computer. The hooked-up one received directives from the elected commander, and the near-sentient ship responded instantly to any impulse it received from its controller. The Bugs were incapable of comprehending that the ship would respond by exploding when the controller realized it was dying, but, then, they thought they were immortal unless cat-face was in the vicinity.

Because the ship was controlled by a living, thinking brain, it was ultra-responsive and could outmaneuver any ship manually controlled by a humanoid pilot. The hooked-up one was fed at regular intervals to replenish the vast amount of energy it used in the process, but they were not original thinkers and never realized that the hooked-up one could become overtired from the constant concentration of keeping the ship operating and on course on very long journeys.

The backlash of the unexpectedly powerful blast had left them confused for vital seconds before they could check the course their fleeing quarry had taken and pursue him. When they checked where the course might end up, they hastily linked to confer in a fit of anxiety.

They immediately assumed the interfering cat-face had somehow learned about the recently discovered desert planet, which was ideal for hatching their eggs. They were desperate to replenish their rapidly dwindling numbers and assumed the cat-face, in desperation to take a last stand, was going there to destroy the precious planet in an effort to save his miserable life. Their elected fleet commander had been killed by the cat-faced human even before its ship exploded, and they hastily designated the oldest survivor to lead and take decisions. It immediately snapped a mental order: *We must follow at the maximum speed we can coach out of our ships. That eternally damned cat-face must not escape now that we know where he's headed! We must stop the creature at all costs since we've searched everywhere and might not find another planet suitable for hatching our eggs. Cat-face must be destroyed even if we forgo our much anticipated vengeance. Go!*

The nineteen ships took off in pursuit, and Kryger saw the cluster of blips on his subspace monitor screen. They were roughly two light-years behind, but his ship was still accelerating. He hoped to outdistance them but was too exhausted to worry whether he could. He didn't even wonder what kind of genius they had enlisted or, more probably, coerced to concoct the ingenious trap as he dropped off into an exhausted sleep. His instruments had calculated the exact distance, and he'd set the alarm to wake him two hours prior to pop-out. That should give him sufficient time to wake up and take stock of the situation.

He reluctantly rubbed his eyes to get them open when the insistent alarm at last managed to irritate him enough to realize he must get back to reality, that he couldn't afford the luxury of stopping the alarm and going back to sleep. He forced his eyes open with conscious effort, sucked a couple of mouthfuls of water from a bulb to get a semblance of life back into his body before he switched the alarm off, and then checked his instruments. He was so shocked to see sixteen blips less than a light-hour behind him that he almost stopped yawning. His jaw dropped, and he shook his head because he just couldn't believe the Bugs could gain that much distance in thirteen hours but knew his instruments wouldn't lie.

And the Buggers, the ironic comparison flashed into his mind, *are incapable of thinking that they might be led on a chase that would eventually overtax even their enormous capacities. There are only fifteen blips left, and I'd like to know whether the missing blips destroyed themselves or if they popped out into normal space so fast that the ships' structures burst into flames or just ripped to pieces. One can only hope.*

They were too close for peace of mind, so he must think and plan ahead. He would come out of subspace perilously close to the solar system, and the ship controllers might very well overshoot when his craft started to decelerate before pop-out, unless they had an inkling of his probable destination.

He just couldn't afford to underestimate them because they might start to decelerate at more or less the same time and pop out before him. He must take that likelihood into account and be prepared to fight them off or just dodge them until he could enter a new course into the computer. He just didn't know how much control they still had over their ships and whether they could decelerate drastically enough to save them from breaking up if they hit normal space too fast.

If they were scattered at emergence, he would have a chance to take some of their ships out before he entered subspace again, but he must take into account that their ships were fractionally faster in subspace and that they might outmaneuver him in normal space.

They, because of their different makeup, could withstand as many gravities as he could, if not more, but it was highly unlikely they were able to unhook a controller during subspace flight. The ship-controlling Bugs must be pretty exhausted by now, and another few hours in subspace might be too much for them. It was a pity he couldn't punch fictitious destinations into the control computer since he might not survive a long journey or could end up in another galaxy and never find his way back.

It was worrying that the Bugs overcame their natural antipathy toward one another to band together, and he must warn his father through Mike, the artificial intelligence that claimed its telepathic ability could keep track and contact a bracelet-bearer anywhere in the universe.

He settled down to make contact with Mike. He'd contacted the AI many times before in subspace to transmit information he'd gleaned from a Bug's mind and was surprised that he received no immediate response. He tried for ten minutes before giving up, concluding that Mike wasn't as powerful as it claimed or that he was still too tired to transmit or receive thoughts over such a vast distance.

Kryger was disappointed, but there was nothing he could do but try again in normal space when he got the chance. The only consolation was that, if and when the constant surveillance began to fade or ceased, Mike would inform Quarr or his father and give them the direction in which Kryger's signal was lost. If contact wasn't reestablished within a reasonable time, his disappearance would be investigated.

When the vicious deceleration began, he set about readying all missiles and counter-missiles the craft carried. It wasn't a chancy thing to do because they were cushioned and would only detonate on contact at high speed. Then he switched on the front and rear Matter Annihilator Guns so they too would be ready to fire. He had done all that could be done and settled down to endure the rest of the thirty-minute severe deceleration. Then he noticed that six blips were passing; four kept parallel and five stayed close behind him. He grimly thought that they planned to box him in and almost smiled.

Kryger was tense as pop-out approached and unconsciously began humming the signature tune of the Golden People as he was wont to do under stress. His right hand was on the push button for the short subspace jump as he couldn't know what was waiting for him, and his left hand was clamped around the joystick.

The sickening lurch into normal space didn't bother him, and his eyes rapidly alternated between the monitors and the space before him. The fourth planet, the only one in this out-of-the-way system capable of sustaining life, was a little to his left, just about two million kilometers away, and the automatic deceleration continued to reduce speed for rapid atmospheric entry. He disengaged the automatic action since he wasn't going to land and quickly switched the craft's shields on for safety's sake. He had a decent look around to see if it was safe and then took a moment to check and punch new coordinates into the control computer.

Kryger almost felt elated when the front monitor screen showed two explosions quite close together on the planet. To be picked up so clearly at this distance, they must be quite enormous, he thought with grim satisfaction. *Two ships and sixteen Bugs fewer to worry about without lifting a finger, he thought happily. It improves the odds so much more in my favor.*

But the elation was short-lived. Even as the explosions occurred, a warning shrilled sharply in the cockpit. A quick glance at the relevant monitors showed a swarm of dots rapidly closing in from the right-hand side. They could only be heat-homing missiles—too many to be deflected by the shields. He fired all counter-missiles on his right-hand side to intercept them, then quickly did a half roll and fired all the interceptor missiles on his left side, hoping that would be enough to stop most of them, but the alarm kept shrilling and he hastily stabbed the jump button, which unfortunately would switch the shields off an instant before the craft entered subspace. It was unavoidable as some peculiarity in the shield generators would not allow a ship to enter subspace.

But as the familiar stomach-churning lurch began, he felt the ship shudder, and the next thing he knew, he was back in normal space with missiles flashing past a little to his rear. He punched the all-shield button and was thankful when the shields flashed into place. *A one-in-a-million chance of being hit by a missile in the rear just as the ship entered subspace,* he thought as he calmly accepted the misfortune. He was thankful the rear missiles didn't explode because he and the fighter would have been scattered debris, which would have been a source of delirious delight for the Bugs.

Missiles began to splash against the shields, and the fighter shuddered continuously. The shields would overheat very soon, and then he'd be a goner. Then a Bug ship tried to ram him, but by applying power, it was easy to avoid the immense bulk. He realized they meant to kill him by any means, even by sacrificing themselves. Did they really hate him this much, or were they trying to prevent him from reaching the planet? And if they were, what's so important about this sandy, barren-looking planet? There must be a very good reason for them to be so uncharacteristically suicidal.

Just to be certain, he stabbed the jump button again, but nothing happened. He quickly punched another destination into the computer, but there was no response. He sighed; the subspace nexus must be damaged, but other than that, the fighter responded quite normally to its controls, and he could fight as long as the shields held. Whether he originally intended to or not, he now had no choice but to land on the lifeless-looking planet. His fighter might be crippled, but it still had enough teeth left to take a lot of Bugs with him.

Three ships approached extremely fast around the curve of the planet just as he turned the fighter in that direction. The ships were quite close together as he aimed the forward big MAG and rapidly activated the trigger three times. Three silent explosions followed in quick succession, which Kryger found strange because a big MAG bolt left only a small hole about a centimeter wide in its path. He noted the unusual phenomenon only because he was executing a tight loop to confront the ships that had crept up behind him. First he fired all forward counter-missiles to intercept approaching missiles and then shot both ships with the big MAG. Again he realized that the ships exploded instead of just becoming lifeless driftage as they should. Perhaps it was the type of metal used, he thought and shrugged. It was none of his concern but a very convenient way to get rid of eight Bugs at one go.

His instruments bleeped twice and showed another four ships approaching, but they were still far away. He thought that they might very well be the only survivors of the six ships that had surged ahead and might have overshot the solar system. He could afford to disregard them because he would land long before they were close enough to enter the thin atmosphere in pursuit. He turned the fighter toward the nameless planet again and increased speed.

As he entered the atmosphere, an alarm began to bleep. He checked the monitors and saw a single ship closing in fast from behind as it was firing a swarm of missiles. *There must be some Bug ships stationed on this planet,* he thought, *and every single one of them seems to be equipped with a surplus of missiles.* He took a chance and fired the rear counter-missiles as well as the rear MAG. He felt the slight, rapid bumps as the missiles left their tubes, but then there was an explosion. The fighter shuddered briefly and then tumbled out of control.

When he flipped the antigravity switch on, it unaccountably didn't respond. *Damn,* he thought viciously as he fought to stabilize the craft, *how in all the hells of creation did that happen?* There wasn't much time because the atmosphere wasn't thick, and he activated reverse thrust at maximum as he fought the craft for control. Fortunately the craft was equipped with Quarr's invention — the joystick was coupled to the thrusters as well — but for some unknown reason, response was tardier than it should have been.

He tried every trick he knew of to level out, but by the time the heavy fighter responded, he was already too close to the surface. The belly hit deep sand, and the craft bounced high into the air. Fortunately the craft stayed level, and Kryger briefly glimpsed a fairly wide fissure in the far distance but couldn't see how deep it was before the craft hit the sand again.

Reverse thrust cut out. Perhaps it had been damaged by the second impact. He could eject — if that still worked — when the fighter shot over the edge of the fissure, but that meant he would be left without survival equipment, provisions, and precious water. Kryger calmly accepted the dire prospects because it had happened many times before, and somehow he always came through.

The situations had been similar but never on a seemingly lifeless planet like this, and with such well-equipped and ruthless enemies determined to rub him out while he was within reach. These thoughts flashed through his mind as he flipped switches off to prevent an explosion or fire if the craft went over the edge or hit an immovable obstacle head-on. Maybe something could still be salvaged after the crash because the ready-packed rucksacks were in cushioned compartments for just such an eventuality.

The fighter slid along as if it were on a greased surface but suddenly began to bounce and lurch as it hit uneven, roughly formed, low dunes. He knew the fighter was designed to survive forced landings and extremely rough conditions but could only hope it would veer off course to miss the none-too-inviting fissure. That same fissure might be the only place to find water and a place to hide, but it was also the most likely place for the Bugs to search for him. So it would be better to stay out of it for a few days and find some other means of evading them.

The trail of billowing dust must be visible from space, he thought despairingly and surmised that one or more Bug ships would arrive soon enough to finish off what they'd started if he didn't get away from the fighter in time. He also knew that, if they didn't see or detect his presence, they would assume he was either dead or unconscious and head for the craft because they'd been trying to get hold of shield technology for a number of years.

The craft must have reached deep, loose sand because Kryger suddenly felt it slowing down quite drastically. The long dust cloud overtook the craft and began to obscure his forward view, but there was nothing he could do except prepare to eject, if he could, when the craft sailed over the edge. He grabbed the ejection lever next to the seat in his left hand, ready to pull it up the moment he felt the familiar sinking sensation and saw a bit of clear sky above.

Then there was a heart-stopping bump. The fighter bounced and then lurched slightly sideways before hitting an immovable object. The restraining straps bit into Kryger's body as the craft came to a dead halt at a slightly downward angle. The swirling dust cloud obscured his sight, and when he tried to open the canopy, it refused to budge. As the opening mechanism quickly overloaded, a warning light flashed a few times before the motor cut out.

Kryger undid the straps and pulled the recessed lever to unlock the emergency door next to him, then forced it halfway open with his legs before it refused to budge any farther. Hot sand and dust poured into the cockpit as he turned on his stomach to blindly grope for the rucksacks with emergency supplies and survival equipment. The cockpit was partly filled with sand when he pulled both bags by their straps and began forcing his way out, backside first. He felt the cascade slow to a trickle as he pulled his shoulders through the half-opened door.

Dust billowed thickly around the craft, and Kryger couldn't wait for it to disperse to see properly since a Bug ship might already be close. By touch he clawed enough sand out for the door to shut. The ship must be destroyed along with its secret weapons, he thought, but it might as well take a Bug or two with it.

Kryger made sure he had the remote control with him to destroy the ship from a distance if the mechanism for autodestruct on forced entry had been damaged, and that the door was properly closed again so only he could open it or the canopy safely with his voice or a bare hand on the lock plate.

Although the urge to run was hellishly strong, he cautiously crawled on hands and knees since he didn't know how far he was from the fissure. Dragging the rucksacks with one hand, he patted the hot sand before him with his free hand to feel his way out. When the dust thinned enough to see a few steps ahead, he came to his feet and checked the sky for ships before he looked around. The fighter had bounced over one of the last fairly big dunes, and its angle and momentum had been just right to make it end up, nose first, in the side of a dune about fifty meters from the uneven edge of the fissure. He quietly thanked whatever higher entity had taken pity on him because the fighter had nearly missed the last dune and would have sailed right into the deep fissure.

He shouldered the rucksacks and ran some distance along the rim as fast as his stiff muscles and the terrain allowed. He wasn't concerned about the tracks he was leaving since the Bugs would naturally home in on the fighter first. Kryger knew they were incapable of considering consequences and followed only their natural instincts but couldn't keep a wolfish grin from his lips when he thought of the deadly trap they wouldn't be able to resist.

The weapon strapped to his side in a holster—called Big MAG by his twin sisters, the inventors—although not heavy or big, was powerful enough to bring a battleship down. The original little experimental MAG, which he always kept in a special pocket on the inside of his shorts, could also do the job, so he wasn't worried about ships spotting him.

The kilometers-long dust trail the fighter had left behind was slowly settling down in the hot, windless atmosphere. After checking the sky again, he stopped for a moment on the gradually rising slope to lift the faceplate of the transparent flight helmet that had kept the dust from entering. He turned the oxygen off and took a short cautious sniff. Although the dry, overly hot air smelled dusty, it was breathable. He breathed faster to get enough oxygen and then removed the helmet completely but didn't discard it since he might need it as protection against poisonous gas if the Bugs resorted to that. He perused the sky again and then continued sprinting along the edge to get as far away from the immediate area as he could.

3

Kryger estimated that he was a little more than a kilometer away from the fighter when he sensed the probing thoughts of Bugs approaching swiftly. He realized he couldn't reach the few scattered boulders about a hundred meters away, on what could be the crest of the gradual rise, in time to hide among them. He therefore sat immediately with his head between his half-drawn-up knees, which covered the transparent helmet, facing the intact-looking fighter, and made sure his mind was completely shielded. His flight suit was covered with dust, and he could easily be mistaken for an odd-shaped rock from high above. He suddenly felt uncomfortable, as if he was being scanned, but couldn't detect any intrusion into his mind. He vaguely sensed mild curiosity as if he was of passing interest, but since it wasn't intrusive, he kept the peephole in his mental shield open in order not to be cut off from any threatening emanations he might pick up. *The feeling must be caused by my weariness,* he thought irritably, *as this is a barren, seemingly uninhabited world.*

Two ships descended rapidly, and from the swaying, awkward way they dropped from an unsafe height, he deduced they were from the original group of pursuers. *Those ship-controlling Bugs are just about done,* he thought with satisfaction.

While the ships came to a teetering halt, he sprinted for the boulders as they offered additional protection, and the blast caused by the exploding fighter wouldn't be as vicious at that distance. If the Bugs spotted him, he could always destroy the fighter with the remote and shoot the ships as they rose; it would be an easy way to get rid of sixteen more noisome Bugs.

He was thoroughly weary and sat on a roundish, roughly flat rock behind a seemingly solid big boulder that was low enough to watch what the Bugs were up to without straining his neck or any other part of his anatomy.

Fourteen Bugs descended from the ships, and Kryger grinned when they fanned out rapidly like frightened rats scattering because of a suspicious shadow. Although the dust almost hid them from sight, they acted warily as they converged on the fighter. Kryger was amused by the thought that a group of such huge creatures could be so scared of a puny human being.

They reached the half-buried craft and seemed to confer as they surrounded it. Then, while the others stood slightly back, two of them started to dig furiously with all four claws, and sand flew in all directions. Within seconds the cockpit was exposed, and Kryger saw one of them getting into position to break the cockpit canopy open with its steel-hard claws even before the dust could settle.

He knew they were enormously strong and wasn't surprised when the canopy flew open after only a few seconds. He immediately pulled his head down behind the boulder, covered his ears with his palms, and hoped the boulders were immovable. The fighter self-destructed as it was programmed to do on forced entry, but he distinctly heard another two almost simultaneous thunderclaps.

Kryger was puzzled, but when he peeked over the boulder, he saw a triplet of dust clouds expanding rapidly in the hot atmosphere. He shrugged his shoulders. Perhaps the mental link between the Bugs caused the deaths of the ships' overtaxed controllers, which in turn triggered a sympathetic explosion in the ships, or perhaps debris caused the explosions since the ships had come down quite close to the fighter.

He thought there should be about seven hundred Bugs left, unless they'd started to breed to replace those he'd disposed of. He sincerely hoped they would assume he had expired with his ship; otherwise they might destroy the planet just to make double sure. One could only hope the Bugs had informed others that they had found his ship intact with its nose buried in the sand before they blew themselves up. They must have believed he was still inside because they had stirred up even more obscuring dust with their furious digging.

The weariness took hold anew when he sat again on the curiously round, benchlike rock to decide his next move. Other ships, if any were close enough, would definitely come to check what had caused the automatic broadcasting from the investigators to cease abruptly. On the other hand, the momentary shock as the fighter exploded should have been felt by others, especially the ships' controllers. They could have had time to transmit the catastrophe that befell the investigators.

Kryger thought the rock on which he sat trembled a little, or it might be a slight tremor caused by the tremendous explosions a minute ago, but it could also be his imagination. He was perspiring profusely and knew he should be concerned about dehydration.

Get your heavy butt off this damn trapdoor, boy, or the Bugs will roast it. Dammit, boy! Move it! Now!

Was he so exhausted that his subconscious mind had to invent an urgent voice in his head to get his rear into gear? He wasn't sure, but it was time to get going anyway. He rose and shouldered his rucksacks, took two steps forward, and then whirled around when there was a slight scraping noise behind him. His heart raced, and the MAG appeared in his hand without conscious thought when he saw the flat rock he'd sat on rotate slowly for half a turn before it lifted up and tilted to one side.

Easy with that toy gun, boy. I don't mind being shot at for a legitimate reason, but when it's by an uncalled-for nervous reaction, I detest it. It's only me, and I mean you no harm. On the contrary, I came to save your butt because the Bugs will be here in force within minutes, and they'll find you since there's no place to hide.

The dry, humorous tone relaxed Kryger's taught nerves, and he lowered the gun. He didn't put it away because his keen ears detected the faint whistle of speeding ships in the far distance.

A spry, middle-age-looking humanoid, about half his size, climbed out of the trapdoor and smiled impishly up at him, but the brown eyes registered surprise. He was an ash blond, well built, and wore only shorts.

Sheeza! They really grow them big where you come from, youngster, but as you undoubtedly can hear, the Bugs are in a hell of a hurry to arrive. Now hand me the lightest of those bags and squeeze in after me as fast as you can. The tunnel may be a bit too low for you, and you'll have to stoop a little, but it gets a bit wider and higher further on. Hurry up, will you? There isn't much time.

The whistling noise suddenly became less, an indication that the ships were drastically slowing down for a quick landing.

Kryger instinctively trusted the tiny human, who backed into the trapdoor and then scurried down as soon as he was handed a bag. Kryger holstered the gun and followed the example of the manikin, feetfirst. The trapdoor was really narrow, but he managed to squeeze through with his rucksack dangling awkwardly by the straps from the crook of an elbow. His feet found a rung, and he scraped down a narrow shaft into a small chamber about six meters down. He turned around and, in the faint light that filtered in, saw the little man pull a lever down. The trapdoor maneuvered smoothly back into position, and a dim light turned on when there was an audible click as the door locked.

With a curt command to Kryger to follow as fast as possible, the humanoid turned and walked down the tunnel, which angled steeply down. Kryger had to crouch quite low, but fortunately the tunnel was fairly smooth, and he dragged the rucksack by its straps as it was too awkward to carry.

We have a number of observation tunnels like this one scattered all over the planet, his rescuer explained. *Because of an ancient prediction, we were ordered to rush to our assigned tunnels when a skirmish and unusual number of Bug ships were detected. We could only hope that, if you were the one in the prophecy, your disabled ship would land close enough to one of the observation posts so that you could be rescued, and I barely made it in time.*

He chuckled. *Fortunately you were already waiting for me; otherwise we'd both be history. Oh, and yes, this planet is hollow. We live on the tropical inside, which is quite a contrast to the desolation you've seen. The Bugs have some pretty sophisticated instruments to detect warm-blooded life, and although our tunnels are shielded to an extent, we don't take chances when a Bug ship's in the vicinity.*

My name's Getik. Kryger sensed the loneliness in the small humanoid. He would later learn that Getik's wife and son had passed away in a freak accident some years before. Lights came on and turned off behind them as they advanced. After a few minutes, Kryger's back began to ache and his legs cramped.

Just a few steps more, boy, came Getik's reassurance, *and you'll be able to walk upright and stretch. I believe that the Bugs' purloined instruments can't reach this far down, so you're welcome to groan or yell if that will help. It's obvious that we don't need the headroom you do, but our tunnels were dug out wide and high enough to allow for air circulation, except for the last hundred meters or so to the outer surface. We never venture away from this planet, so we've never encountered a human race similar to us as big as you are.*

Although the ceiling was only a few centimeters above his head, when Kryger at last rose to his full length, he stopped and arched his aching back and neck. He shook his legs one by one to ease the cramps.

That feels better, he exclaimed. *Thank you for your timely rescue. My name is Kryger. It means "warrior." Maybe my parents had foreknowledge of what I would become out of necessity, and, oh…yes, this toy gun I pointed at you can easily take out a Bug ship, so I wasn't really helpless out there, although they are annoyed enough with me to use missile bombs to get rid of me. I won't be surprised if they destroy the planet to make sure they get me at last. I've been a constant pain in their…well…safety valves for the last couple of years.*

As if to emphasize his words, the earth suddenly trembled. Kryger stiffened, but Getik only smiled.

Relax, boy. They've used a percussion bomb, which may have collapsed a few hundred meters (Kryger translated the measurement to meters, which wasn't quite accurate but close enough) *of fissure wall where your craft came down. That's their way of making sure that you haven't escaped the explosion of your craft and that of their ships. Yes, I can read their satisfied thoughts at this distance. They won't destroy the planet because they won't find another one in this galaxy so suitable for hatching their painfully laid eggs. We have a long way to go to the inner world, and you should be able to get a little sleep in before we get there. We're safe now, but let's get going before you fall asleep on me. I'm not strong enough to drag your bulk to the intersurface elevator. This one pack is heavy enough.* Getik smiled.

I like you, sir, and sense that I can trust you. Kryger was sincere. *One immediate question, though: Are you scanning my brain?*

Please call me Getik; everyone does. No, I'm not scanning since I can sense your thoughts. Why?

Kryger shrugged his shoulders as if confused. *Before I left my fighter, it felt as if someone was unobtrusively scanning my thoughts as if mildly interested. Maybe it was just my imagination, but it's a bothering nuisance because I can't sense what it was and can't shake the feeling.*

Getik was quiet for a moment as if he was searching mentally. *I checked all the frequencies I can reach, but I don't sense any other thoughts. So you can be sure that it's not the Bugs, but don't let it worry you until you've had a good rest. We'll reach the elevator in a few minutes, and then you can strip if you feel more comfortable without the flight suit. Nudity doesn't embarrass us, and it's never cold down there. We only cover strategic places when we feel it's necessary or when we need pockets.*

Kryger shouldered the rucksack as they trod on down the rapidly descending tunnel. He felt a very slight breeze on his face, so he opened the front of the overly hot, oppressive flight suit. He immediately felt better.

There were unpadded bunks on three sides of the roomy elevator, and although Kryger could sit on them, they were too low and narrow to be comfortable. Getik told him there was a reversal of gravity about halfway down and that the elevator would tilt over. Otherwise they would end up on their heads after the gravity shift. He'd have to strap in for the drop down and the turn over, and the rise to the inner world would also be quite fast. The journey would take about three hours, and there were no stops.

It sounds strange to me, but it's logical, Getik, sir. I was prepared to stay awake to evade the Bugs for about fourteen days, even though I don't know how long the days are here, but now that I'm safe, I don't think I'll be able to keep my eyes open, even for only three hours. I sincerely hope that you won't pass out when I remove this flight suit. Would you please wake me up when we slow down for tilt-over? I must warn you, though: don't touch me or try to enter my mind to wake me up. I'm trained to kill immediately without thought when the latter happens. Just call my name in a normal tone of voice. It's not difficult to pronounce.

When he stripped to his shorts, he expected Getik to at least cover his nose, but Getik only smiled and remarked that he'd endured worse odors in his lifetime and that the air in the elevator would change rapidly once they got moving. Kryger gratefully folded the suit and then stuffed it halfway into a rucksack before strapping himself in for the journey.

Getik pressed the only button after he too had strapped in. Kryger felt the bottom drop out underneath him; the straps creaked, and he swallowed his stomach back into place. He was used to fast drops, but this was real scary because it was out of his control. He didn't have a joystick in his hand to get out of the drop, nor could he brace his legs against something. All thoughts of sleep were lost somewhere up above in the shaft, and it felt like minutes before the straps relaxed and he dropped back onto the narrow bench.

I apologize for my oversight, boy. One never really gets used to it, but I've been doing it for more than two hundred years on and off, and it never occurred to me to warn you as you're the first visitor from outside we've ever had.

The elevators are rounded on the outside, and all functions are automated. The ball form allows it to slowly turn around in the zero-gravity zone, and one only feels the uplifting sensation—maybe a little too rapid for comfort, I suppose—when an elevator slows down to a halt on the other side. Not one has ever failed between stations, but in the unlikely event that it does, in theory it will eventually rock to a stop where gravity is neutral. Getik smiled mischievously. *There it can be reached and repaired, but it'll take some time.*

Kryger grinned. *Thank you. It's very reassuring because there's always a first time for everything. I can only hope that this isn't it.*

Getik returned the smile. *About two thousand years ago, after millennia of wandering, we found this world by chance and decided to settle down permanently. We expected that the Bugs would eventually find it and prepared for the event by closing the* two entry points to the inner world and melting out quite a few of these tunnels to the outside surface, especially along the fissure where the only water on the outer surface can be found. We check every tunnel once a year to make sure that the entrances aren't blocked by sand or other elements.

Where we blocked the natural entrances at the North and South Pole, we built observation stations with sophisticated instruments that continuously monitor the universe for as far as they can reach, which is a number of light-years. Thus, we are prepared for physical threats that can't be detected by our Sensitives. Seeing that your exhaustion is temporarily scared away, let me briefly give you a rundown of our history to pass some of the time.

About a hundred thousand years ago, we lived on a planet called Ekur, in a solar system about a million light-years from here. Roughly about half the population was dedicated to the physical sciences, and most of the other half was investigating the finer sciences of the mind. Of course, there were many who practiced both because there were an amazing number of ideas and principles which could be put to practical use. The physical science adherents were trying to develop an organic computer for storing and easy retrieval of vast volumes of accumulated scientific data because after multiple centuries, some inventions were lost due to mechanical failure or other reasons. It took ages to retrieve the information one was looking for, if one was lucky enough to find it at all.

Then one day, a colony of semi-intelligent Bugs, about the size of house cats and omnivorous, were discovered on one of the other semi-arid planets. Experiments revealed that the moment one Bug experienced or was taught anything new, the rest of the group knew it within moments. The "in-between" scientists thought that nature had provided them with ready-made organic storage computers and experimented further. They found that although the creatures stored every bit of information, they could only retrieve it after one was shown by telepathy how to do it, but they memorized that information as well and promptly forgot about it.

Although the pure mental scientists criticized and cautioned the in-between scientists, they went ahead and artificially increased the size of the creatures. The new creatures quickly became predators in order to get enough energy for their bulk. The mental and most of the physical scientist groups foresaw disaster coming and built big ships and subsequently departed for safer planets and other solar systems.

When things started to go awry, the experimenters tried to eliminate the new Bugs, but their carapaces had hardened to such an extent that bullets and rays just bounced off. Bombs and fire had some effect, but the bugs started to retaliate by killing and eating humans because they found that they could overwhelm animals and humans by linking their enhanced minds.

Those who stayed behind to monitor the situation fled when the creatures began to strip the planet of life, but the original experimenters refused to leave, for they intended to eradicate their mistakes. When the Bugs eventually broke into their stronghold, they were killed and devoured one by one. We know this because one of them took time to broadcast a mental message while the Bugs broke down the door of the strong room he locked himself into.

The giant breed of Bug was only interested in eating and nothing more. They starved when they denuded the planet of life but didn't die because they could survive on almost any kind of vegetation. Eventually a starship of another civilization landed there in all innocence and thus provided the Bugs with the means to reach and take over other planets. Unless they're stopped in time, they will eventually denude the universe of life and then find a way to reach other universes.

The narrative was familiar, and Kryger said that he seemed to have been born to hunt Bugs and that he only hoped he would live long enough to eliminate every single one of them. He detested the almost continuous danger because he had been driven to become a lone wolf, as very few could resist a Bug's dreadful mental power. He estimated there may be less than seven hundred left because he'd killed eighty-three over about twenty months and suspected that at least seventy-two had perished in their own trap.

That's an impressive number for a mere boy, and maybe that's why they're using this planet to replenish their numbers because it's naturally hot enough to incubate their tough hard-shell eggs. We've managed to destroy quite a few eggs with certain rays that render them infertile, but they're getting suspicious, and we have to be very careful. As I previously mentioned, to them egg-laying is a painful process which they dislike, and the process leaves them vulnerable to a sharpshooter when they bend over because that's the only opening that may be penetrated by a missile or an energy bolt. They first try to lay their eggs in an upright position but eventually have to bend over to force it out. It's an ideal opportunity but unfortunately one we can't use because it would be folly to let them know of our presence.

As it is, they got suspicious and started to guard newly laid eggs after the first batch didn't hatch because they instinctively know when an egg is not fertilized and destroy it immediately, which is a very rare occurrence. Now that they've had so many losses, they're likely to have more than one guard constantly monitoring and watching for interference with their eggs, which are laid close to the biggest and the only permanent waterhole in the fissure because a newly hatched bug immediately needs water.

"You seem to be watching them closely. How do you accomplish that?" Kryger wondered out loud.

Because of our planet's unique outer surface and the water, we expected them sooner or later. We therefore excavated tunnels to just about every waterhole in the fissure and installed mechanical eyes as well. There are other desertlike planets, but they can't sustain life. The Bugs made a permanent camp at the choicest water source close to the end of the fissure, and they didn't block access for the few hardy creatures that are dependent on the water, for they will serve as prey for the little Bugs. The little Bugs run wild for the first few months until their brains start to develop and they can be brought under control. If any hatch, we won't be able to destroy them, for the Bugs might just be irresponsible enough to use a planet-buster when they find that there's more to this planet than they suspected and can't locate us.

Getik saw that Kryger was relaxed, that he found it hard to keep his eyes open, and that he was thinking about his wife and child. Perhaps the cat-faced boy had adapted to the silent, smooth drop because gravity was normal again, and he sensed that the youngster required plenty of rest.

Lie down in a corner on your favorite side, boy. I'll strap you down so that the changeover won't disturb you too much. Give me Quarr's frequency, and I'll let her know that you're okay. I have the ability to home in on any frequency anywhere in this galaxy. I see that you're not surprised that I know of her, but it's uppermost in your thoughts that she would be worried by your inexplicable disappearance.

Kryger thanked him, opened his shield wide enough to transmit the frequency, closed it again, and was asleep within seconds.

4

A week before, because she had a finely trained mind and could ferret out closely guarded secrets, Quarr had been asked to investigate riots and incidents of unrest allegedly caused by an as-yet-unknown subversive group or cult. She welcomed the distraction because it helped alleviate the worry about Kryger's fate—where he'd ended up and whether he was still alive. Mike, the artificial intelligence with an acquired personality, had in his usual abrupt and matter-of-fact way, reported that contact with Kryger had gradually faded because of increased distance beyond Mike's reach.

Quarr, after a much-needed shower, stretched out naked on her bed. The weather was unusually hot, and her one-year-old son was with his grandmother until the case was solved. She was tired from constantly rushing around to investigate reported riots and so far had always arrived too late and, thus, hadn't picked up a single clue as to who had organized the disrupting incidences or for what purpose.

She was awakened from a dreamless sleep by a voice that repeatedly said in her sleeping mind, *Knock, knock, beautiful Quarr; wake up and listen to me.* She was alarmed because her mind was always shielded, even while she was sleeping. *Who are you, and how did you get through my shield?*

Trade secrets, lovely girl. I'm Getik, and I live on a planet we call Faraway, appropriately named so because it's far off the way of galactic traffic routes. I didn't intrude on your privacy, just wanted to get your attention to put your mind at ease. Kryger crash-landed on Faraway a few hours ago after one hell of a fight with a number of Bug ships. Please don't worry about him as we will take care of him and provide him with a new ship in a few weeks. I must add that the boy is quite a fighter. He was sent into a trap and narrowly escaped, but the Bugs followed right on his heels. I'm glad to inform you that quite a number of them expired when they caught up with him as he exited into normal space.

Thank you for the wonderful news, Mr. Getik. You truly have an exceptionally powerful mind to reach me. She put a warm feeling in her thoughts to show her appreciation, then was puzzled when she sensed a presence in the room.

Think nothing of it, love. We are masters of the mental and physical sciences, and we hope that the ship we are building will last longer than the last Bug. To explain briefly, I'm using a slightly different method of communication, and I'm here in the room with you in my astral form. If I get the time, I'll teach Kryger this method because it uses only a fraction of the energy expended in pure thought-exchange over very long distances.

Quarr didn't cover her body because it was clearly too late. If the entity was there in person, it would already have had an eyeful. She wasn't self-conscious, and it wouldn't make any difference to her dignity. A great worry had been taken from her mind, and now she could concentrate on her task. She had a sudden inspiration.

If you're that good, Mr. Getik, can you perhaps sense who or what is causing the unrest in our city?

We usually leave other people's problems for them to solve unless it directly concerns us, but I really like your husband. Give me a moment and I'll see what I can do as my time is very limited.

Quarr felt the presence disappear, but it was back almost immediately.

I have to leave right now to check up on Kryger, but I'll visit you in my physical form sometime if I can persuade your husband to let me tag along. I'll give Kryger your love, for I can sense it. As for your problem, I suggest that you check the Bug frequency right away. Bye now.

Before she could thank him, Quarr sensed she was alone again. *How did he know that I can reach the Bug frequency?* But she was wide-awake and decided to do what her surprise visitor had suggested.

She carefully tuned in to the Bug frequency and was just in time to intercept the last part of a fearful, strained conversation:...*Why do you punish your humble servant so severely because he doesn't know the location of his planet, Master? You already know, for you are omniscient. Why do you still have to test me? I'll do my utmost to find out to please you, just as I've gathered followers to do your will as you commanded. What more can you expect me to do?*

After a lengthy pause: *Gontstrat, you really test my patience to the utmost! I set you a simple task to teach you, and you fail me! I'll give you three of your days to obtain the coordinates of your planet, and if you fail me again, you will feel my displeasure. That's not too much to ask, is it? If I must do your thinking for you, I suggest that your followers create havoc at the place of such knowledge and that you break in under cover of it to acquaint yourself as to where in the universe you are! I command you to do so, and you must obey if you want the power to rule your planet, which only I can give you.*

The Bug abruptly cut communication to terrorize its so-called servant, but Quarr's wispy feeler stayed with the servant. She must know who he really was and where he lived. Bugs lacked the ability to reason and were incapable of that type of cunning. The pause indicated that it had a human adviser knowledgeable enough to advise it during such interrogations. The deception obviously was to locate the planet of their nemesis, Kryger.

When she was sure the Bug was gone from the mind of the duped traitor, she entered. She found bewilderment in an arrogant but anxious-to-please mind. Although she was repulsed by the horrible imaginations of brutal carnal orgies that would follow his rise to power, she delved deeper to find memories that could be of use to her to locate him. The man must be a criminal moron, she thought, to think he would get away with such disgusting acts. The most likely reward this half-wit would receive would be obliteration by a planet-busting bomb since the Bugs would go all out to destroy the planet and its population once they knew the location of Nevus.

Quarr had no compunction about delving deeply into the would-be world ruler's memories. This unscrupulous, egotistic character seemed to have below-average intelligence and was trying his best to boost his conceitedness by betraying a planet for imagined gain.

What she learned was, the dupe was a librarian with a knack for old languages. Years ago he had found some forgotten metaphysical books brought from Earth which he avidly studied. Believing he was specially favored because he had been brought up by a fanatically religious mother who doted on her only child, he began to experiment without adequate knowledge and preparation—and it backfired. He suffered a breakdown and his mind was impaired. He began to hear voices he believed to be especially for him from the Infinite Father. After a few weeks, during such conversations when he inadvertently formed an image of a cat-faced man in his mind and expressed his envy, the multitudinous voices suddenly stopped, and a single voice that asked penetrating questions regarding the cat-faced man he'd visualized took over.

Gontstrat was led to believe he was a favorite of the gods, that he would be given special powers on condition that he obeyed the voice of his master. He was promised unlimited power and any reward he might wish for, but first he had to come up with the galactic coordinates of the planet he lived on, which fortunately was withheld from the general population for just such an eventuality. When he told the voice that such information was closely guarded, he was instructed to gather followers and create incidents of unrest until he had enough influence to obtain the information. Rewards would follow success, and punishments for failures.

Quarr also gathered that he dearly wanted to fly like a bird to demonstrate his power to his small number of followers and quickly attract more, especially women. Feeling remorseless toward the unthinking, self-centered traitor of life on Nevus and ultimately the galaxy, she ruthlessly reinforced the wish to fly by planting the belief that he could do so when his followers gathered at ten that same morning in front of the six-story library building. He would appear on the roof, jump, and soar like an eagle to prove he was the chosen one to his still doubtful followers and all mockers. It was merciless but the only quick solution to squash the movement before it gathered momentum.

If he was only arrested along with his followers, he could still serve as a homing beacon when and if the Bug's adviser realized it could be done. The fall would be a fitting end for the destructive prophet, and an inglorious death would serve the purpose of destroying any belief that might linger on.

***

Quarr was up early, and first she cautiously touched the mind of the disgusting Gontstrat to make sure he was going to "demonstrate" the reinforced fancy that he could fly. She found that he was calling his adherents to gather at the library, promising they would see a demonstration of his bestowed powers precisely at ten o'clock. She arranged for a company of peacekeepers to meet her at a certain place a block away from the library at nine o'clock. While she was having breakfast, she reconsidered her decision to let Gontstrat leap to his death but came to the same conclusion.

Apparently the news had spread, for quite a crowd was gathered in the square when Quarr and the company of peacekeepers surreptitiously approached just after nine thirty. She noticed a tight, isolated group of about forty people off to one side who chased anyone away who approached too close. She scanned the mind of one to confirm her conclusion that they were Gontstrat's flock. Yes, they believed the drivel spewed forth by their self-proclaimed prophet and were keeping apart from the laity because, after this morning, they would be the proud elite.

Quarr directed the commander to have his people discreetly surround the group but close in and arrest them only when the "special event" they were waiting for ended in disaster.

At one minute to ten, a gaunt man clad only in a flimsy white toga appeared on top of the building. The sun was behind him and silhouetted his naked, scrawny body. *Oh my,* Quarr thought. *He wants the crowd to see that he doesn't have an antigravity device strapped on.*

Gontstrat proudly looked over the crowd and then at his watch. At precisely ten o'clock, he shouted in a commanding, carrying voice, "I am the chosen one! Behold the power given to me!"

He spread his arms, and the toga lifted like wings because it was fastened at his wrists and ankles. Then he leaped from the building. The toga billowed out like the wings of a bat as he plunged down—and then his plunge leveled out into flight. The crowd gasped. Perhaps it was because his naked, overly developed appendage was accentuated like a cancerous growth by the gauzy toga or because he really soared before he began to rise rapidly, straight up. His fading yell of terror was mistaken for a yell of exuberance, and his followers cheered.

Quarr too was momentarily taken by surprise. *Maybe my reinforcing his wish to soar freely was so potent that he suddenly acquired levitation,* she thought fleetingly, *but he doesn't know how to control it.*

Gontstrat was first going to freeze and then suffocate in the upper atmosphere long before he drifted into a low orbit.

But it wouldn't do because it could start a new cult, and the destructive riots might continue with increased vigor. She quickly reached into his terror-filled mind and totally negated the cell-acceleration process. She fortunately knew how to do it since Kryger had taught her what he'd learned from the young priestess on Okryon. Otherwise she would have sent a bolt into his mind to stop him.

He stopped rising and then plunged straight down, screaming his head off in terror. The suddenly panicked crowd scattered in all directions because it seemed to everyone that the screaming man would fall on top of them. Quarr signaled the commander to arrest the group before they scattered. As the peacekeepers surrounded the group, there was a sickening splat toward the edge of the square.

The body had narrowly missed a man who hopped away like a jumping hare while he continuously tried to scream his lungs out with shock. Quarr reached into his mind and calmed him down. *That should curb his inquisitiveness permanently*, she thought and then went to make sure no innocents were trapped with the late Gontstrat's followers.

She briefly pitied Gontstrat's mother—if she was still alive—but the planet's safety was at stake. The best people were fighting and dying out there to keep this planet from being rediscovered by the enemy's minions. She silently thanked the entity who called himself Getik and who, apparently with little effort, gave her such an easy solution. *That guy really knows his stuff*, she thought. *Nevus might have been betrayed within the next couple of days.*

She couldn't help smiling when she overheard the captain, quite seriously, tell one of his men to "get a shovel and a bucket and scrape this mess off the pavement." Then she took a broken miniature antigravity device out of one of her pockets and asked the captain to let the media know it was found in the impostor's body.

5

Getik, when he returned to the elevator, felt elated because chance had given him a reason to start living again and not to just slog along for the rest of his life. He wondered where Kryger and Quarr came from because he knew of no cat-faced race without tails, but that was private information he couldn't dig for. He really liked the respectful boy, and he'd sensed that the lovely Quarr really appreciated the news and the little push in the right direction. She was an exceptional beauty with an astonishingly advanced mind.

He felt changeover beginning and visually checked that the sleeping boy was strapped down properly. He was intrigued and wondered what the boy had gone through to make him such a dangerous being—ever alert even when he was sleeping—but he also sensed an innate gentleness and a great respect for life. He became aware that Kryger was disturbed and beginning to wake up. He took a chance and sent a wispy, calming thought into Kryger's mind.

There's nothing to worry about, boy; stay asleep. It's only the changeover starting, and you're adequately protected. Then he instinctively shielded his mind tightly, for he expected a backlash.

But he saw Kryger relax was surprised by the gratefulness he felt. Getik felt protective toward the unique young Bug destroyer more than twice his size. He wished the boy, his wife, and his son could be his new family and his deceased family could now rest in peace. He settled down to pass the next hour or so in contemplative thought.

When he cautiously told Kryger to wake up a few minutes before the elevator arrived on the inner surface, he was impressed by the boy's immediate alertness. Getik's people had never been in any kind of war, and he wondered what kind of upbringing or circumstances could make someone so instantly vigilant.

You aren't shielded, sir. It depends on where I am and what I sense as I wake up. It's a subconscious, automatic instinct drilled into me from early childhood that has kept me alive. I only fear killing a non-Sensitive by mistake, but so far it hasn't happened.

Getik smiled. *I was able to contact Quarr, son. I sensed her love for you, and she was relieved to hear that you're still in one piece. We're going to stop in a moment. Mind your head because our doorways are on the low side.*

He didn't mind Getik calling him son because he'd sensed the man's kindness and respect. The elevator came to a gradual, silent standstill. They traversed a fairly long corridor that, Getik explained, was carved out of a low mountain, the perception depending on one's size, of course. Kryger appreciated the dry humorous tone.

As they turned a corner and reached the outside, Kryger saw a fairly large boat resting under a huge tree close to the exit. He wondered what a boat was doing so far from water, and he thought Getik was joking when he went straight to it, got in, and seated himself at the controls.

Seeing Kryger's perplexity, Getik laughed and said, *Get in and drop your bags. We used to have flying platforms but changed to boat form when a child fell overboard and lost his life. We don't have many children, for we don't intend to overcrowd this planet. We have a long life span and don't want to draw attention by expanding to other planets and live on the outside exposed to Bugs, seasons, and all that go with it. And yes, this flying boat can land on water too if you want to go for a swim or do some fishing. It uses antigravity principles, and we didn't make it fast, as we never rush anywhere.*

Kryger smiled, then yawned hugely, politely hiding it behind a hand.

We don't have far to go, son. The decrepit councilors can't wait to meet you, and then I'll see to it that you sleep afterward until you wake up naturally. They'll want to explain a few things they think you need to know right away.

Kryger was glad he wasn't dodging Bugs on the outer surface and accepted where destiny had temporarily taken him. These tiny humans seemed to know more about the Hullenii Bugs than Quarr's people or what his own people could deduce so far from analysis of the carcasses. He intuited that he could learn a few things that might help him drastically reduce the Bug population.

As the boat rose above the lofty trees, Kryger saw the sun, which was about the size of a ten-story building. *Your sun is bright, but I scarcely feel any heat on my skin.*

Our sun has no harmful rays, and one can get quite close to it—with one's eyes protected, of course. There are no seasons here, but we have a nighttime period as we haven't adapted to perpetual sunlight. Even the native races – those we know of – rest at regular intervals. They crawl under a heavily shaded bush or into a hut, but we darken our houses. I'll show you around later.

The boat was similar to the sleds Kryger was used to. Even the controls were more or less the same. He sensed that Getik expected a few questions about the boat that soared effortlessly above the huge old trees of a seemingly endless forest, but he felt disinclined to talk, although he commented on the seemingly untouched forest. The trees were abnormally huge, even more so than those in "Mike's jungle".

Getik seemed pleased. *Yes, they've been untouched for unknown millennia. We do not want to disturb the natural balance and only take what we need from the forest, usually only fallen giants. We leave the rest alone as there are a few native races in the developing stages that inhabit the forest. Our city is hidden by the trees, and only a few buildings can be seen from the air.*

As if it was an afterthought, he added, *We leave the other races alone to develop naturally at their own pace, in their own way. As you know, we learned a very expensive lesson with the Bugs.*

After a few minutes, Getik pointed ahead. *The antennae-covered building in front of us is our central control station. It also houses our council because they need to be close to make so-called instant decisions if any threat that may concern us is encountered by the spotter stations at the two entrances.* He chuckled. *So far it hasn't happened.*

Don't let the senile old fossils bully you, son. You're important to us and the universe, and if you need anything, just let me know, and we'll see what can be done. The ship that will take you anywhere in the universe is almost ready, and I'll take you to it soon enough.

Kryger managed to grin. *I gather that you don't like the council much.*

Oh, I can tolerate them—in a way—but it's a question of respect. They think they know all there is to know about human nature and that no one else does, and they're far too arrogant for their own good. Although I'm the designing engineer of your ship, they treat me as if I can't think for myself. You'll see in a moment what I mean. By the way, we'll stay in the building until you're rested and have been educated in our language and customs.

Getik's tone was more amused than aggrieved. He took the boat down quite sharply and landed in front of the small building. Getik explained that most of the building was underground, as was the rest of the city.

Kryger followed Getik up the few stairs and through a maze of corridors he automatically memorized. After a few minutes, they arrived before a closed door that Getik, with a mischievous grin at Kryger, just opened without knocking and walked through, leaving the door wide-open behind him. The three councilors, who seemed to be busy doing nothing at all, looked up at the ill-mannered intrusion and were visibly irritated when they saw who it was.

"Oh, it's the half-naked, uncivilized recluse again. Can't you learn to at least knock before you enter," one of the two men remarked sharply in an unfamiliar language, but Kryger understood the supercilious thoughts behind the sarcastic words.

"I'm addled in the top story; don't you remember, respected *Councilor*?" His tone was mockingly ironic. "I was under the impression that you were overly anxious to meet the prodigy from outer space, *Councilors*, so I brought the boy directly to you as we were instructed to do. His name is Kryger."

At that moment, Kryger, who'd sensed the unspoken request to delay an instant, shuffled in slowly. He heard three audible gasps and then clicks as their mouths snapped shut. They hadn't expected such a young superbly muscled giant, and the trio were evidently caught by surprise. They were overly dressed as befitted their office, Kryger thought. He stopped next to Getik and made a small bow with his upper body while maintaining eye contact. They were clearly advanced in age, and he respected that but dropped the rucksacks with a thud as he detested their attitude of moral superiority. He sensed Getik's approval.

"Welcome, young giant. We were expecting you," the elderly woman who completed the threesome said in an authoritative voice.

Kryger again understood the thoughts behind the words, but following Getik's cue, he replied politely in his own language, "Sorry, I don't speak your language." He sensed that Getik had a hard time suppressing an amused giggle.

The old woman developed a slightly pink tinge in the face but didn't apologize. She sent a direct thought to Kryger instead: *Can you mind-converse, young giant?*

Of course, Councilor, he kept the tone of his thoughts respectful as it would be impolite to antagonize the councilor. *It's the only way one can overcome the language barrier, and it's how my guide, Getik, contacted me at first to explain the situation;*

otherwise I would have taken my chances with the Bugs on the outer surface.

Ah, you're a headstrong, independent youngster. I like that. The woman smiled for the first time, and it almost made her attractive. *We seldom mind-speak to each other, and I sometimes forget that strangers may not be conversant in our language. Oh, my manners! I'm Tirr, and this is Councilors Pebis and Kolvak.* She pointed to each in turn. Kryger nodded and locked eyes briefly with each of them as they were introduced. *Welcome, Kryger.*

Her authoritative manner had changed, and Kryger smiled at her, but the smile turned into a huge yawn he hastily hid behind an open hand.

I'm sorry, Kryger; we won't keep you. We'll teach you our language while you're sleeping, and your developing brain could be enhanced as well.

Kryger interrupted her by raising a hand. *Please don't. I must warn you in all seriousness that to try and enter my mind or physically touch me when I'm asleep would be suicide. I am trained to automatically react violently. I agree that I still have a lot to learn, but please do your teaching when I'm awake, and even then only with my prior knowledge. Please take this warning seriously.*

The councilors looked at one another in disbelief. Getik knew that anything he said would be taken as a challenge. Kryger sensed their doubt. *I understand your disbelief, Councilors. You won't stop a mind-bolt, however powerful you are. It's the way I've killed many Bugs, and I can't control the automatic responses unless I'm fully conscious. My people live in constant danger, and we've learned to protect ourselves in a number of ways.*

Tirr looked at him again, but the disbelief was plainly written on her face. She decided to humor the youngster. *Okay, young man; if that's the way you want it, I'll respect your warning. Getik, I take it that you'll see to the boy's needs. Apartment five has been set aside for you, complete with cook and housekeeper. You may go now.* She smiled at Kryger again. *We'll talk again when you're rested.*

6

Getik gave them an inscrutable look and turned without a word. He gestured Kryger to precede him out. This time he closed the door, but hardly gently. Getik hastily passed Kryger and led him to a nearby unit that had been prepared for their huge—to them—guest.

The heavy curtains were already drawn, and Kryger dropped his rucksacks and weapons in a corner, warned Getik not to touch the personalized weapons, and stretched out on the double layer of piled-together mattresses. He sunk deeply into the bedding but ignored the resilience and went to sleep as soon as his head touched the attempt for a pillow.

Getik took a thorough look at the young man's face for the first time. He saw a tired, stern, yet kind half-feline, half-human face. Even in sleep his full lips were firmly, determinedly pressed together, and his mouth—as a matter of fact, his whole face—showed a rock-hard resoluteness that would chill any enemy to the bone. *I'd hate to see you angry, son, and I'm glad we got off on the right foot,* he thought. *I can't help but respect and admire you, boy.*

He was about to close the door as a precaution when the housekeeper entered the apartment. He knew her quite well. "Hi, Gorsmat," he said in a whisper, holding his forefinger against his mouth in the universal signal for silence. "The boy just fell asleep and mustn't be disturbed for any reason. I'm guessing he'll sleep for at least two sleeping periods, so you might as well go about your own business, and I'll let you know when he wakes up. Is that okay?"

"Sure, no problem," she whispered. "Can I take a quick peek at him before I go? I'm dying to see my first alien, and it's hard to believe that he's still a boy, as you pointed out."

Getik suddenly realized that the door couldn't be locked for various reasons and that she might arrive and open it to satisfy her curiosity when he might not be around—with possible fatal consequences. He must let her see Kryger and then try to trust her. "Okay, but give me your word that you won't open this door whether I'm here or not?" He stood aside, holding the door half-open, and she nodded and then tiptoed closer.

To her credit, she suppressed an astonished gasp, and Kryger stayed motionless because his subconscious sensed Getik's friendly thoughts and presence. She drew back after a few seconds, and Getik silently pulled the door closed.

"Thank you, Getik," Gorsmat whispered with awe in her voice. "He's a giant, but strangely, very beautiful. I like him. He'll be starved when he wakes because, although I can see the exhaustion on his face, I sense that he sleeps as wary as one of those big jungle cats when it's hungry. I think I'm going to enjoy cooking for him. What's his name?"

Getik was surprised by her perceptiveness. He relaxed and smiled. "And I can assure you that your cooking skills will be thoroughly tested. I know that he's hungry, but he would have fallen asleep with his face in the dish after the first bite, and even with your help I won't have the strength to drag him. If you're asked, just tell your friends that he's big, and don't invent anything because you might have to swallow your words later on. Okay?"

Gorsmat smiled too. "Yes, and thank you again. There are enough ready-to-use supplies here to feed two huge starved jungle cats for a day or two. I know you can cook a little if need be, so if you have to wait for me for any reason, you can help yourself, or you can order something from the restaurant."

"I will." Getik lifted a hand in farewell as he turned into the kitchen. After all the talking about food, he was also quite hungry.

When the door closed behind Getik, Kolvak snorted through his nose. "That youngster sure has an inflated opinion of himself and his mental abilities. *'Please believe me; I'll fry your brains,'*" he mimicked and derisively snorted once again. "He's plainly unaware that he's a mental infant compared to us. Won't he be surprised when he wakes up and speaks our language," he said and cackled.

"Strangely enough...I believed him in the end," Tirr replied. "I sensed his utter sincerity, that he was convinced of what he said. Although he'll sleep like a log, I really think we should take the warning seriously and let him be. He developed on different lines than ours and might be capable of doing just what he said. I'm not in favor of taking chances just to prove a point."

"Okay, stay out of it, then. What's your stance, Pebis?"

"That unmannered, despicable moron seems to have taken a liking to the boy. To teach him a lesson he won't forget, I'll link with you as we've done many times before when we had to teach a half savage the basics of our language within minutes. If we detect or sense the so-called mind-bolt coming, we'll merge our shields and deflect whatever it is easily enough. After all, we are the very best."

"You think? I wish you luck, but if your brains do get fried, then what?" Tirr replied icily as she realized the two were envious of Getik. "Why endanger yourselves to prove something of no importance? There are other ways—faster and more thorough—to teach the young giant what we think he should be taught."

"We won't be blasted, sweetheart, and we'll take the credit and rub the boy's, Getik's, and your noses in it."

"I've never realized what arrogant braggarts both of you idiots are!" This time it was Tirr who snorted derisively. "Remember the Bugs? Our ancestors were sure they could handle them too...and this boy fries their brains with his mind power when he confronts one of them. That should make you morons think twice."

"You've been told a lot of nonsense. It's not the same, and we're not Bugs; we can reason. Just wait and see."

"While I wait, I might as well start thinking of replacements for two senile old clunkers," she shot back, then got up and walked out of the room when they laughed mockingly.

She met Getik outside the apartment assigned to him and Kryger. The door that led to one bedroom was closed. In a fierce whisper, he said, "I hope you're not here to disturb the boy's sleep with stupid questions. Don't you have enough intelligence to heed the boy's warning?"

"No, I came to ask you a sincere question," she quietly replied. "If the occasion warrants it, would you serve as councilor, even if it's just temporarily?"

Getik looked at her as if she'd taken leave of her senses. "What are you talking about, Councilor Tirr? I'm not in the mood for jokes even though you think that I'm muddle-headed."

"I'm serious, Getik. I'm forever annoyed with your deliberate bad manners, but I know you have exceptional insight and talents."

"The answer would be an emphatic no. Why do you ask?"

Tirr's face turned pink because Getik's tone was a brush-off and a little too impolite. He might at least have considered the honor of being approached for such a prominent appointment at his age. She replied brusquely but kept her voice down: "Because those arrogant imbeciles won't heed the boy's warning and are going to stimulate his brain while he's asleep." She finished the sentence although Getik had left her in a run, heading for the very room she had just left. She followed as speedily as she could manage, wondering what he was going to do. Nothing too violent, she hoped.

She bumped into his back and knocked him forward with her momentum because he was standing just inside the opened door. Then she could see what had brought him to such an abrupt halt. Kolvak and Pebis were sprawled on their backs on the floor, still half seated in their overturned easy chairs. It was quite obvious that they were lifeless, but the expressions of astonishment were equally noticeable on their faces. Both were lying in spreading pools of urine, and there was an unpleasant smell in the large room.

"They only had enough time to be surprised," Tirr almost screamed with mounting agitation. "What am I going to do? I don't know how to handle this."

"If you implicate the boy in any way, I'll pin you on your back and bash you to death as slowly and as painfully as I possibly can; you hear me? The oldsters can't complain because they were warned, and they just got what they asked for. Let's go check on the boy first and then decide how to handle this mess. I say 'we' because I'll accept your invitation, but only on a temporary basis as an adviser while we look for suitable replacements for these two has-beens." He pulled the door shut as a precaution although there were rarely any visitors for the councilors. His mind was in a spin with worry about Kryger. He didn't know how to handle the situation either but realized he needed time to gather his wits and think it through after he'd checked up on his ward.

Tirr marveled at Getik's resolute calmness and wondered why she had ignored the middle-aged man for so long since his mind power was visibly superior to that of her late colleagues. Perhaps she was influenced by their intolerance of the quiet scientist she had first met. It could be that they had sensed and recognized Getik's superior intelligence long before she did. Anyway, that was water under the bridge, and she'd better follow Getik's lead until she was over the mind-numbing shock.

She was quiet as she accompanied the scientist to his and Kryger's temporary quarters. Getik listened in front of Kryger's door but was careful not to create the impression that he was doing it furtively when he quietly opened it. The boy was tossing agitatedly in his sleep, and his face was drained of color and energy. Getik calmly, quietly projected a thought at the boy as he'd done in the transit elevator.

It's okay, son; it was just an unfortunate nightmare. Go back to sleep. Kryger visibly relaxed and quieted down immediately. Getik gently closed the door again when Tirr, who'd peeped over his shoulder, had backed out of the way.

"You have the boy's trust, it seems," she whispered. "I misjudged you all along, until a short time ago when you presented him to us. I'm sorry, Getik. I blame those two envious ex-colleagues of mine. I now understand clearly that I allowed them to influence me. As I belatedly realize—they were afraid of being asked to stand down and lose the privileges and respect they enjoyed as councilors. I can only offer you my sincere apologies."

"It's irrelevant," Getik replied in a normal voice since they were halfway back to the council chamber. "What is important to me is, How are we going to explain two simultaneous deaths without involving the boy? Because that boy is more important than a billion decrepit old fossils. In fact, the boy is the only one in this galaxy capable of totally destroying the monsters our ancestors created. You know the predictions and how we are preparing to help Kryger do what we should have done millennia ago."

"Yes. I'm still in shock, I guess, and I can't think coherently. Have you any suggestions?"

"I have to think it through thoroughly because my mind is in a spin. Let's go to the canteen and have something to eat and drink, and don't disturb me with idle talk while we're there. The door to the council chamber must be left unlocked because it would be suspicious if someone comes around and finds it locked. In fact, I think it might be fortunate if someone finds them while we are at the canteen because then we can act flabbergasted."

She nodded and, without a word, turned and led the way to the canteen as befitted her status.

There was no crime and no police of any kind on Faraway, just a number of individuals halfheartedly trained in specific tasks in the event that those duties were called for. Still, two simultaneous deaths in a council of three were most unusual and might raise awkward questions. The cause of their demise could not be made public since there were always those holier-than-thou moralists who—if they heard about Kryger's strange ability and his warning to the meddlesome old coots—would clamor for investigation and retribution just to feel important because they were too ignorant to think or care about the consequences. They'd dismiss the fact that the duo were responsible for their own deaths. In addition, there were professional medics who could establish the cause of death in suspicious or unusual circumstances. It was this dilemma that was thrust upon Getik to find a plausible solution for.

He told Tirr, "Treat me as if you're the reluctant host and order yourself something to eat. I'd also like a substantial meal because I haven't eaten anything for the last twenty hours or more, and I've been on my feet for double that time. Don't behave out of character since it would arouse suspicion if we're suddenly chummy-chummy. If we're talking when someone comes within earshot, we'll say something about the just arrived sleeping boy or our progress with the ship." Then something clicked in his mind, and he had an inkling of what they should do.

"Okay, and I'll force myself to eat although I'm really not up for it." Now that she looked closely, she could see the tiredness in his eyes.

"That's important and essential! You do the ordering and the talking while I do the thinking. Don't be upset if I don't answer when you address me."

A waitress approached immediately, her eyes riveted on Tirr because she was the most important person on the planet. Luckily the canteen was almost empty, and she took them to a secluded table at the back when they asked for privacy.

As soon as the waitress left to fulfill Tirr's order, Getik said in a soft voice, "I'm more tired than I realized because the solution is so obvious that I nearly overlooked it. The boy is asleep—you, Gorsmat, and I are witness to that—so nobody can point a finger at him. We can only hope that someone else discovers the deceased yesteryears; otherwise you'll have to 'discover' them when you leave here. Just don't scream loud enough to wake the boy.

"Act upset, and don't say anything about Kryger's warning. Don't even think about it! You don't have the faintest idea of how they died so suddenly in your absence or what they were doing while you treated me to a meal for bringing the boy in. Is that clear enough, and can you manage it?"

"Yes, and thank you. I'll be really upset when I see their stupid faces again, so I won't have to act." Tirr looked up and smiled at the approaching waitress to warn Getik.

Getik also heard the pitter-patter of the waitress's sandals as she approached and wasn't caught off guard. "Ah, yes," he said as if replying to a question, "the boy can sleep until he wakes up naturally since the first test of the ship won't be until three or four weeks from now. It may be a good deed to manufacture a hard, appropriately sized mattress as he said he snores on such soft, hastily sewn-together bedding," he said when the waitress placed a platter of food and a glass of wine before Tirr and then before him. He thanked her and then asked Tirr's permission to start eating, adding that he knew it was impolite but that he was starved.

Tirr smiled and nodded, but the waitress didn't move. She said "Excuse me, Councilor Tirr. The rumor that the alien had arrived seems to be true, and we'd all like to see him. Will there be an opportunity?"

It was an ideal opportunity, and Getik waited to see how Tirr would handle it.

Tirr smiled again and said in a regretful voice, "He's not here for show, but there will be many opportunities for people to gape at him. He's still a very young man but big, more than twice our size. Unfortunately he was so tired that he almost went to sleep on his feet when we councilors tried to talk to him. He just made it to his makeshift bed and summarily fell asleep. We expect that he'll sleep for a few working periods; he's that tired." She smiled again, and Getik thought the smile suited her.

The waitress thanked her and then left with a happy half-grin. She was the talkative kind. Getik stopped chewing, swallowed, and told her, "You handled that perfectly. The news will spread rapidly, so that's one worry off our minds. We also have curious onlookers that clearly overheard the conversation. Now eat, even if you choke on the salad. Have my glass of wine if you want."

She smiled broadly. "You're enough to drive me to drink at my age. Pass it over; I'm beginning to like your impertinence."

7

By the surprised looks on their faces, the medics concluded that the deceased councilors had probably experimented with something they couldn't handle. They didn't find any signs that pointed to an unnatural cause of death, so there were no autopsies or repercussions.

Kryger slept for nearly thirty hours. As soon as he was awake, he checked if the vague, impersonal presence he'd felt since he crash-landed was still bothering him but found no trace of anything unusual. He was sure it wasn't his imagination. He also had an uneasy feeling that something had happened during his sleep but shrugged it off since he couldn't remember and it didn't seem important.

He washed his face in a small basin in a corner of the room and then opened the door. His nose led him to the kitchen, where he found Getik in the company of a plumpish woman who introduced herself as Gorsmat, one of the best cooks on the planet.

Gorsmat gave Kryger her best smile and said that, although it was deemed only midmorning, she was ready with enough of a meal to satisfy any hungry giant. True to his upbringing, Kryger acted so politely and respectfully toward her that she hovered around him like a broody hen seeing to the needs of her giant chicken. If Getik was amused, it wasn't obvious, but pride of his ward showed in his attitude, as if he were taking credit for Kryger's courteous manners.

After Kryger took a brisk walk to get the stiffness out of his body, Getik took him to Tirr. On Getik's advice, she had moved to a different room from the previous day so as not to remind Kryger of the two "docs," which, Getik had explained to her, was short for "deceased old codgers." Tirr didn't mention them at all when she asked pertinent questions to test the extent of Kryger's expertise and training and was astounded by his wide-ranging, in-depth knowledge.

She felt ashamed when she realized the bigoted, superior attitude she and her ex-colleagues had so arrogantly adopted and hesitantly recommended that Kryger first learn their language to be at ease with people he'd meet. She'd learned her lesson the hard way and, rather than evoke Getik's biting sarcasm, asked him to evaluate Kryger and then arrange for education in whatever he deemed necessary.

The language session took only five hours, after which they went back to their temporary quarters. Getik was astounded by the effort Gorsmat had put into the preparation of an early supper but wisely kept his mouth shut and listened while Kryger did the complimenting in his newly acquired language. After the sumptuous meal, Getik took him to the museum, which was situated on the edge of an open, parklike space where people came to relax, let their children play in organized games, or just simply gossip.

"Having been born on the inside and living here for generation after generation, most people are afraid to venture to the outer surface, especially at night," Getik explained. "For first-timers, it's really intimidating to see the far horizon dropping away into a haze of heat waves instead of curving upward, and in the near pitch darkness of night, the faraway stars and the great void above are frightening for the uninitiated. Most collapse at the sight of nothing above them except emptiness and a distant sun. Then they refuse to ever venture topside again, and we call them permanent insiders. It takes a courageous, adventurous type of person to volunteer for topside duty, but there's no shortage of such individuals, men or women."

"I guess it's not difficult to understand. I know quite a few people who won't get into any type of vehicle that leaves the ground," Kryger mused. "It's a question of how a person is raised, how their parents indoctrinated them. I would, for instance, find it difficult to adapt to a peaceful, humdrum existence. I can't imagine a life free of conflict and, for instance, trying to farm for a livelihood, although I love the solitude of what us Nevusians call the Wasteland. Am I explaining things clearly and effectively in your language?"

"Yes, quite well. You seem to even think in it already. I should teach you a few swear words so you can properly express your opinion when needed."

Kryger laughed. "Yes, that will be useful. It's usually the first words I learn in any language."

Getik grinned mischievously as they entered the huge museum. The first thing Kryger saw on the left-side wall of the entrance was a series of life-size paintings. The first one presented a human, roughly Getik's size, shining a multicolored ray of light over an egg a little larger than a pigeon's, while a Hullenii Bug, about the size of a fully grown rabbit standing on its hind legs, looked on. The next picture depicted the egg hatching, and successive pictures showed the Bug increase in size until it dwarfed the human.

"These pictures are to remind us of our ancestors' folly," Getik said. "They used a growth ray on Hullenii eggs. Now we can't even risk destroying Hullenii eggs for fear of being discovered."

"Is it possible to reverse the process? I mean, develop a ray to reverse the little bugger's growth before it hatches?"

Getik stopped so suddenly that Kryger bumped into him and had to grab him by the shoulders to prevent him from being knocked over. Getik continued as if he didn't even notice the bumping and grabbing.

"You know, son, we focused so much on destroying them that none of us thought of such a logical solution. Such tampering with their eggs won't be noticed or suspected in broad daylight. Awesome! Excuse me a moment." He sat on one of the numerous benches and closed his eyes.

Kryger wandered away to look at some of the other exhibitions. Getik was quiet and motionless for a few minutes. Then he opened his eyes and got up to join Kryger. "I was asked to thank you. The scientists concerned think that it should take about thirty to forty hours to get such a ray operational and into position. It led to another thought, namely to develop another ray to render the Bugs themselves infertile, but they might sense such a ray, so it will be tried only if your idea fails."

"Quarr calls it overlooking the obvious, which happened to us quite a number of times and led to pretty useful inventions."

"She's a lovely woman blessed with a superb brain, but let's forget history for the moment and go soak up sunlight for a while. I suddenly need it."

"That would suit me perfectly, sir, especially since I'm cooped up in narrow cockpits for extended periods. I should take advantage of your 'special' sun while I can. I might never be back to enjoy it." He was still clad in his shorts and had nothing else to wear.

"I'd like to go with you when you leave. No one else knows the ship inside out like me. I designed every component of it down to the bolts and rivets. If you permit me, it's quite possible that we will never return. The ship will soon be ready for its first test flight. Then we only need to identify and assemble your crew on the various planets as per the prophecy, although the entities concerned are not aware of their destiny and might need some persuasion.

"Okay, it's quite a complicated story," he added when Kryger looked at him as if he'd lost his marbles, "but all will be explained by Councilor Tirr in due course. The ship needs four gunners and maybe a cook and an engineer. Our problem was that we don't have any knowledge or record of real warfare, so we had to guess what would be needed by studying old adventure novels left behind by older generations. I suspect that we might have miscalculated, but you can tell us where we have to make corrections."

Kryger got the impression that he was regarded as a willing pawn in a preordained cosmic game, and although the so-called prediction amused him, it also annoyed him a little. They, whoever "they" were, would find out he was his own person with ideas backed by knowledge and experience. However, he would play along for the time being since he wanted to get home.

"Prophecies, to my knowledge, are only probabilities that might occur when certain conditions are met or adhered to without deviation and circumstances don't change. It implies no free choice. It's all very well for you to speculate about a fighting ship and a crew, sir, but only people born on Nevus can withstand the gravities that have to be endured in what we call a dogfight, which is a vicious free-for-all-comers battle between fighting craft. Of what use will an unconscious crew be?"

"Hah, but you see, that is what makes the ship we are building so unique. Every position, including the pilot's and copilot's areas, even the small kitchen, has individual gravity neutralizers that can be preset to a preferred gravity because the individuals we are to collect would be used to different gravities. Nobody will feel any increase in gravitational pressure once it is set, no matter what the pilot does or what happens to the ship, as long as the power source isn't damaged, which is extremely unlikely. Only the cook will have to be careful of spillage during fighting maneuvers, and the others may become a bit dizzy if you get a little too wild. That's all there is to it!"

"So it's a big ungainly ship, an easy target for beams and missiles?"

"No, not at all. Okay, to us it's fairly big but compact and functional—no wasted space. It's got advanced shielding technology for protection," Getik announced proudly.

"I hope the shield or shields automatically create holes when a gun or missile is fired from inside instead of having to switch the entire shield off first."

Getik stopped in his tracks. "What are you talking about? That's not possible."

"It is, and we've been using the technology on all our ships for the last two years since Quarr came up with the idea. It's really quite a simple technique."

"Okay, so how is it supposed to work?"

"Let me ask you the obvious: If your ship can fly with its shield or shields on, how do you create an opening for the propellant to escape to push the ship?"

"I know what you're talking about, but we don't use that type of engine or shield. Our engines work on a different principle to accelerate."

"Okay, but if I have to switch off a shield or shields to be able to fight, then the craft is useless because it will be too vulnerable, especially when the ship is surrounded by a host of enemies vying with each other to be the one who destroys it. I'd rather have the type of shield I'm used to because the opening for firing a gun or missile works on the same principle as the permanent opening for the driving force to push the craft forward. The moment you fire a gun or a missile, an opening is automatically created, lasting only long enough to let the bolt or missile through. The majority of our fights are not against Bug ships but against huge fleets of their suicidal minions with ships of all sizes armed to the teeth. It's only on my forced flight here to escape certain death that the Bugs, for the first time, exposed their precious carapaces to danger because they thought that they had me cornered. If they had the ability to think ahead, they'd have had me. Only ability and pure luck saved me."

When they reached the park, Getik stopped and turned around. "Wait a moment while I consult with the shield experts. Our armament could very well be inadequate. I think you should see the ship as soon as possible and give us your opinion and advice. If we can't adapt our shield, we should still have records of the older types of shields. I have to sit down since this needs concentration and may take a while." He sat out of the way on the grass close to a shrub and closed his eyes.

Kryger didn't sense anything but heard a stealthy tread close behind him and felt a slight displacement of air. There wasn't time to think. He instinctively whipped around while raising his left arm as if to fend off a blow to his face. He wasn't surprised when he blocked a descending arm. He automatically turned his wrist, grabbed the attacker's arm, and pulled forward with all his strength to unbalance his assailant.

The body attached to the arm was quite heavy, but its momentum helped him to pull it over his hip. He didn't let go when it landed in front of him on its back with a loud *whop* and a forced expelling of breath. His right fist was already traveling to where the neck should be to deliver a killing blow when he realized it was a naked female of a catlike species and that the hand was only a fist without a weapon. He sensed no hostility, but his fist touched her silky neck before he could stop and stayed there for a breathless second before he released his hold, took a deep breath, straightened warily, and stepped back without taking his eyes off her while his senses ranged about the immediate area.

Humanlike brown eyes wide with shock looked up at him, but Getik yelled angrily, "Dammit, Sheeftag! Why did you have to choose this moment to play your silly games? Couldn't you sense that I was starting an important conversation? You nearly got killed, and for what?"

The catlike girl turned her face toward Getik. "I'm sorry. It was an ideal opportunity and I couldn't resist. When I saw the two of you approaching, deep in conversation, I removed my weapons belt to be noiseless. This human proved far superior. I will follow him." She looked up at Kryger. "You are faster and more powerful than I imagined. I felt the power of your nearly landed punch, and I'm shocked at my narrow escape from certain death. I can't believe that you had the control to stop when you did." She leaped up with a catlike jump, away from Kryger, arching and swishing her long tail as if shaking the dust off.

"You're one of the few lucky ones as I'm not used to silly pranks. Next time you might not be so lucky." He was angry, but it was under control, and only a slight tightening of his lips showed it.

"We're disturbing Getik, so let's move away." He walked farther into the open space with Sheeftag on his heels. He might as well be occupied while Getik found out if their ship was of any use as a fighting craft. "Physical strength is only important when personal survival depends on it," he continued, "but a leader must be able to outthink opposition and adversaries. He must plan ahead, anticipate possible problems, and be ready for emergencies. I can't judge because I don't know your people, but that's more or less what we require from a leader before we will follow him. Brute strength isn't of any use to a leader, except maybe in a primitive society to keep underlings from stepping out of line. What did you mean when you said that you'll follow me?"

"I'll be your copilot, and I'll follow your instructions because you bested me. You won't have any back talk from me, I promise."

Kryger's heart sank through his bare feet into the strange matted grass because he sensed and knew from experience that she lacked the fierce fighting spirit that refused to surrender, as required in a war pilot, but he asked, "How long and what have you been flying, and can you shoot a gun with any accuracy while dodging enemies?"

"I've been practicing in a simulator and flying airboats. Yes, I have used a gun, but my ears are sensitive, so I prefer silent weapons such as spears, knives, or a silent ray gun. I only fought against opponents about a dozen times in personal combat," she told him quite innocently but sincerely.

He turned away and had a hard time not laughing aloud but disguised it as a fit of coughing. He didn't know whether he should laugh uproariously or cry. Come to think of it, How much did Getik's people know about combat in the sky or in space? The answer was, of course, sweet blow all.

"Let's wait here for Getik," he managed to say with a straight face and a tight clamp on his thoughts just on the off chance this artless creature might be a good Sensitive. He flopped down on crossed legs, and she followed his example.

8

Getik joined them a few minutes later. "If you are ready, we should go to the workshop so that you can see the craft. The shield is an impenetrable field of force, and they don't think that holes can be created to fire any type of gun or missiles through. There's a boat here at the museum we can use, and if we go as we are, we should be there in a little over two hours."

Kryger suggested that Sheeftag take control but wasn't impressed by the delicate way she handled the boat as if she was afraid she might do something wrong. He didn't know how to broach the subject of her inexperience and unsuitableness to be a space pilot without making an enemy. He'd have to wait for the appropriate moment when they were alone to ask Getik how in the world they expected such a timid creature to handle a spacecraft in battle. She'd very likely fall to pieces when things got too hectic.

Worried about his own inexperience with controlling a crew, he didn't enjoy the unusual other-world scenery and was relieved when they arrived at the remote site, situated under enormous trees. He asked the obvious question: "Why so far from the city?"

"The special ore used to construct the craft is mined and smelted close by. The sheets must be shaped while it is poured because the strange metal, once set, cannot be cut or reshaped by any means we know of. It was thought to be more inexpensive to do it here, away from interference, and the huge hangar was already here, built ages ago by a long-vanished civilization and still in excellent working order. So we find it convenient to use." He seemed quite proud of their accomplishment.

Kryger nodded. They were expected, and as soon as Sheeftag landed the boat in front of the huge doors, a side door opened, and a friendly group emerged as if on cue.

They were obviously taken aback by Kryger's size when he stood to step out of the boat. He smiled when he heard a few whistles of surprise but knew how to put people at ease.

"Don't be intimidated by my size, sirs and ladies. Believe it or not, where I come from, I'm considered a shorty," which was close to the truth and evoked laughter as intended. "I am Kryger, as you undoubtedly already know."

Kryger's easy manner helped them relax, and he immediately made friends. A proud Getik introduced them one by one. They eventually entered the hangar through the same side door, and to Kryger's surprise, he didn't have to stoop. He thought the constructors of the hangar must have been people close to his own height.

The hangar was gigantic, and from that distance the craft looked completed, but like a hideous, streamlined box with a cockpit added. It seemed too ungainly to maneuver in atmosphere.

Getik sensed his disappointment and quickly said that appearances could be deceiving. The craft didn't need an aerodynamic shape or wings to fly because of the unique antigravity drive.

Kryger had to stoop quite low to get through the doorway of the craft and had to keep that posture as they proceeded through a narrow, low passage to the cockpit. The passage was covered with innumerable gauges and switches, enough to make your head spin. He thought it would take a number of hours to do a preflight check, which was impractical for a warcraft that might be required to take off in a moment's notice. It was quite clear that these people had no idea what was required for warfare, but he kept his silence. *It should at least get me home,* he thought as he listened to the incessant explanations of the construction engineer.

The cockpit contained two seats close to each other with no control levers between them. The construction engineer immediately noticed the blunder. "Uh-oh!" he exclaimed with a red face. "We badly miscalculated the pilot's size, Getik. Sheeftag fits, and we thought that would be big enough. We'll have to remove the cockpit, build a new one, weld it on, and redo the circuits. I'm very sorry, Kryger, but it will take a few weeks. You might as well inspect the rest of the ship and give us your comments because I suspect we slipped up just about everywhere."

Kryger didn't comment until the end of the tour: "I appreciate the effort and time you folks put into building this ship, but it's not a functional warship." He knew Getik was devastated. "It's not totally useless, though. I can sit or lie down if you have an experienced enough pilot to take Getik and me to my people. If you remove the gun platforms and put a few overly large beds there, it could be converted into a small rescue ship—for which it would be ideal. In the first place, this ship is too compacted"—he didn't want to use the word "cramped" — "and even your people, if they are cooped up in it for long periods, will begin to stress because there is not enough space to move about. It's only in a one-man fighting craft that space can be minimized," he said, softening the blow.

"There must be much more headroom as well, about three times your own height, and a warship must be extremely automated with only essential instruments visible in front of the pilot or pilots so that the craft can get operational without any delay. No enemy will ever be polite enough to wait for you. On the contrary, they'd appreciate your craft's tardiness."

He elaborated for a few minutes as politely as possible despite the dismay on their faces. They were clearly very proud of their first ship, which they had deemed indestructible.

"Permit me to go into a little detail regarding shielding. As I understand it, your force field is impenetrable as it quite correctly should be, but so are our shields, unless they are overloaded by a constantly heavy barrage. If a nervous rookie or an overeager gunner starts firing before a shield is deactivated, the bolt or missile starts to ricochet around inside, creating an extremely deadly situation. That is why we now design our weapons to create an opening in the shield where they are pointed the moment the trigger is pulled. Of course, there is a split-second delay after the trigger is depressed. We originally designed overlays of curved shields so that a shield can be switched off during a battle on the side facing the enemy. We kept the overlay design in the event of malfunction or damage of a shield generator to leave a way for mistuned and other ricocheting missiles to exit."

"Ah, that makes sense! Now I understand," the chief engineer exclaimed. "So perhaps we should think along that line—that is, if we have to. Let's retreat to the back of the hangar where our design offices are, Kryger, and it's also suppertime."

Kryger and Getik tagged along behind the others. Then Kryger suddenly stopped in his tracks because his eyes were drawn to a faint bluish shimmer floating about the height of his knees in the far corner to their left, and he saw the outline of what looked like a stubby-winged aircraft a little bigger than the fighter he'd scrapped on the outer surface. He asked, "What's the craft on our left for?"

"You've got very good eyesight, son. I only see the barely discernible shimmer because I know it's there. We don't know the history of that craft. We found it here when we discovered the hangar and the open-surface mine. Perhaps it was built right here by the vanished civilization we haven't found any traces of yet. We can only hypothesize that the hangar was built to manufacture and store craft like that."

The group, who had been speculating about ways to change the rejected ship to something useable, halted when Kryger and Getik came to a standstill. When Getik stopped speaking, the head engineer continued, "We tried to enter it many times, but we can't because the glimmer is a sort of force field that repels any object thrown at it, and it stops anyone from touching the door or any part of its frame. It's a weird sensation and feels as if it pushes one's hand away when one tries to touch the surface."

Kryger was intrigued and moved closer to the craft. He tried to use his third eye by a process of looking at a thing but not really gazing directly at it. His dear friend, Pgabys, had explained the principles of the natural gift the Shadows were born with, but he never had the time to practice. He saw only a recessed lever next to the door and was astonished when his hesitant hand went right through the shield with only a scarcely noticeable tingling sensation. He was reaching for the lever to either push or pull when an urgent alien thought told him not to do it.

The warning voice was friendly but sounded weary. *Don't even touch it! The ship is protected by a very advanced force field, but because of its rudimentary sentience, the ship recognizes you as a warrior capable of flying it. It therefore will let you in, but it won't allow you to leave unless you can speak to it and know what to say. Yes, I'm the presence you became aware of when you crash-landed. I am known by various names, but the Ancient One seems to be more widely used. I was still evaluating your character and potential when you released the lightning bolt as those crude minds tried to force entry while you were sleeping. The backlash almost scrambled what little brains I have left. I was only half-prepared because I picked up the warning you gave your rescuer, so I got what I deserved.*

That fighter was built for me and my late companion. It's the only one of its kind, but I never had a chance to fly it in battle because I was disabled when I tried to reach it. I am too weak to

transmit all the information you need, so I must ask you to come to me for detailed instructions. My time in this round of existence is nearly at an end, and I would like to explain the reason for the ship's construction while I instruct you in its proper use. And yes, you might as well bring Getik along if he wants to come since a few alterations are necessary, and he's had a little experience in that area. I sense your sincere interest, and I think the ship will take to you.

I reside in the place Getik's people know as the dead zone. The locals call it the Place of Great Silences. The journey through the surrounding jungle is fraught with danger because you'll have to proceed on foot when your vehicle stops functioning, but I know that you can look after yourself. Bear in mind that energy weapons won't function in the dead zone and that some of the creatures are big, primitive, fierce, and don't die readily. Don't rely on your special weapons as they use energy too, but consider sharp cutting weapons and muscle power.

You might find my appearance a bit out of the ordinary, but you are used to all kinds of strange creatures. Since my accident many centuries ago, I've been looking for an honest, trustworthy fighter to entrust the deadly craft to because another type of destroyer from another galaxy, more intelligent and vicious than the Bugs, could very well arrive in the near future. This ship was the first prototype of a fleet we planned, but our enemy found us before we had a chance to thoroughly test its only weapon, which is even more deadly than your personal weapons. That is one of the reasons you must be instructed in its operation, and Getik should also be instructed on the science to make changes to the ship. Think about what you've just been told, and when you're sure, just call my name, Maksika, mentally because I'll be aware of you all the time.

The alien presence withdrew quickly when the chief construction engineer asked, "Why did you stop, Kryger? Your arm was through the protective field—something we've been unable to do. Perhaps you could use this ship, and from what little we can see, it seems more or less the right size for you."

Kryger was ready with an answer since he was a quick thinker. "Something occurred to me at the last moment. The ship is protected for a reason, and I must try to study it before I think of entering it. It may do something very unpleasant or explode as our ships do when entry is unauthorized or forced. Let's leave it alone for a while longer because Getik and I have some other business to attend to first."

Getik sensed that Kryger had held something back but wisely kept his silence. The boy would tell him when he felt like it.

The back room of the hangar contained all sorts of manufacturing equipment; in fact, it was a comprehensive workshop. Kryger was taken to a desk where he had to go down on his knees so as not to bend over awkwardly. First he drew the outlines of a fighter—underside, top, one side, and dimensions. Then he drew details as he remembered them—the guns, the missile tubes—explaining as he drew while everyone made notes. He admitted that he knew very little of how the frames were reinforced to take extreme stresses but related what he did know. Then he did the same with a light cruiser as the subject, which the rejected ship was meant to be.

Sheeftag elected to stay behind when they left after a sumptuous meal, saying she'd learn more if she could help rebuild the ship. Kryger mentally wished her luck but, when they were in the air, told Getik, "That girl will never make a good pilot as she lacks a vital ingredient. Perhaps it's a characteristic of her tribe, but a bully lacks courage."

9

Getik flew the boat back to the city. When they were well away, Kryger told him what really had stopped him when he touched the alien craft. Getik was gray faced but said he would go with Kryger as everyone had somehow heard of the ancient recluse, but no one had ever met him, and no one knew what or how old he was. More than a hundred years ago, an expedition had ventured into the dead zone to find him, but they'd reported that their boats had crashed just after passing what appeared to be a pink-tinted mountain and that their guns had failed to function when huge reptilian creatures attacked ferociously without warning. They'd stayed silent after flashing the warning and were never heard from them again. Since then nobody had ventured into the dead zone.

Kryger thought awhile and then said, "I'm good with a bow and arrow, but the bow should be very strong to accommodate enormous creatures, and I'm proficient with a battle-ax as well. Even a sword might help, but it would be more effective to make a strong battle-ax, since it is swung with both hands and I'll be able to put all my power into the swing. I've got to try. The ship is drawing me and asking me to take it into battle."

Getik abruptly turned the boat back to where they had come from. "I practiced with a bow and arrow when I was a youngster and taught my late son how to shoot accurately. I keep fit and often swing an ax to chop wood for a cooking fire when I'm away from home. So I won't be a completely helpless burden to you."

"Why are we going back?"

"The metal we built the ship with can be cast into an ax and sharpened before it cools down. It is a lightweight metal, and the ax can be molded with a good grip and a long handle that will be virtually unbreakable. It'd be everlasting and will never be blunted. The arrows will be the easiest to cast. You just have to draw them for me and indicate how big and long they should be. I'll make the mold and do the rest, unless someone more knowledgeable volunteers to help. A thin, flat bar is resilient, and we can experiment with different bows as well. It will only take a day or two, or what goes for a day around here. I'll get someone to bring a roll of synthetic string for the bows, thin but strong enough not to break at an inconvenient time.

"One thing, though: don't say a word about where we're going. I'll tell them we want the contraptions for fun and to take along as indestructible souvenirs."

Kryger had been wondering where saplings strong enough to make a battle-ax handle and a bow could be found in this forest that seemed to consist only of huge old trees, but Getik's idea could save their lives. It should also take less time and effort than shaping a suitable stick, but he'd wait and see.

Kryger drew a battle-ax the size he thought might suit him best and hoped it wouldn't be too light or too heavy. He added a long spearhead on top of the blade and indicated that the handle should be about two and a half meters long and four centimeters thick to suit his handgrip. Then he tried a few available flat bars and found that, although they were resilient, they bent too easily. After stacking three together, he felt that the flexibility was just about right and showed this to Getik, who measured the thickness and made a note of it. Then Kryger drew the type of bow he preferred and told Getik it should be about a meter and a half long, tapering from the handle to a thinner end on both sides, with deep notches at the ends to take the string. He then drew the size of the arrowheads.

There were plenty of eager expert hands to help, and the molds were quickly prepared and filled with a kind of plastic that melted and set quickly, was about the same weight as the metal, and was used as a cheap method to check what shape a sheet should be so as not to waste the special metal.

Kryger hefted the first sample battle-ax and swung it around a few times but found it much too light and unbalanced. He suggested that the head be weighted, if possible, to about the equivalent of five kilograms, the haft a little thicker, with a rounded knob at the end and the lower half finely grooved for a nonslip, two-handed grip. He tested another two prototypes and was satisfied with the third, and the experts set about producing the real thing.

The bow felt right the first time, but he'd have to test the real thing.

They measured Kryger's reach and suggested arrows of the same metal with weighted heads and slits for feathers at the rear end, should such things be required for more accuracy. He was quite happy to leave the work to them since most of them used bows and arrows for recreational purposes.

Since it would be suspicious if they didn't study the alien craft, they borrowed two long stepladders and checked it from all angles while they waited.

Kryger liked what he saw. Remarkably it was more or less the same shape, though somewhat broader and longer, than the heavy fighter he'd scrapped and seemed to seat four, two abreast, with a spacious compartment behind the rear seats. The seats were big enough to accommodate his proportions but weren't made to be comfortable for human bodies. Presumably this was one of the changes Maksika had hinted at.

There weren't obvious weapons or holes that hinted at hidden weapons. But the stubby wings ended with what looked like rods, a little thicker and longer than the tips of the wings, with tapering knobs on the forward-facing ends, which could be the deadly weapons Maksika had mentioned. Kryger knew it was useless to speculate since their function would be explained soon enough.

He was determined that nothing would stop him from trying to reach Maksika. This sleek and deadly looking alien craft was the first of its kind ever encountered that he was aware of. He had to fly it even though it's capability as a fighter was in question, but if the big MAG could be mounted in front of the cockpit, he could surely make it home.

The head of the first battle-ax was too light again and not quite balanced, but the second one he accepted as just about right. The first bow bent too easily and didn't drive an arrow hard enough to penetrate deeply; the second one snapped the string but was just the right size, and he wanted it since it was just the right power he was after. A rolled double string didn't snap but was a bit too thick for his liking. Getik was also satisfied with his second effort. Each received an indestructible lightweight quiver with a bundle of fifty metal arrows and thirty extra arrowheads.

A much appreciated, unexpected gift was a long hunting knife of the same metal for each of them. Kryger was at a loss to express his heartfelt appreciation and said so. The creator smiled, patted him on the arm, and told him good-naturedly to go and practice somewhere where his personnel wouldn't be accidental victims.

They went in among the giant trees and practiced their swings on one that had fallen. Kryger was surprised at the penetrating depth he could achieve with the sharp blade. The only arrow he tried at the same target from a hundred steps away went in so deep that he had to cut halfway through the hard trunk to free it. That was enough practice for him. Getik had the same fate but fortunately didn't have to cut as deep since his bow had less driving power.

They said a temporary goodbye to everyone and went back to the city. Getik obtained a roll of heavy-duty string that twanged musically on the bow when Kryger tried it a few times without an arrow. He cut and made a dozen spare bowstrings. The rest of the roll he wrapped around the ax shaft for a better nonslip grip, leaving a loop at the knob to push his left wrist through, retain his grip on the handle, and prevent it from being pulled out of his hands.

Of course, Getik did the same as he was learning from a master. Kryger told him to get camouflage clothing for both of them and a backpack for himself large enough to hold an emergency kit, emergency supplies, and whatever else he thought they would need. Kryger packed what he would need into one of his own rucksacks and asked Gorsmat to take care of the other one for him. When he was ready, he went still and thought, *Maksika*, and received directions. They dressed in the new clothing specially made for them, but Kryger preferred his own soft, durable shoes.

Getik had acquired a fast airboat, and they reached the foot of the bare, distinctive pink peak at the edge of the dead zone after about eight hours. He was worried about finding the place again, but Kryger assured him he could home in on the peak. It was an acquired ability that never failed him. The peak should be visible from afar as they seemed to be in a veritable jungle free from the giant old trees, although the trees still seemed quite tall but slender enough to be climbable in an emergency.

Kryger needed a distinctive beacon where they could leave the boat. He asked Getik to fly slowly along the peak while he looked for an easily recognizable place to park the boat. After only a few minutes, he saw a darker-colored crack on the side facing the dead zone and directed Getik toward it. They parked under a dense tree close to the shallow crack, removed their gear, and covered the boat with a mottled green sheet.

Kryger first fired the little MAG at a boulder close to them, and a small hole appeared. He meant to use it at intervals until it malfunctioned as predicted by Maksika. It paid to make certain and might save a few physical fights as long as it functioned, and if they were pursued when they returned, he would know when to start using it again.

"Using the bows while carrying our rucksacks won't be a problem," he said as they shouldered their bags. "I hope we don't encounter something we need the axes for in a hurry because it may be awkward to defend ourselves against something big or nimble when there isn't time to drop our bags." They'd attached the axes to harnesses over their shoulders so they could be out of the way but within easy reach, and they had practiced removing them quite fast.

"I have full confidence in you, son, because your reaction time is faster than mine and you've had more experience than I'll ever have. Well, let's get going and see what awaits us. I wonder why the Ancient One chose to reside here instead of somewhere more accessible."

"I've encountered very strange things on many planets, but never anything as…well…alien as this area where only primitive science works. I suppose it can only occur on the inside of a hollow planet." He started off, taking the lead. "From now on we don't talk aloud. Don't walk too close to me, and watch my hands for signals when I stop suddenly. Try to walk as silently as I do. We should try not to attract unnecessary attention."

"Okay, son. I'll follow three steps behind you, keep my eyes and ears open, and listen with my mind as well." Getik wasn't clumsy, and their progress was almost soundless.

Less than ten minutes later, Kryger sensed a subtle change in the atmosphere. It didn't feel menacing but made him feel uneasy. The woods were unnaturally quiet, and he found it unnerving not to hear a bird chirping now and then. Even pestering insects were absent, and he could hear only the slight rustle caused by a breeze in the tree tops. The trees were also becoming smaller as if the soil quality was poorer. There were old, rotting, fallen tree trunks here and there, but none were giants. The undergrowth was also getting denser, impeding rapid progress, and it became difficult to move silently because of the dry, leafy carpet. He also smelled water.

It was time to test the little MAG again. He stopped and pointed it at a branch high up in the tree before him. The energy bolt would penetrate anything for more than two hundred kilometers, and he didn't want to kill anything inadvertently with a lower shot. He pulled the trigger, but no hole appeared. He pointed pulled the trigger again, but nothing happened. He put the little MAG away.

It seems that we landed close to the dead zone, he flashed his thoughts to Getik. *We'll have to rely on muscle power from now on.*

He changed the bow to his right hand because he preferred to use it that way and took an arrow with his left hand from the quiver on his back. He immediately transferred it to the fingers of his right hand and did so twice more. He would be ready to shoot all three rapidly at a moment's notice.

I felt the ambience change but ascribed it to my highly strung nerves, Getik replied. *Why the three arrows?*

It could mean the difference between life and death to have arrows ready in your bow hand instead of grabbing one at a time from the quiver. I might be a bit rusty right now, but years ago I was taught to shoot rapidly this way with as many arrows as I could hold together with the bow, and it saved my rear in quite a few situations. So I became somewhat of a toxophilite.

Getik shook his head. *You seem to have had quite a hectic life. It would never have occurred to me as I've never been in a situation where I didn't have recourse to a gun, but I'm not too old to learn. Archery is just a recreational sport for us, and no one takes it seriously.*

Stepping around a dense bush, Kryger abruptly came upon an extensive grassy clearing. A rill meandered along the edge, bordered by knee-high yellowish grass. He stepped to one side to let Getik catch up with him and said, *I have an uneasy feeling about crossing this meadowlike place. It doesn't look like a swamp, but I sense a hostile vibe, and there might be unpleasant surprises since there's not even a dwarf tree growing anywhere.*

Getik replied that it looked peaceful and natural enough to him. Kryger's roving eyes just then caught a movement toward the middle of the meadow, and he pointed to it. A yellow lionlike predator that reminded him of a sand cat rose slowly from the camouflaging grass about two hundred meters away and tested the still air as if it had heard something but wasn't sure what it was. Its head turned slowly to scan the area until its eyes fixed on them. Then it cautiously turned around and began a slow stalk, placing its feet carefully in the grass and keeping its eyes intently on them.

I wonder if that creature thinks that we're shortsighted or what. I'm reluctant to kill it, but if it keeps on coming, I'll have no other choice. Kryger already had an arrow fitted to his bowstring. He'd see when it tensed its muscles for the charge since predator behavior on all the planets he'd been stranded on were more or less always the same. Out of the corner of an eye, he saw Getik fit an arrow to his bowstring as well.

It's known as a deng. As far as we know, it's the fastest land animal over short distances, but it seems to lack stamina because it prefers flat open grasslands. It will charge the moment we turn and be here in less than five seconds—long before we can scramble up the nearest tree. I hope you don't miss when it starts its charge.

The deng had covered about half the distance, and Kryger, seeing signs of its muscles tensing, was about to draw the bow when, eye-blindingly fast, an unusually large, perfectly camouflaged snake leapt from the grass next to the deng, bit it on the neck, and speedily coiled around the animal before it could react. Perhaps the deng had been too intent on its prospective prey because it didn't even have time to squeal.

"From now on we don't even consider crossing clearings," Kryger whispered. "Let's veer right. It looks like the quickest way around this." He looked at the hapless deng again and saw only part of its head protruding from thick mottled coils. *I've seen a lot of constrictors in my time, but none of them match this one for speed or size,* he projected at Getik. *I dread these creatures because they're too strong to fight. I don't ever want to tangle with one.* Kryger involuntarily shuddered, and he wasn't ashamed to show it.

He realized anew that a wilderness could hide many unpleasant surprises as he warily took the next step. He kept an arrow notched in the bow, ready to let fly at a moment's notice. His brilliant green eyes flashed to every possible hiding place that could conceal something, especially overhanging branches, but they circled the clearing without mishap and continued through the fairly dense jungle. Soon, though, the undergrowth thinned out, and the trees became bigger and spaced farther apart.

After a while, they came upon a well-used game trail, and Kryger remarked that it would be easier to follow but pointed to a well-camouflaged python draped over a branch a little way off. *That's their usual method, although lazy or injured cats do the same thing since a well-used path is an ideal place to waylay prey. Prey animals can't reason, and even if they escape a trap, they will return and follow the established trail.*

They crossed the trail while Getik commented. *It wouldn't surprise me to find big cats and other predator types around. The ones I know of usually hunt in pairs or as a family before the grown-up pups are forced to leave, and most of them have retractable claws to climb trees. We can only pray that we'll be fortunate enough not to come across those types.*

10

They'd been walking some distance off the trail but following its general direction for about an hour when they heard furious roars some distance in front and a little to their right, and equally furious yelling that sounded female, desperate, but not fearful. Kryger started to move in that direction.

They came across a strange scene. A humanoid, unmistakably female, was up in a low tree, and two gray speckled lionlike predators were jumping up at her, almost reaching her, but she hit them across the eyes with what looked like a slim stick as soon as they clawed at the branch on which she was standing close to the trunk. Their attention was riveted on her and hers on them.

Kryger was within thirty meters of them when he pulled the bowstring back and shot the nearest predator in the back. It had just jumped onto a lower branch and was rearing up to reach the girl. The arrow entered between its shoulders and pinned the uncomprehending creature to the trunk. It seemed surprised, but Kryger's attention was on the second one as he notched another arrow to his bowstring.

Kryger aimed at the other creature as it dropped back to the ground, shaking its head and blinking its eyes rapidly. It was facing him, but its attention was riveted on its intended prey, and it didn't notice that its mate was rearing backward in an effort to get away from the suddenly hostile tree. The arrow went into the soft part where the neck joined the breast, and the beast dropped in its tracks since the arrow went through its heart, severed its spine, and stuck just about three-quarters through its body.

The first creature was free at last but fell on its side as it twisted to land on its feet. It was up immediately, but Getik's arrow smashed into its skull just as Kryger drew his bow and discharged his third arrow.

"Damn!" Getik exclaimed. "I almost missed, but these arrows are sharp, aren't they? It went right into the hoodah's thick skull."

"So that's what they're called," Kryger remarked as he lowered the bow and beckoned the unarmed female to come down, hoping she wouldn't misinterpret the gesture. She scrutinized them for a moment, apparently undecided whether to trust the strangers or flee, and then lithely slithered down with her face toward them, watching for signs of hostility. Sensing they weren't going to harm her, she approached slowly with her tail twitching slightly from side to side.

Getik spoke to her in a language that sounded faintly familiar to Kryger.

She suddenly smiled, and Kryger saw that her face was almost human. It was a light-gold color and devoid of hair, but her nose was too short and blunt to be attractive to humans. The top and back of her head, neck, and body were covered with short, fine, golden, silky-looking hair, and her eyes were light brown. She too had hairy feline ears, and they were twitching backward and forward as if she distrusted the silent jungle and was constantly on the alert for sounds that could spell danger.

His eyes shifted to her naked body, to her magnificently muscled, humanlike legs, and he could see the muscles ripple with every step. She was much taller than Getik, and Kryger estimated that the top of her head would touch his chin. Her hands and toes were humanlike, and she appeared to be quite robust. She had four breasts: the upper two small but developed, the lower two just nipples. Kryger thought that, physically, she was better developed than Sheeftag since she moved with an easy grace that portrayed speed and power.

There was a seemingly empty sack made of soft skin and a quiver with a couple of arrows in it slung over her shoulders, but no bow. The only clothing she wore was what looked like a belt tied tightly around her narrow hips with a knot. It supported a short flint knife in a half scabbard and a few small pouches, some empty and others bulging. To Kryger's trained ears, she replied in a language that seemed slightly different from the one used by Getik, but they seemed to understand each other, for they continued to converse while he retrieved his arrows.

The arrow protruding from the second creature's back would be messy but relatively easy to remove. The first arrow was lodged firmly into the tree trunk, which had enabled the savage hoodah to pull itself free. Shrugging his shoulders, he proceeded to chop deep notches above and below the arrow with his battle-ax to dislodge it. He was prepared to cut through the trunk if necessary, which wouldn't take long as the ax was heavy and went in deep with every chop, but he didn't want to damage the tree more than necessary.

At the first chop, the female stopped talking, but Kryger was unaware she was looking at the ax and the arrow in amazement. She asked something in an awed voice, and Getik answered at length while she walked closer, pulled the other arrow from the hoodah, and inspected it closely.

"The female is impressed with your ax and arrows. She asks if she can keep this one to make a spear with. She's surprisingly intelligent."

"Of course she can. I can cut a shaft for it when we find suitable saplings. She seems to have lost her bow, so I'll make her another one."

"Her bow is the bent, unshaped stick in her hand she beat the hoodahs with. She said the string broke just as they began charging her. I'll give her one of mine as hers is made of hand-rolled plant fibers, which can't be very strong or durable."

Getik said something, reached into a pocket, and gave her a spare string. She immediately strung her crude bow and tested it. By the dull sound of the twang, Kryger knew it didn't have much driving power, but she made happy sounds like a child to show her appreciation.

We might as well get going, Getik. I'm not tired yet, but I think we should rest at least every twelve hours. Otherwise we might start making stupid mistakes. We already made too much noise with my chopping and the chatting, which might attract unwelcome attention. The girl seems at home here. Ask her if she's on her way somewhere or if she would like to accompany us.

He had habitually reverted to mind communication, which he projected to both without giving it a thought and barely suppressed his surprise when he received an answer directly from the catlike female.

Yes, I'd like to come with you. There's a pack of droogs roaming around this area. Their sense of smell is superb. We must run to put distance between us and these carcasses. Oh, by the way, my name is Protvor. The Strange Old One taught me to mind-speak. He said that I had potential—whatever that means. Call me Prot if you like.

I'm Kryger, and my companion is Getik. We're actually on our way to meet this Old One who told me that he was known by many names.

It's too late, Protvor said urgently and pointed to a fairly dense tree with easily reachable branches about thirty steps away. *I hear the pack approaching fast from downwind, but we might make it to that tree. Droogs are not climbers, but they can jump as high as a hoodah.*

Kryger heard eager yelps and what curiously sounded like low-pitched baying. By the rapidly increasing volume, he realized they were closing in very fast. He let Getik and Protvor get ahead while he put the arrows away, slung the bow over one shoulder, and snatched the battle-ax from the other. He was about five steps from the sanctuary when he heard heavy breathing and a rapid stampede close behind him. He jumped forward, and when his feet touched the ground, he turned with his back against the tree just as Protvor swung into the lower branches and pulled Getik up with her tail under his arms and around his chest.

Kryger swung the ax and cleaved the oversize head of a huge wolflike creature open as it leaped for his throat. The fleeting thought that such powerful jaws could take an arm or leg off with a single bite faded as he speared the next one in the chest and assisted it over his head past the tree trunk.

By that time Getik and Protvor had scrambled out of reach, but there was no break in the attack so that he could jump up and try to reach sanctuary too. He dispatched another droog with a backhanded sweep of the ax, and suddenly there seemed to be hundreds running around the tree, getting in one another's way to get at him. He just stabbed, swiped, and chopped as fast as he could on all sides in one continuous movement. The pack seemed indomitable, and Kryger was beginning to feel the effects of the furious exertion. Just as he thought he was about to be overwhelmed, someone dropped down on the other side of the tree and began to mow down droogs as fast as he did. He felt grateful for the help and briefly, out of the corner of an eye, saw that it was Protvor with Getik's ax.

The powerful, nimble droogs continued to attack ferociously, and carcasses piled up quickly in a half circle in front of them. Kryger was covered in blood, and his footing became slippery, but he rooted himself in a fighting stance and seemingly effortlessly swung the broadax as he twisted his upper body as far as necessary, although the heavy backpack was a hindrance. There seemed to be no end to the droog pack, and he heard Protvor's heavy breathing while she uttered sounds that, judging by the tone of her voice, could be only imprecations.

Kryger was breathing heavily too, when suddenly it was over. He glanced around. Not a single droog moved. He climbed over the wall of carcasses and saw Protvor leaning tiredly with her back against the tree. She was unharmed, her eyes shining, and grinning contentedly as her chest heaved rapidly up and down. He smiled at her, and she could see the gratitude and relief written all over his face.

Her smile broadened. *I've wished for a very long time that I could do something like this, even with only a sturdy club. Hopefully Getik isn't too upset that I grabbed his ax because this was an opportunity I couldn't resist.*

Getik hesitated to take the ax back as he climbed down and looked at Kryger, who sensed what he wanted to say. He nodded and Getik told her, *You're a natural, almost as good as Kryger with the battle-ax, and might as well keep it with you for as long as you're with us.* Protvor smiled happily.

My tribe left me with the Old One when I was little. I guess I was always a bit of an outcast. The Old One taught me everything I know. I can take you to him. We should have some peace for a while because every living thing that can run departs when the dreaded droogs hunt—with the exception of the giant reptiles that happily gobble them up. The droogs fear them.

They reached the brook a few minutes later, and Protvor signaled for them to wait while she walked along the stream about ten steps from the bank until she found a deeper pool. They watched as she carefully inspected the pool and the sparse vegetation along the banks. Protvor warily slunk downstream to where the pool overflowed into a shallow, half-overgrown rivulet. She suddenly backed off slowly, quietly put the ax down, and removed her bow and one of the primitive arrows while her eyes remained fixed on the rivulet. She fitted the arrow to her bow, pulled it back, and quietly stepped closer.

She angled the arrow downward into the rivulet, let go of the bowstring, and then nimbly jumped away, landing next to the ax. Her eyes remained riveted on the stream as she felt for the ax with a naked foot and then quickly bent over to pick it up just as a huge mottled snake surged out of the water, splashing waterdrops everywhere as it thrashed about. The arrow was embedded in its head, just behind its ratlike ears, and the snake's strikingly long body coiled out of the rivulet in a weird sort of death ritual. After a few seconds, a shudder ran down its core and it went lax.

Protvor looked at Kryger, who had jumped closer with his ax ready when the snake's head emerged from the water. *These snakes* (he translated the unpronounceable name she used) *have a nasty habit of lying in wait at the outlet of a shallow pool, especially in the open grasslands, and as soon as activity is transmitted through the water, they glide into the pool and attack. Their poison almost immediately paralyzes the victim. It might come in handy if we put some of it on our arrows.*

Kryger shook his head. *I had no idea that such a poison existed. We use other types of weapons that kill from a distance, but they don't function here in what Getik's people call the dead zone. The Old One told me that people who live here call it the Place of Great Silences.*

Protvor nodded. *Yes, we do because the stinging, noisome flying insects don't come here. We're not sure why. That's why we like it here, and most of us never venture outside the zone because some insect bites bring death or sicknesses we cannot cure. It is now safe to go wash because these snakes travel solo. Interestingly, when they encounter other snakes, they communicate by flashing colors across their skin.*

She put her bow and arrows down, undid the rope belt and carefully stowed it with the attached pouches out of harm's way, walked into the pool up to her knees, bent over watchfully while she washed the battle-ax, and then stuck it within easy reach by the spearhead into the pool next to her. Then she cautiously proceeded to wash her whole body, but she never relaxed her vigilance. She was clearly self-reliant and used to being alone.

Although he was using his senses to scan the area, Kryger asked Getik to watch for possible danger while he cleaned his ax, then stripped and joined Protvor in the pool. Later he rinsed his clothes, shook some shape back into them, and donned them again thinking they might dry quicker that way. Getik only rinsed the dirt from his hands and then refilled their canteens at the pool's inlet.

While Protvor, enjoying the use of the ever-sharp battle-ax, cut branches to build a platform in a selected tree, Kryger wandered around looking for saplings or straight branches strong and supple enough for a bow and a suitable straight handle to make a short spear for Getik in place of the ax, figuring he should at least have something besides a knife to defend himself. As always, he scanned the area continuously with his eyes and senses as he tested likely shoots and saplings before cutting them. At last he found what he was looking for, cut suitable lengths, and tested them again before he returned to his companions.

I'm nearly finished with our platform, Protvor said when she saw Kryger. He retrieved his rucksack, poured some of his dry rations into her and Getik's hands, removed a few for himself, and offered Protvor his canteen when she began to chew hers. She swallowed and made a face but smiled at him. *It tastes like dry grass, but I already feel less hungry.*

Protvor grabbed a heavy branch with her tail and nimbly scrambled to the top of the tree while Kryger started on the crude spear by whittling one end so that an arrowhead could be screwed on. Protvor finished the platform long before he tightly wound a spare bowstring around the end of the arrowhead to make sure it stayed in place.

11

The wooden tree platform felt sturdy, but Kryger sat close to the main trunk and was careful not to make any sudden moves. Protvor smiled and told him she was going to dip the tips of their arrows in the poison that was available just in case they were disturbed by one or more of the bigger animals who weren't easily killed by other means.

Occasionally one encounters a really big cold-blooded reptilian creature away from the lake area. One can only escape if it stays unaware of one's presence or if one is nimble enough to scramble up a huge tree out of its reach. There are some omnivores, but the majority are predators who prey upon anything that moves.

My arrows don't even scratch their thickly scaled hides, but you, with your heavy bow, your power, and sharp metal arrows that do not break, should be able to drive an arrow deep enough for the poison to take effect. I don't think that even you can kill one with your ax unless it is tipped with poison, but then it might not die fast enough for you to survive its ferocious attack. It even gulps down its prey while alive.

She took a wooden jar with a stopper from one of her pouches.

Kryger told Getik to get some sleep for a few hours so that he could take over the watch because Protvor seemed overly tired and should sleep too. Getik stretched out on his side with his face under a shady branch, away from the ever-present sun, and went to sleep.

Kryger handed Protvor the crude but strong spear and his quiver, then started to whittle the bow with the new daggerlike knife, which was sharper than his old hunting knife.

When Protvor was finished with Getik's arrows and ax, Kryger told her, *For now, only put poison on the spear tip of my ax. I'll keep watch until Getik wakes up, and he can take the watch while I sleep. I sense that you are a light sleeper, so you'll wake up if anything happens, but otherwise sleep until you are fully rested. It's important that you get enough rest since you will lead us and therefore be the first one to be exposed to predators in hiding.*

Kryger warned her not to touch him while asleep and was beginning to like and respect the self-reliant girl. He didn't think of her as a female of another species but as a companion.

I'll remember, Kryger. The Old One taught me many things and told me many true stories to educate me. I feel that you are telling me the truth. I like your knife as it cuts so easily. I've seen something like it before because the Old One has a bigger one, but he only uses it to cut up meat. It takes us a long time to chip a new knife, and it breaks easily if we have to use it roughly.

Kryger smiled and almost reluctantly retrieved his trusty old hunting knife in its worn sheath from the backpack and held it out to her. *Here, you can keep this one. It saved my life many times when I had nothing else to use as a weapon. You put your belt through these slits. This clip secures the knife in the sheath, and you unclip it like this.* (He showed her how to do it.) *This flat surface attached to the back of the sheath is used to sharpen the cutting edge when needed.* He watched the undisguised joy on her face as she wonderingly took the knife from its sheath. He loved the knife he'd had for many years but sensed that its new owner would treasure it more.

I can touch you when you are awake, she said as she moved over to him on her hands and knees, threw her arms around his neck, and pressed her upper body against his, and he was quite sure that she purred. It was her way of thanking him because the words "thank you" didn't exist in her culture. He gave her a hug and told her to go to sleep, which she did with a pleased look on her face after she'd hung the knife on her belt. She slept with her hand on the knife as if she were afraid it would be taken away if she let go of it. Kryger smiled because he knew how he would have felt in her place.

While he tapered the ends of the bow, he let his senses roam around to check life-forms that came within range. Most were warm-blooded, and they seemed too apprehensive to approach the pool or the tree. Perhaps it was the strong smell of droogs or maybe the blood that bothered them since he didn't sense other droogs. Perhaps the droogs were territorial and kept other packs away. So far he hadn't seen or heard any avian species in this Place of Great Silences.

He felt tired, but Getik and the girl needed the rest more than him, and he knew how to stay awake when it was required. He finished the bow after a few hours and tested the way it bent. Then he whittled some more in the right places until he was satisfied. He used a spare string and tested the bending of the bow by pulling the string to his shoulder a few times but didn't let go of the string because the twang would wake Prot up. The pull was too light for him, but it should be okay for the girl. Then he unstrung the bow so it could dry out more before use. He put it down beside him in the full sunlight. He was sure that Protvor would like it because it looked beautiful, bent evenly, and would be much more accurate than her unshaped stick.

He yawned but didn't relax his vigilance because he still didn't know what to expect in this strange, almost ominously silent forest. He hadn't seen any fruit or berry trees, which might explain the absence of birds because, as far as he knew, forest birds usually were fruit or nut eaters. The patch of grassland they'd bypassed might have supported a few tiny grass warblers in the distant past, but they wouldn't have survived for long.

To while away the time until Getik woke up, he thought of the incomparable Quarr and wondered what she and his son were doing. His thoughts wandered from them to Maksika, the Strange Old One as referred to by Protvor, and he wondered what he, or it, looked like. Then he thought of the ship and speculated what it could do and what it would be like to fly. It would be a novel experience to fly a truly alien craft.

At long last Getik woke up, wiped his eyes with a splash of water into a hand from his canteen, and quietly told Kryger he was rested and ready to take the watch. Kryger immediately stretched out on his right side and went to sleep.

He woke up abruptly but didn't open his eyes because his subconscious mind would awaken him only if something had changed. He sensed nothing close except his two companions but felt cold and clammy. Kryger slowly opened his eyes and found that the perpetual sunlight was obscured by a dense, damp fog. He sat up and yawned hugely with his hand in front of his mouth. Protvor was also awake.

"What's happening, Getik?" he asked immediately after the yawn. "This is very strange."

"Oh, you mean the weather. This is our version of rain. We don't get clouds, showers, or thunderstorms as on the outer surface of planets. The fog forms over the seas and is driven across the planet by the breeze until it thins out and is dispersed by the heat of the sun. It doesn't happen regularly but often enough to keep the vegetation growing. It usually only lasts for a few hours. You've only slept for about two hours, so you might as well try to go back to sleep. I'll cover you with the waterproof sheet I brought along."

Kryger slowly drifted back into a deep sleep but woke up again several hours later, hearing an unfamiliar noise.

What's that knocking sound? It sounds like it's coming from below.

All three peeked curiously over the edge of the platform. They stared straight into the green eyes of a hairless rodentlike creature about four feet long and with a tail twice as long as its body. Its eyes, with noticeably small pupils, looked like they were about to pop out of its head. Its skin was an unflattering mulberry color.

"Look at its teeth," Getik blurted out. The animal moved slightly, and they could now see that it had a really peculiar thin middle finger.

It's a yep-ya, Protvor announced. *Their teeth grow perpetually. It's tapping on the tree to find bugs. It will then gnaw a small hole in the wood using its forward slanting incisors and insert its narrow middle finger to pull the bugs out.*

It looks like an adorable vampire, Kryger thought. Growing up he had read stories and seen pictures of vampires in the archives on Nevus of a planet known as Earth.

If you think a yep-ya is ugly, you should see some of the other creatures. Protvor chuckled.

"Not a sight that's conducive to a good night's sleep," Getik muttered.

Kryger told Protvor that the bow was finished but that it was better to let it dry out longer before she tested it. She hefted it and said it was longer than hers but felt comfortable weight-wise. She'd keep it to test when it looked dry enough and then decide whether it was better than the one she had made herself.

Kryger smiled secretly while he scanned the area with his senses and then climbed down first. Protvor followed, her tail wrapped around the new bow and Getik's spear. She smiled at Kryger and said she didn't want Getik, or anyone else, killed by his own spear if he accidentally dropped it because he required both hands to climb down with his heavy and awkward pack and weapons.

They went to the pool and washed after Protvor checked for snakes, then refilled their canteens. They drank their fill, which was the prudent thing to do.

As Kryger walked away, meaning to cross the stream and continue the journey, Protvor stopped him from jumping across.

She spoke, and although she used different words, their meaning was clear: *The direct way to the Old One is too dangerous. I don't think we will live very long as only a little way from here, almost straight ahead of us, is a large lake surrounded by extensive grasslands where the great cats and the enormous reptiles hunt, often killing a weaker one of their own kind. You may kill a few, but there are too many, and the cats often hunt in packs of six or more to overcome some of the bigger, more difficult-to-kill prey. There are hills to our right where very few of them wander because there's little water in that region, and the reptiles do not like to go too far from the lake since they like to lie in deep water.*

The wind was blowing toward them, driving the remnants of fog patches to other parts of the world, and as if to give weight to the girl's words, Kryger heard the faraway screams of some creature in utter agony.

The reptiles don't kill cleanly like the cats. They rip chunks out of their catch and eat it alive until it dies of pain and blood loss. That's what you're hearing.

Kryger involuntary shivered. He couldn't imagine the hellish pain when an animal was being torn piece by piece from the rear to the front. He would definitely not like to die that way.

Okay, I'm convinced. You lead the way, Getik follows, and I'll cover our backs. If you smell, hear, or see anything you think you can't handle, stop and warn me; I'll scan with my senses, ears, and eyes, so I should know if something lurks ahead, unless it's a cold-blooded reptile. I can't sense those things at all.

Cool! I wish I could do something like that.

"And so do I," Getik echoed her words aloud.

It's not hard to do, Kryger replied, *but I'll have to enter a certain part of your minds to show you how it's done. It'll take less than a minute each, and then you can practice as we go.*

Protvor said she wanted to be first, and Kryger told her to sit as there was nothing menacing he could sense. He entered her mind and was once again surprised by the exceptional intelligence, although a little alien, he found. He stimulated the appropriate center and then showed her how to let her senses roam as he had been taught. *But don't ever depend too much on your senses alone,* he cautioned. *Use your ears and eyes at the same time, for there are those who can stop their minds from emitting, and you must always be on the lookout for snakes and other reptiles since their thoughts are too coldly alien to pick up.*

He did the same with Getik. Then they began the roundabout journey, and Kryger was extra vigilant because he realized the other two would at first be distracted, focused on exercising their novel new abilities—and it was just as well he did. He had shouldered the battle-ax and had the bow and three arrows in his hand as usual. Protvor was almost beneath a tree when he saw a well-camouflaged big snake getting ready to drop on her. Without aiming consciously, he let go with an arrow. As she glanced up to see what had caused the thud, some coils dropped on her shoulders, and she jumped away with a startled yelp. Getik also jumped and screamed, for some of the coils hit him too as the snake thrashed for a few seconds, its head pinned to the branch.

Your poison is really lethal, Prot, Kryger managed to say with a straight face before he succumbed to uncontrolled laughter. After a minute he was able to say, *I'm sorry, but it was really funny to see you two jump so high and so far almost in tandem. Do you now see what I meant when I said that you must use your eyes and ears at the same time you use your senses?*

Getik laughed embarrassedly but was still a bit shaken up. "It could have been a fatal lesson for the girl if you weren't so experienced. Thanks, son. I should learn to use my eyes."

Protvor came up to Kryger and gave him a fierce hug since it was her way of expressing appreciation. Kryger looked up at the snake's head.

"That's one arrow I must say goodbye to. It'll just be too much trouble to try to retrieve it."

I'll retrieve it for you, Protvor said as she prepared to scale the tree.

No, the branch is very thick, and the arrow is too firmly embedded. The noise of chopping it down may attract inimical attention. Let's go; I have enough arrows.

You're right, but I feel negligent because I should have seen or smelled it. There are many of them waiting in unexpected places, and I know it.

It's okay, Prot. There's no need to feel guilty. Please continue to lead the way, and yes, I should have told you to scan only at intervals, not the entire time. It comes naturally after practice, but you must train yourself to do all four things simultaneously.

I won't forget, she assured him and then took the lead again, now much more alert to the sights, smells, and sounds of the primeval jungle.

Kryger, true to his training, never relaxed his vigilance because the ability to scan for a considerable distance around him was highly developed. After an hour or two, he told the other two to climb the nearest tree. Something had picked up their trail and was approaching way too rapidly for peace of mind.

Protvor didn't hesitate. She pointed to a tree close by, and they ran for it. She assisted Getik into the tree with her tail, while Kryger turned around to see if the creature that had developed such an interest in them was in sight yet. He expected the creature to charge the moment it saw them, as he sensed a raging hunger. Then Protvor told him there was just enough time for him to get into the tree, for she could hear it running. Her hearing must be much keener than his, he thought as he hurriedly put his arrows away and slung the bow over a shoulder. He jumped for the lowest branch and climbed rapidly to where the girl sat nonchalantly a little below Getik, holding on to another branch with her tail.

It's one of the powerful big cats. Perch a little above me, for I'm going to prick it with Getik's spear. I'm anchored with my tail so I can swing away because it can jump high and climb but never dies fast enough. Don't spear it with your ax as it might grab it with its mouth and pull you from the branch. Rather, get an arrow ready to stick into its throat if it scrambles higher up. It should just about reach us with its jump, and remember that it's very fast and vicious when it's hungry.

Kryger gasped silently when the cat loped into view with its nose close to the ground because it was as big as a fully grown horse. It was lean, and muscles rippled under its gray, orange-striped pelt. It stopped under the tree and looked up with ferocious bright-yellow eyes. Seeing them, it growled and leaped past the lowest branch, almost touching the girl. She stuck the spear deep into its exposed neck and left it there as she immediately swung away to grab the branch around which her tail was wrapped. The cat roared, and its shoulder muscles bunched as it prepared to leap after its prey.

Kryger knew that severe pain in an eye might make a predator hesitate long enough for him to blind the other eye as well. Under normal circumstances, a blinded predator would still be focused on killing, and this would be only a delaying action to give the poison a few seconds to paralyze such an enormous body. Anchored by his left hand to a branch, he leaned sideways and stuck the arrow, held ready in his right hand, deep into one of the cat's eyes, pulled it out, and stuck it into the other eye. He could sense the cat was hesitating, and the distraction gave the poison enough time to paralyze the savage heart of the ferocious killer. Its bunched muscles relaxed slowly, its claws retracted reluctantly, and the cat fell backward and bounced limply from a lower branch before it tumbled to the ground.

"Yowza! I'd be very happy if I never come across another one of these. The six seconds it took to die felt like an eternity," Kryger exclaimed.

He climbed down to inspect the big cat. Its legs were all sinew and muscle and almost as thick as his own. Its claws were the size of dinner plates, and its jaws were big enough to bite his head off. He pulled the spear from its neck, wiped it on its pelt, and gave it to Getik when they joined him. Kryger, with a wealth of foreign thought at his disposal, explained, *I'm inspecting it because one should know one's enemy. The only soft place I can see is the spot where the neck joins the breast, where Prot's spear penetrated. All animals, even humans, have it, but it's protected when the head isn't up in the air. So if it is exposed, aim for this area because an arrow or a spear would penetrate deep and maybe reach its heart. An arrow would go in between the ribs too, if you are lucky. The skull looks hard, but I'm going to see how hard. Would you have a go first, Prot? See if you can cleave its forehead between the ears. Its head would normally be raised because it would be going for your throat. Just swing your ax, and don't aim since you won't have time to do it in any confrontation.* He stood aside as she quickly moved in front of the cat and swung her ax in a half circle. The ax went halfway through the skull right in the center.

Good girl, he praised. *That should either kill it or stun it long enough for a second chop, should it be necessary. Now stand back.*

From his side he swung his ax with all his power in a sideways swipe at the head, as he would normally do in a fight. He wasn't surprised that the jaw was cleanly severed just below the eyes.

Just remember that it can still use its claws to maim or kill you in its death throes. In my experience, an animal doesn't thrash around if you cleave its brainpan, but always make sure that it's dead. If you thrust an arrow, spear, or a knife upward through an eye, it should reach the brain because bone behind eyes is never thick.

I'll remember, Kryger. Protvor was serious.

Getik just nodded. He'd seen Kryger push the arrow into the cat's eyes and would remember it for the rest of his life. Yes, it was callous, but necessary to keep a giant dying but still persistent predator at bay.

12

When they resumed their journey, Protvor used her eyes, ears, and nose as she was wont to do and scanned the area with her finer senses only when she was sure it was safe to do so. Kryger approved since that was the proper way for a beginner to develop his or her finer senses. Quite a number of times she scented or saw a snake and then took a detour.

Kryger sensed quite a variety of warm-blooded life-forms. The predators were hunting or alertly at rest. Prey animals were timid and started at any slight sound.

After hours of surprisingly uneventful travel, the ground gradually rose, the trees grew closer together, and the undergrowth was denser. Protvor remarked that they were approaching a densely bushed, hilly area but that they must soon look for a resting place, for she was getting hungry and would like freshly fried meat for a change.

Kryger sensed a grazing prey animal a little distance off to their right and said he would go and get supper if they could find an open place for a fire and a climbable tree nearby. Protvor immediately pointed to a tree in front of them. She said she'd gather firewood while he was away, and when he told her his hunt was successful, she could start cutting branches for a platform if he wanted one.

No, the tree is for you and Getik to climb into if one of you becomes aware of danger. You just get a fire going to fry the meat, and then we'll rest farther along because the smell of roasting meat will entice a variety of hunters and scavengers to investigate. We won't get any rest—oh damn, something…I think a snake because I can't sense it, just caught our potential supper. He paused. *Ah, another one is moving this way, and I don't sense predators nearby.*

I agree with moving on after our meal because I know from experience that what you just said is true, and most of the time one isn't even allowed to leisurely finish or enjoy your meal if a predator is near enough to investigate the source of the smell. I sense some life-forms too, but I can't tell prey from predator. How do you know which is which?

I'll show you the difference when you can scan, smell, see, and hear at the same time. Kryger put his rucksack on the lowest branch against the trunk and asked them to take it up higher if they had to scramble into the tree. He didn't leave the battle-ax behind because he might need it, and it wouldn't cause any giveaway noises. Then he stalked off in the direction he sensed the approaching animal. He usually didn't stoop so low as to sense the location of his prey since, according to his upbringing, it wasn't fair, but this environment was different, and he had to be constantly on the alert.

The animal was just about thirty meters away when he stepped from behind a bush with his bow ready. The long-necked animal, which vaguely reminded him of a malformed gazelle, stood with its head turned back over a shoulder as if it had heard a noise behind it and was trying to see what caused it. Its nostrils were distended as it tested the still air. He put the arrow into the soft spot formed by the v-cavity of its chest just below the neck because the arrow would also pierce the heart, assuming it was located in the normal place. The bucklike creature dropped without a sound. He was about to retrieve it when he heard a stealthy footfall.

He stopped warily, fitted another arrow to his bow, and quested about. He sensed nothing but discerned dull thuds as if something heavy was trying to sneak closer. His eyes wandered to where the bucklike animal had been looking—and his heart almost stopped beating. A gigantic lizardlike beast, about twenty meters high on its tree trunk-size hind legs, reared and seemed to be sizing him up with cold black eyes in an overly big head attached to a muscular neck. It had small three-fingered claw hands with a ridiculously small opposing thumb attached to equally ridiculously thin but strong-looking arms. Its long powerful jaws, armed with razor-sharp teeth, would cut him in half with one bite, and the long heavy tail would crush him to pulp with a single swipe. These things flashed through his head as he instantly put the arrow right into the softer v-spot in the huge chest where the neck started.

The creature cocked its head to one side as if it was puzzled by the slight itch, giving Kryger the impression that it didn't feel the arrow that had disappeared completely into its chest cavity. The soft throat below the chin wasn't exposed, so he aimed carefully and put the other arrow through the eye that seemed to be sizing him up. It penetrated quite deeply, and the creature shook its head; bellowed in anger; lowered its upper body, neck, and head; and charged with astonishing speed.

Kryger realized it would be useless to run, for even he couldn't outrun such unstoppable momentum. He therefore stood ready until the monster was almost upon him before he jumped sideways and then sprinted to the nearest tree. Maybe he could elude it among the trees, for such bulk, in his experience, couldn't execute a tight turn, but he heard it thundering on, breaking branches as it carried on in almost a straight line. He was relieved but found it incomprehensible that the beast had decided to flee instead of turning back to make a snack of him. Maybe Protvor's poison didn't have an immediate effect on such gigantic reptile bodies, or perhaps it was immune to the poison.

He strained his eyes and ears to check if more reptiles were in the vicinity and detecting nothing suspicious, warily returned to his kill, and cut off its hind quarters without skinning it first. It would be enough for all three of them. Then he jogged along the trail left by the reptile to gather sticks thin enough to use for skewers. Since he knew exactly where he had left his party, he calculated that the monster would miss them by a wide margin if it kept on in more or less a straight line.

He found them high up in the tree and told them they could come down and start the fire; the big reptile had decided to leave them alone.

"We heard it coming from the direction you took, son. How come it missed you? Prot said that the big reptiles have a keen sense of smell, and we were almost out of our minds believing that it couldn't miss you. She told me that carnivorous reptiles have excellent eyesight too, although they're a bit limited in the brain department."

"You should have used your sixth sense to scan for me as I showed you. It was stalking the same prey, but I was there just before it. I couldn't sense it, so maybe it gobbled up the first prey that I thought was caught by a snake. I don't know if we can kill such a monstrous thing. I put an arrow through its chest that it barely seemed to notice and then charged off when I put another one through its eye."

Ah, but you did, Kryger, Protvor answered his spoken words. *The Old One said that such big reptiles have two brains: one in the head that controls the instincts and one in its hindquarters that controls the body. He said that it doesn't feel pain the way we do, that it's just something like a warning itch. The poisoned arrow in its head immediately killed that brain, and the arrow in its body will slowly kill the other brain as the poison circulates. The running will help, and we'll find it not far from here. I've never seen one from close up, and maybe we can retrieve your arrows. But first we eat because it can wait. It is said that scavengers and predators are so afraid of these reptiles that they will only feed on one when it starts to decompose.*

This one may have been driven this way by a bigger one because they prefer to hunt in the swamps and grass fields around the lake. They lay their eggs in the open, and the male and female take turns to guard their nest. They spend a lot of time in deep water; I think it's to take the weight off their feet, although they grab and devour any smaller water creatures they come across. That's all I know about them.

Kryger was careful with his thoughts since he'd already realized this self-reliant girl was more sensitive than she'd let on. Getik lighted the fire while he started to cut the meat into easily handled portions. Protvor sprinkled the pieces with salt and herbs from her numerous pouches before skewering them one by one and passing them on to Getik to roast when the stick was nearly full.

After a tasty, satisfying meal, they gathered their things and followed the branch-strewn trail. They found the reptile where it had succumbed on its stomach a few hundred steps away, and only then did Kryger notice that its finely scaled hide was a mottled, well-camouflaging range of colors with green and brown predominant. He pulled his slightly bent arrow from its eye but didn't see any sign of the other when he inspected the entry point. He decided that it wasn't worth the effort of cutting the enormous belly open to look for it.

Protvor kicked its backside, saying that it was something she wanted to do for a very long time. Kryger told her to string her new bow and try it out since it should be dry enough. Getik gave her ten of his arrows since her new bow was about the same size as his.

She happily accepted the arrows and then strung the bow. Kryger told her to aim for the area where his arrow had gone in, but he and Getik stood well away. She did so from about thirty steps and jumped up and down in a weird dance when the arrow went in halfway. Then she ran to the carcass and managed to pull the arrow out with both hands and a joyous smile on her face.

I never dreamed that a bow could be as strong and accurate as this one you made for me. I had doubts, but this is the best one I've ever had. She took the string from her old bow, dumped the unshaped stick on the carcass, and hugged both of them in turn.

They killed two more of the big reptiles, a few snakes at streams, and a number of other predators between the next four resting periods. Then, after the fourth sleeping period, Protvor announced they were close to the Old One's area and that they should reach him before their next sleeping period if they weren't unduly delayed.

Kryger, contrary to his usual approach of tackling things as they came, was tired. Getik was good and never took a back seat when trouble came their way. The girl was better, but Kryger felt responsible for both of them and was always the first to sense trouble coming their way, except for reptiles, which she heard first or sniffed out because her sense of smell was well developed. He still preferred to be on his own because that was the way he had grown up. After the two years with Quarr as his navigator, he had again reverted to being a loner since new technology took care of that precision chore within seconds.

When Getik noticed his unusual quietness and became concerned, Kryger told him a very old joke to explain what was troubling him. He used equivalent words translated into Getik's language: "A crop farmer took on a drifter who passed by and asked for a job. The farmer didn't like the looks of the drifter but hired the guy after being urged by his wife, who took pity on the down-and-out human being. After a huge meal, he gave the drifter a spade, took him to a big field, and asked him if he would start digging, for he must plant the field with vegetables before the season changed. His old plow horse had recently died, and he was in the process of looking for a reliable one. He expected the guy to start walking after he was out of sight.

"To his surprise, the drifter finished half the field before sunset and finished the rest the next day. The farmer felt guilty about treating the fellow unfairly and decided to give him an easy job. The next morning, he took him to a shed to sort potatoes into different sizes for the market. At noon he went to check on the guy and found him unconscious with only a few small heaps of potatoes around him.

"Now feeling thoroughly guilty, he shouldered the man and took him to the house, where he put him to bed. Together with his wife, they resuscitated the drifter.

"'I'm very sorry. I overtaxed you with all that digging,' the farmer apologized.

"'No, no, I liked the hard work,' he replied, 'but it's making them decisions that are killing me!'"

Protvor, who didn't know what a drifter, a market, a day, decisions, or potatoes were, just shrugged and looked at him uncomprehendingly. Getik laughed because he saw the humor and knew how lazy some people were. After a while, when he finally realized what his friend was trying to tell him, he said, "You'll get used to responsibility, son, but don't shoulder all the decisions that must be taken. Just as I have taken responsibility for designing your miniature spaceship, I've delegated the work to others who must make their own decisions and take responsibility for what they do. You can't watch everyone and do everything for them. You have to trust them to do their part. Do you see what I mean?

"You've given Protvor the responsibility to lead us, and she does it to the best of her abilities, but you are still trying to help her when she doesn't need help. We're learning from you as you're learning from us. I've realized that you're trained to depend only on yourself to stay alive. Yet we value our own lives and try to stay alive to the best of our abilities. Protvor trusts her instincts because she grew up in this environment. Okay, I admit that we still make stupid mistakes because we haven't got your iron discipline, but we're learning all the time. You have to learn to let go now and then."

Okay, my friend, Protvor continued. *I've been through the territory we're entering now, and I will avoid the most dangerous places, but I can't guarantee the unpredictable. The problem, as I see it, is that we have become too reliant on you to warn us of danger. Luckily the worst of the really dangerous is behind us. Trust me to do my best to get you to the Old One intact.*

Kryger smiled. *I've trusted you since we first met, Prot, and I trust Getik too. But I cannot afford to relax my constant vigilance because it will become a dangerous habit, and both of you should remember and make it a habit to scan the area while you're talking or doing anything else. Lead the way, please, and I'll follow after Getik as usual. My job is to cover our backs.*

As she turned around to face the way they were going, Kryger shot the leopardlike cat that had just started its charge from thirty meters away in the chest. It fell dead a few meters in front of Protvor. She turned back and smiled at him.

Thank you, she said calmly. Getik had been teaching her the meanings of words and the customs of his people to pass the time while Kryger slept during rest periods. *I see what you mean.*

Kryger smiled back. *You're welcome.* Protvor glanced at Getik, and he explained what the words meant.

Kryger was once more impressed with the girl's unperturbed calmness. She would make a great warrior, he thought, and wondered if she would prefer to stay here or join him to be trained as a pilot. She would never be Quarr's equal, but in time, and with enough practice and experience, she could come quite close.

13

By the time they reached the spacious stronghold with high walls of stone, built against a perpendicular cliff of a high outcropping of bare sandstone, Kryger was tired and also sensed the exhaustion in Getik. Protvor had pushed the pace more than usual after telling them it wasn't necessary to spend another resting period out in the wild when they were so close to their destination. A heavily reinforced narrow wooden gate opened as they approached and closed behind them.

Most of the arable area inside the wall was cultivated with what seemed to be vegetables and some fruit trees. There was even a small rill meandering through the middle of the area before vanishing through a narrow opening in a sidewall. It reminded Kryger of a small self-sufficient hamlet. The open ground and footpaths were neatly kept, and a few tailed gardeners were busy doing some unnecessary chores, or so it seemed to Kryger. They were of different hues, and he thought they might be from different tribes of the same species as Protvor. If so, he thought, they must be quite civilized to keep gardens instead of hunting for a living.

The gardeners waved to Protvor, and she acknowledged their greetings while she made her way along a well-trodden path to the numerous caves against the cliff. Tailless humans seemed to be unusual, and Kryger's size aroused questions, but Protvor ignored the queries, and her companions followed her lead. She entered the widest opening without announcing their arrival.

The rather huge cave was divided by well-fitted timber walls into a number of room partitions on both sides of the broad passage. At the far end of the straight passage was an elongated spot of sunlight, let in through a wide crack high up in the roof. A weird-looking, at least from a distance, creature was seated on what looked like a padded armchair and seemed to be a primitive throne. Kryger sensed the mental power emanating from the strange being.

As they came closer, he noticed it was a naked humanlike lizard with a big braincase and a fairly flat face. It was a little bigger than Kryger but much heavier and broader, especially in the abdomen area. Its shoulders were small in comparison, and its hands were humanlike, but it had only three fingers and an opposing thumb. Its right leg, from the knee down, was missing, and the foot of its intact leg had four toes. Otherwise it was as humanoid as could be.

Next to the chair was a pair of crude thick crutches. He noticed that the big chair, made of sturdy timber, was shaped like the seats he had seen in the craft. *This guy must have a spinal ridge like a chameleon,* he thought, *but he's not that weird at all. He's much better looking than the Shadow Ycagabys, for instance, although his rough skin looks a bit on the dry side.* Kryger became friends with Ycagabys on a planet invaded by the Hullenii bugs. It was his first encounter with a giant bug that went by the name of Gorrel.

That was a quick and accurate evaluation, Kryger, and essentially correct, but what you can't see is that I have a stumpy knob—no doubt the result of evolution—where my remote ancestors must have sported a tail. Welcome to my abode, Kryger, Getik, Prot. You traveled quite fast—and with not even one scratch to show for the perilous journey. The benches may not be very comfortable, but sit down for a while. Prot, you've already heard what I'm going to tell them, so you can go and sleep in your old room after you've placed a good meal in that growling stomach of yours. Please ask Hotvrol to bring meals for us also.

When Protvor was gone, Maksika continued, *You must know some background before your education can start. To get directly to the point, by means of hypnosis I must teach you my language first, written as well as oral, because the symbols in the craft are in my language, and the semi-intelligent craft responds* only to questions and commands spoken in my language, and of course, it replies in the same language. The language requirement can be changed if you know how, but my language may now no longer exist, so I recommend—unless there is a compelling reason to do so—that you don't change it to prevent theft of the craft. Anyway, I'll implant the knowledge in your brains when we get to it.

Other weapons and gadgets can be installed in addition to the two—let me call them death rays, for that's what they really are. The invisible-ray weapons were designed to turn any living creature they touch into a scarcely noticeable heap of ash, so as you both realize, one who controls it can intentionally destroy his fellow beings instantly without leaving traceable evidence. The weapons disperse the atoms of any living body they touch, even inside a closed building or spacecraft within their range. If you target a spacecraft, for instance, every living thing inside will vanish without a trace, but the ship itself isn't affected and will continue until it crashes or malfunctions.

In other words, it doesn't destroy inanimate things, so, to disable a spacecraft void of enemies, you might add that little weapon of yours that creates holes in everything, even planets. My personal opinion is that that is the most useful little weapon ever invented, although you have to aim it accurately.

After essential changes have been made to enable you to comfortably fly the craft, you must take it to your people to add other weapons and gadgets you may need and, naturally, change the controls to what you are used to, which Getik and his people can start doing.

Just then a middle age-looking cat-woman entered with three meals on outsize plates on a crude cart. Beginning with Maksika, she handed each of them a plate and a thin wooden spoon. All thanked her politely and dug in as she left. The heaps of vegetables were strange but tasty, and the stew was superbly spiced.

Maksika was pleased with their enjoyment. *I've succeeded in domesticating some members of different tribes. Previously they were hunters only, but some of them now actually enjoy cultivating different tubers, herbs, and other vegetables. My life-mate started the project and tried to civilize the locals before she was killed by a stray giant reptile a couple of thousand years ago.* Kryger and Getik made appropriate noises of sympathy, but Maksika shrugged it off as of no consequence. After all, it had happened so long ago.

I still reckon time by the outside standards since there are no seasons or nights here. I'll let you in on a secret—why we remained in this dangerous region which is called the Place of Great Silences by the locals, although it's not really silent. Some peculiarity in the sun's makeup cast an extraordinary influence over this area. Our scientists found that life is prolonged here, but we didn't know by how much.

Kryger, you live by a code that essentially says, "I won't die until I give up." That is quite true, you know, even in an ordinary, uneventful life. You trained your subconscious mind to be positive, never to yield to anything detrimental to your well-being, even sickness or strife. We did the same type of thing. I am close to twenty thousand years old, which is about fifty times longer than our normal life span. I've endured all that time, telling myself that I won't give up and die while I'm waiting for a warrior to be born or to arrive who has integrity and is caring, honest and capable of using my fighting spacecraft exclusively for the purpose for which it was invented, because the enemy to life, who destroyed the outside of this planet, will return and begin to populate this galaxy.

I watched you in my spirit form when you fought the Bugs, Kryger, and I was impressed by your fortitudinous and exceptional performance. I've never imagined that someone can do so many things almost simultaneously and stay unperturbed. I'm very pleased that you are here because I know that the end of my life is near. That's why I had this chair placed here, where I can enjoy the sun in privacy and never move too much a distance from the sun to my bed. Oh yes, Kryger, I'm as warm-blooded as you are, but the indignity of advanced age paired with disabilities has many drawbacks.

Please bear with me for a while because I feel the need to talk and tell my story to someone who'd know what I'm talking about. I want to tell you about my people. I am the last of the Scrii, as far as I know, and someone else should know of the menace that may arrive—unless the murderous race of beings who followed us from the next galaxy have met their deserved end. When you've rested, it will be all business because I have much knowledge to transfer to you. If you both will let me into your minds while you sleep, I can teach you my language because it will save time.

Kryger said he would allow it as long as there was no prying into secrets that would automatically trigger the bolt, and Getik dryly said he didn't have the ability or inclination to stop Maksika.

Maksika continued, We weren't an aggressive race. Like yours, Getik, we were rather interested in the physical sciences and the development of mind power. In time we explored our galaxy, met many interesting races, and settled on a few other suitable planets over centuries as we increased in numbers and also just because the planets were there and devoid of intelligent life.

Then one day, one of our planets was attacked by a race similar to ours, but with slit eyes and more red of color than gray. There was no apparent reason for their attack, but according to mind-sends we received, they were extremely cruel and aggressive. Once they had their fill of cruelty, which they called sport, they had destroyed all life on the surface of that planet.

On our home world, we frantically developed all kinds of weapons, but they proved ineffective in the first battle. Our fleet was almost totally destroyed within a few hours, but one ship escaped and returned via a roundabout route. While they were indulging in murder, destruction, and pillage, a volunteer scout boarded one of their temporarily abandoned ships and sent us information about its numerous types of weapons, which we copied and improved upon in record time.

In the next encounter, we destroyed most of their fleet, but then a few years later, thousands of their ships arrived and destroyed the planet as well as our fleet. Subsequently they systematically searched and destroyed inhabited planets one by one. By that time we had built huge ships capable of doing hundreds of light-years per hour because we had decided to leave the galaxy to escape them, which we did. Only a couple of thousand elected to stay behind to defend the planet and to deceive the enemy by fierce resistance.

After years of searching, we found this planet, similar to our old home, and decided to stay. Research and tests of new weapons started again, but after a few hundred years of peaceful existence, most of us became too complacent when the expected enemy didn't come. The general belief was that we escaped them.

I was still a youngster when the inner world was discovered, and also the unique, almost indestructible metal the ship was constructed from. Our rulers, just in case the enemy migrated to this galaxy, decided to build a few hundred special fighting ships that could not be detected by any kind of instrument and that protected themselves from destruction, for our science had developed rapidly during the war years and after we settled here, although thereafter it slowed down due to our undisturbed, peaceful existence.

The outer world was our preferred home because of the day and night cycle we were accustomed to, stars we could look at, and seasons we could experience. We came to the inner world to work, taking our time to build the first ship since we had to experiment with the super hard metal. Testing the finished prototype was me and my companion's task. It surpassed our expectations. The two ray guns worked fine, and the ship reached something like nine hundred and eighty-three light-years per standard hour. A beacon was created for the ship to home in on because we could've gotten lost in the vastness of space on the test run if we had sustained the expected maximum speed for more than an hour.

Then our executives conferred at length to decide, with our input, if we needed bigger ships with more weapons and if it was worth the effort. Just after we decided that four-seat ships with a few extra weapons were adequate, the enemy arrived unexpectedly and attacked immediately with incendiary hell-bombs. It seemed that they were determined to wipe us out once and for all.

My mate and I were in an air-car at the time, and we headed for the opening to the inner planet at ground level in an effort to reach our ship. Unfortunately, just as we reached the half-concealed entrance, we were spotted by a small patrol ship. They, of course, gave chase and were rapidly overtaking us. We were unarmed and headed here in the hope of luring them into the dead zone. By the time we reached the dead zone, they were above and close behind us and opened fire just as I veered away when I recognized the pinkish hill which marks the edge of the dead zone. The single salvo miraculously missed my companion, but I lost my right leg just below the knee. The air-car lost power, and my companion grabbed control while I hastily applied a tourniquet to stop the bleeding.

The car rapidly lost altitude, and my mate descended into the dead zone. They followed higher up, perhaps in anticipation of seeing our craft crash into the jungle so that they could gloat before finishing us up leisurely, or perhaps they were astounded by the inner world. Their ship's engines cut out, and we think that they crashed close to the reptile lake.

We were almost at ground level and my mate miraculously managed to land. I'll skip the irrelevant details of our initial struggle to survive. My mate later repaired the car and warily returned to the outer surface to look for survivors, but the once fair planet was a scorched desert. Even the lakes and seas were just sand and rock, but a few hardy animals and plants survived in the deep fissure. Life-giving air seeps into the fissure, and that is why the surface has acquired a livable atmosphere again. We were grateful *that the inner planet was not discovered or reported by the crew of that scout ship.*

Now you have the background of how and why the outer planet was devastated. If you're interested, you might find what may be left of the air-car in a cave in the pink peak.

It will be easier to embed what I know of our sciences in both of you, and I'll provide you with all the knowledge about the ship and how it operates. I've asked Hotvrol to show you to your rooms, which are actually only partitions, as you've noticed. Just remember to open your mind and await me, Kryger, for I don't want to be blasted again.

Maksika's face contorted into some sort of grimace, which Kryger interpreted as a smile. The cat-woman arrived and took them to separate rooms with stuffed sleeping mats of animal skins that were just long enough to accommodate Kryger's big frame, perhaps because there were no short humanoids in the compound.

After wishing Getik a pleasant sleeping period, he shed his clothes and stretched out on the soft mat. He felt pleasure at being able to sleep safely for a change. Then he relaxed, prepared his mind not to retaliate to any intrusion, and drifted off to sleep. He was aware when Maksika entered his mind but fell into a deep, hypnotic sleep when commanded to do so.

He woke immediately when Getik, in the company of Protvor, called his name from a distance. He felt surprisingly refreshed, dressed himself, and was led to the kitchen, where they were served a meal by another female of a local catlike species who introduced herself as Nobruk.

As they finished, Protvor said in a language consisting of clicks and other strange sounds, "Maksika wants to see you alone, Kryger. He says you're first because your instruction is more difficult and will take longer than that of Getik."

Kryger was surprised he understood, then realized it was Maksika's lingo. He found he could reply in the same language without too much thought.

14

Protvor directed Kryger to the same place where they'd met the alien before. There was a sleeping mat in front of Maksika, and he told Kryger to lie down because it would be easier to relax. He had to be hypnotized again; otherwise it would take ages to transfer the knowledge he would need to control the semi-sentient craft. He had to understand the science behind it as well and how to change whatever had to be changed to suit his requirements.

Kryger trusted Maksika not to tinker with his mind or to extract secrets. He sat and then toppled over onto his back. He relaxed as he had been taught to do and then told Maksika to proceed. He instantly lost awareness when he felt the alien touch his mind.

When he was brought back to consciousness, he felt drained of all energy. Maksika looked a bit worn out too but grinned and then said in his own language, "It took more time than I anticipated, but the knowledge is transferred. You're exhausted and should sleep after you've had a meal because your subconscious mind must integrate the new knowledge, which you will recall whenever you have a need for it. I must rest for a few hours too before I impart knowledge to Getik. After your rest period, Prot will show you around while you reflect on what I've taught you. It is necessary to do so because you must consciously know what knowledge you have. Otherwise you will make unnecessary and perhaps fatal mistakes. You must bear in mind that it's an alien craft for you and that it's intelligent enough to execute oral commands. After the necessary changes, fly it, get used to it, and use the weapons on one of your legitimate enemies to check their range and how deadly they are. And think twice and consider all the possible consequences before you make other changes since not all might be beneficial.

"I find your people's automatic aiming through the helmet intriguing and think that it's an essential addition for your special weapon. I will, after I'm finished with Getik, show you how and where to make changes so that you can instruct your wizards, as you call them, to do it safely."

Kryger thanked him and went to ask for a meal. Hotvrol was on duty again and ladled up a generous helping of every dish and then basked in his praise. She was clearly not accustomed to compliments.

His brain was tired, but he went for a leisurely walk around the enclosure to recall what Maksika had taught him about the craft. He found it difficult to believe he needed to tell a ship in an alien language when to start and shut down its engine and ask it to open the door to let him in or out. It sounded a bit silly, but that could be changed, although it was a nonlethal way of safeguarding the deadly craft since the weapons couldn't be activated when the engine was inactive. Maybe he should think about changing the language for Quarr's convenience, but there was plenty of time to make up his mind. He returned to his room and immediately fell asleep.

***

Maksika eventually said he had transferred all he knew about the craft and the little of the old Scrii science he was privileged to have learned. Kryger and Getik decided they would depart after the next rest period.

During their last session, Kryger became concerned because Maksika was visibly showing signs of deteriorating health and, when asked, readily admitted he was letting go because he at last had found someone to take over the task he couldn't complete. He no longer had to cling to life and already had lived much, much longer than was normal. He was looking forward to joining his mate in the hereafter.

Kryger was young, but he understood the loneliness Maksika must have endured after his mate was killed. He thanked the old lizard being for everything and asked if it was appropriate for them to leave after one day of rest.

Maksika smiled and said it was fine and that he appreciated the use of the word "day."

Kryger was awakened by a timid knock on the door of his cubicle. His senses told him it was Nobruk, and he told her to come in. She did so and whispered that the Old One had asked her to bring Kryger to him as soon as possible.

Kryger didn't bother to dress since no one in the compound ever dressed or even owned an article of clothing. As he reached Maksika's cave in the sandstone cliff, he was told to come in and close the door. Maksika was reclined on a comfortable padded bench that apparently could be converted into a bed.

"There is one last task asked of me by an entity from the next stage of existence. She said that I was the only one on this side of life sensitive enough to receive and understand her entreaty. She asked me to memorize words in an unfamiliar language which I had to repeat to you, but I could not pronounce them because the timbre of my vocal cords won't change. She can use me as an anchor in this dimension to speak to you, but it will be a mighty effort even if it lasts for only a minute because apparently there is a time and vibration difference which takes tremendous energy to overcome, even for a short period. You must also be in a supine position since it is quite possible that you might lose consciousness for a few moments.

"She said she was unable to bid this dimension farewell until your memory was restored, and I'm her only means to complete her task. Do you know what this is about?"

Kryger said he was mystified as well. He felt silly but would do as required mainly out of curiosity. He sat on the smooth stone floor and then toppled over onto his back so he could see the Old One, who looked a bit nonplussed.

He watched Maksika close his eyes and then go still. Next to his couch, something began to glow, which increased in brilliance until he saw the form of a very alien but strangely beautiful woman looking down at him. She was about twice his height, and he felt like a naughty young boy looking up at an adult. A vague memory began to stir when she smiled at him.

She mind-spoke, *Hello again, Kryger. You'll remember me in a moment after I've removed the blocks which I put into place to allow you to develop strength of character and purpose through experience. The blocks would have been removed in another two to three years' time, but the catalyst has been killed in a duel because he became too arrogant for his britches. Fortunately a random factor was introduced some years ago by higher forces in that the remainder of the Scrii people fled to this galaxy to avoid extinction, and the only survivor kept himself alive until you arrived, which somewhat changes my people's prediction of more than a billion years ago.*

Maksika's conscious knows what I'm saying, but he'll be drained of energy in the minute or two I'm using him to remain in the third dimension because I cannot use you as an anchor on this side. Now to business!

Suddenly Kryger's senses reeled, his mind went blank, and he blacked out for a long moment. He was back with Quarr behind the cascade, isolated by the water curtain from Gorrel's overpowering mind, which was angrily scouring the ether to reestablish control over his mind after having lost it when Kryger fell into the river. His brain was befuddled, hopelessly entangled with Quarr's, when she threw caution to the wind and merged their minds to save his life. She could shield her brain against the irresistible thoughts of the Hullenii Bugs, and she wanted to transfer the ability to him but was unable to extricate her mind again.

He had just forced her and himself to sleep in the hope that their subconscious minds might untangle the mess. Suddenly an irresistible force entered both their minds and restored their individualities. The soul of the tall, strangely beautiful alien woman then took him on an incredible spirit journey. He relived the beauty of the ancient hidden city, the glimpse of her real body in the stasis unit before it suddenly turned to dust when the unit was deactivated, and what he was told and taught. The vague, tantalizing memories he'd dismissed as fantasies became reality.

It took less than two minutes for Kryger's full mind power and memory to be restored. When he regained consciousness, he felt invincible energy coursing through his veins, and he was humbled by the incredible fortune that had marooned them on Okryon, but the alien woman didn't have time to indulge in his reflections.

I would have stayed a little longer in this life if I knew that your mind would mature enough in less than two years to control the knowledge given to you. Use it wisely and with thought. I just might have enough energy left to remove the block that prevents you from misusing it.

No! What for? It's better to leave it in place! Kryger was most emphatic.

The shining image smiled. *I'm more than pleased with you. Farewell, and thank you, Maksika.* She faded before he had time to express his heartfelt thanks.

He sat up slowly and faced Maksika. The alien's face was gray with fatigue but filled with wonder, for he was sensitive to Kryger's mind and shared his experiences and feelings. *I'm incredibly blessed to have witnessed and been part of what you have experienced, Kryger. It fills me with wonder and gratitude that I can leave the craft to someone with so much integrity. You have had a very interesting life, and it seems that an extraordinary destiny awaits you. It's been my privilege to witness a tiny part of it, and I'll take that knowledge with me to the other side. I don't envy you, though, for your lifestyle would have been too tough for me.*

Kryger slowly got up and went to Maksika. He took the alien's rough-textured hands in his. *There is no way I can thank you enough for everything you've done for me, but I will remember you and the woman entity for as long as I live. The only way I can express a little of my gratitude is to give you some of the energy I feel coursing through me. It won't make up for the energy and time you've spent to transfer your knowledge to us, but it's the only gift I have that is of use to you.*

He then transferred energy and love until he saw the alien's face soften and the tiredness disappear. He was aware that his mind was much stronger and more sensitive than usual.

Maksika's face showed wrinkles that hadn't been noticeable before, but they could sense he was happy. He addressed them in his own language: "I've taught you all I know, but I can't tell you three how happy I am to at long last hand the ship over to a worthy warrior. I know that you will use it well, Kryger, and look after it, although your combat methods are a bit...well...challenging. I would appreciate it, though, if you'd take Prot with you because she doesn't fit in with this primitive society, and she'd make a good pilot if trained properly. She knows as much as you do about the ship, but she needs to be taught how to be a fighter pilot and which end of a gun to point away from her. You know by now that she doesn't lack courage."

He stopped and looked Kryger in the eyes, who in turn looked at Protvor, who was looking hopefully at him.

"I was going to ask you to take me with you."

Kryger smiled. "I apologize for my bad manners, Prot. I just assumed that you were coming with us. Yes, you are most welcome, but you have to realize that you will be in a totally new environment where your old customs will not be tolerated, and you will experience hardships, possibly hunger, the possibility of an early death, and many other things that may discourage you.

"You may regret leaving this world of eternal daylight, for to my knowledge such a world doesn't exist anywhere else, and the periodic darkness outside this world will be frightening at first. I'll do my best to help and teach you when and what I can, and so will Getik and other people. You will be cooped up over many sleeping and waking periods in a confined space where you can barely stretch. Do you really want to endure all those inconveniences?"

She nodded. "I can only do my best to adapt to whatever is required, and I won't complain because I know that I no longer belong here in the Place of Great Silences. Maksika showed me many mind-pictures and told me many stories, so I have a fair idea of what to expect."

"I'm a good teacher, and I'll be patient and understand your courage. Just remember that in other worlds, people will stare at you because you'll be one of a kind. But we are wasting our host's energy. I'm sorry, Maksika, for I can sense your tiredness. I'll keep my mouth shut, but I want to thank you for the legacy and your patience in transferring your knowledge to us. As Prot said, I can only try my best, and I'll be worthy of the fighting ship."

Maksika smiled wanly. "Don't worry about my health. I welcome the fast-approaching end of my way-too-long life span. I'm grateful that you were driven here because I couldn't have staved off death for much longer. Perhaps it was part of our destiny. I've never heard of nor met anyone as courageous as you."

The other two watched in astonishment as Maksika suddenly sat up straight with what was a smile and held out his arms. Kryger stepped forward and briefly embraced the old being, stepped back, lifted his hand in farewell, and abruptly turned away to hide any visible emotion. Getik and Prot quickly followed his example.

They said goodbye to the cooks, collected their weapons and packs, and were let out of the compound. Out of habit they fell into the usual order, Protvor in the lead, and started the journey back.

Kryger forced his thoughts away from reliving the experience with the beautiful alien woman because his life and those of the other two depended on their combined vigilance and undistracted watchfulness. He would recall those specific memories when he was in a safe environment again.

Protvor more or less followed the same route. Kryger soon realized that her scanning ability had improved to such an extent that she could sense predators at some distance and therefore circled downwind around them. They couldn't evade opportunistic predators that followed their scent, though, and once they were treed by a small pack of hoodah they were forced to do away with because they had made themselves at home under the tree in a manner that indicated they weren't in any hurry to leave. Wandering or lost giant reptiles were thankfully absent. When he brought the subject up, Protvor said that only a few wandered this far away from the vicinity of the lake and that they had just been unlucky the previous time.

After eight rest periods, Kryger began to see landmarks that indicated they were nearing the pink cliff where their airboat should be, but out of habit he still scanned the area as far as his senses could reach. He sensed only furtive animals going about the business of feeding, but in the direction they had come from, he detected someone in trouble.

"The way to the boat is clear of troublemakers unless a snake or two are on the lookout for a meal, but about a kilometer and a half back on our trail, someone is in the same sort of trouble as Prot was when we found her. Do we leave him to his fate, or do we take time to go and see if we can help? I'd like to know if he was following us," he said in the Scrii language to keep in practice.

"I sense nothing since I can't reach that far yet," Getik replied. "How do you know it's a male? We're not in a hell of a hurry to get home, and in his place I'd appreciate any help I could get. What do you think, Prot? Shall we go and check who is in trouble?"

"I can't reach that far either, so what the hell?" she replied after a moment's concentration. "Let's go and see if we're in time to rescue the moron. Anyone who has the guts to go it alone might be worth saving."

Kryger pointed the direction, and they set off at a trot. After a kilometer, Getik remarked, *I still can't sense anything out of the ordinary, son. Your scanning range must be extraordinary. And while I think of it, your thoughts have been closed to me since we left Maksika. What happened to you?*

I'm thinking, and I don't want to broadcast what I have to think about. And yes, one's scanning range improves with constant practice. I've done it for more years than I can remember, and I think that my range is about five kilometers, he improvised. It was much more, but he didn't think it advisable to disclose his true range. *The male, for I can even sense gender after all the practice, is less than a kilometer away. He is treed and beating off one determined cat. He is tiring but should last until we get there.*

Then let's put on more speed, Protvor suggested. *We can go much faster than this jog.*

No! You should know the danger of that. We might not see a snake before it strikes. Be extra careful because you're the one in front, Kryger answered.

From then on, Protvor was very alert, but fortunately they didn't meet any other predators and arrived at the scene about five minutes later.

A male, the same race as Protvor, had both feet on the highest sturdy branch of one of the smaller trees and was clinging to the trunk a little higher up in a half-sitting position. He was beating a spotted predator in its face, head, and sometimes on its bleeding nose with a short, thick stick and kicked it with the heel of a bare foot every time it reached the branch just below him.

Getik sent an arrow into the creature's neck as it lunged up again with its claws clinging to the trunk. It shook its neck as if irritated and then fell on its back. The male, who was clinging with his tail and one arm to different branches, looked at it in surprise and almost lost his hold when Protvor shouted a name that sounded like Fekbris to Kryger.

The male shouted her name and rapidly slid down the tree. He was trembling with fatigue but hugged Protvor fiercely when she approached him. Then he looked at Getik and Kryger with hatred in his eyes and rapidly rumbled off a few sentences to Protvor. Kryger couldn't follow as the male's mind was a jumble of conflicting thoughts. He gave up trying to sense what the male's business was at the edge of the dead zone.

Protvor laughed merrily and then said something. She turned to them and explained in the Scrii language, "This is my father. He returned to the compound because he was concerned about my safety.

"Some idiot illogically remarked that I left a few sleeps earlier, followed by two strange, tailless males. He thought that I was being taken away by you against my will and followed our trail as rapidly as he could. I explained that I asked to come with you and that I won't return to the tribe. Now what shall we do? We can't take him with us because the rest of the tribe will start looking for him and get into all sorts of dangerous, unnecessary trouble."

"What happened to his bow, arrows, and other weapons?" Kryger asked.

She turned back to her father, and a brief exchange followed. "He says that he was suddenly attacked by a pair of sondars—what we call these spotted cats—while he was studying our fresh tracks. He shot one, and then his bowstring broke when he fitted another arrow. He threw the bow in the other cat's face to gain time and then ran to the nearest tree. The cat jumped a little too short but got his claws on the quiver, and its weight ripped it off. It then savaged the quiver to shreds, but the remaining arrow had fallen clear. There was only one arrow left anyway, but he says he would have stuck it into the cat's eye if he still had it. His ax broke when he missed the cat's head, but he kept it at bay with the handle. He lost his flint knife as well, but it should be somewhere near."

"Why don't you give him yours, Prot?" Getik said. "You won't need it after we're in the airboat. You can have mine since I won't have any further use for it, except to get youngsters into trouble by bragging with it. But you must warn him that he might get his throat cut for possession of the arrows."

Prot looked at her bow, shrugged, and then reluctantly gave it to her father with a few words. Then she gave him her quiver with about ten arrows in it—six of them metal. Fekbris inspected the bow and arrows delightedly, even jumped up and down like a kid presented with a coveted toy.

Kryger gave her one of the arrowheads and said her father could use it for a skinning knife once he'd fitted a short handle to it. Fekbris tested it and cut his thumb, but he laughed and told Prot he'd have to hide it from the tribe. He bowed to Kryger and Getik, then said something to Prot, who nodded her head. He turned and pulled the arrow from the sondar's neck. He gave Getik a questioning look, and Getik indicated he could keep it. Fekbris bowed to them again, gave Protvor a hug, and then turned away. He didn't even make an effort to look for his flint knife as he trotted back the way he had come.

Getik had been educating Protvor to the best of his ability during rest periods while Kryger slept. She knew what to expect in the city and that she wouldn't need weapons unless she went out into the woods. He described a gun and told her she'd be taught to use it because it was deadlier, more accurate, and easier to use than bows and arrows.

"I'd like to have your bow and arrows, Getik, to keep in practice. But keep it for now until we reach your airboat. Which way do I go, Kryger?"

"The most direct route is to follow our tracks, but we must make a detour. Let me lead this time because one of the really big cats is sniffing at our trail. It may decide to check if we're good enough for an easy meal, although it's not hungry."

Kryger started back at a lope, leaving it to the other two to decide who would be rear guard. Protvor gestured to Getik to follow Kryger and took up position behind him with the ax ready in her hands. Although they scanned the area, they left it to Kryger to warn them of danger.

15

As usual, Kryger clutched three arrows ready for use in his bow hand with his forefinger curled around them and the poisonous tips pointing downward, slightly forward, and sideways. He maintained quite a fast pace because he knew Getik was fitter and could handle it. He kept about a hundred steps downwind from their previous path because if a predator decided to follow their trail, they would see it in time. He killed in self-defense and when hungry, but only when it was absolutely necessary. He hoped the predators were sated because these cats had a role to fulfill in this silent region, and they'd already killed too many of them.

Perhaps he was distracted by the fleeting thought of how to avoid another killing, and although he glanced at the pile of dried leaves, he didn't smell or see the well-camouflaged snake coiled half under it. The snake uncoiled and struck blindingly fast when he passed close to the pile. Its teeth snapped into a shoulder as the coils wrapped swiftly around his body, enclosing his legs and pulling him off his feet.

As fate would have it, one of the coils was pierced by the arrows in his bow hand, but the coils tightened with killing frenzy for a few vital seconds. Kryger instinctively held his breath and tightened his muscles, but it wasn't of any use against the tremendous power of the constrictor. His breath was squeezed out of his lungs, and he felt the mind-numbing sensation of being suffocated; then the tightening paused as the poison began to set in, but Kryger couldn't breathe and his mind was paralyzed with shock.

Protvor jumped past the petrified Getik and stuck the poisoned spearhead of the battle-ax into the snake's body, just below the head at an angle away from Kryger's shoulder, half severing it just as the coils relaxed a fraction. The snake instinctively tried to tighten its coils to suffocate its victim, but the overdose of poison was rapidly paralyzing its nerves, and its coils started to relax.

Kryger was losing consciousness when the pressure around his ribs started to subside. He took a shallow, shuddering breath, but his ribs felt squashed to splinters. He continued the shallow breathing, although it hurt and he couldn't move any part of his aching body. His survival instincts started to kick in again, and he sensed a predator approaching to investigate the prospects of an easy meal.

Getik! The cat's coming fast! Be ready! he shouted with his mind at the little wide-eyed man, who was gazing at him with a bewildered expression.

Getik, with a guilty start, immediately scanned the area and sensed the cat very close to them. He readied his bow and turned that way. He resolved to make doubly sure of his shot since he was the only one who could stop the big cat from reaching them.

When Protvor started to unwind the snake's coils from around his body, Kryger told her to be ready to use her ax on the big cat if it didn't die before it reached them. He was confident that Getik wouldn't miss because his accuracy had improved considerably with practice, but the big cats had the annoying tendency not to die quickly enough. She sensed that there was enough time to untangle the snake from Kryger because she knew she couldn't move him since it would cause agonizing pain. To her it was a miracle he was still breathing—until she noticed the three arrows protruding from the snake's body.

Without realizing it, Kryger took a deeper breath and began to chant the ages-old power song he had been taught by the Golden People on Nevus. The vibrant sound filled the air, and he felt strength return to his battered body before he realized he was hum-chanting the old song, but he didn't stop as the big cat loped into view and then stopped in its tracks when the strange vibration and sound reached it. Getik was tempted to shoot to err on the safe side, but refrained.

Perhaps the unfamiliar sound made the cat nervous, or perhaps it found the strange melody disconcerting. It suddenly jumped sideways as if kicked in the ribs and bounded away among the trees at a dead run.

When the song was finished, Kryger tried to sit up, but he was still too weak, a sensation that was very alarming to him. Getik slung the pack from his back and fished for the emergency kit.

"I'm going to give you an injection, son, since all kinds of harmful bacteria enter the bloodstream because a snake's teeth are contaminated. Infection sets in, and one can still die if it is not treated in time. Then I'll clean and bandage your shoulder wound."

Kryger realized he still couldn't get enough air into his lungs to reply.

Getik carefully cut Kryger's shirt open—and then stared at the snake's bite marks. "I don't believe what I see," he said in an astonished voice while he shook his head. "I've seen constrictor bites before, but these holes are rapidly vanishing, although your whole shoulder is red and swollen."

I told you that I'm a fast healer. It's a legacy from a beautiful lady, but it's a long story, which I may tell you some day. Please cut the shirt away as I can't even lift a finger yet.

Getik completed cutting the shirt off and then pulled it from under Kryger and threw it to one side. He mumbled a few unintelligent words as he injected some kind of fluid into Kryger's shoulder muscle. Then he wiped the area with a small pad and put the syringe back into the kit to dispose of it later.

"You must have some real magic healing power, son, and I'd like to hear the story behind this seemingly automatic ability."

Some other time when I feel better, Kryger replied and concentrated on moving a toe or a finger, anything to keep his mind occupied.

After an indeterminate time, he could move an arm and managed to roll over onto his stomach, uttering gasping grunts. He asked Getik to remove the weapons on his back. Then he pushed with his arms and came upright on his knees—and stayed that way, swaying backward and forward but determined not to give in. Protvor grabbed him by the unwounded shoulder to steady him.

He groaned. *That damn snake just had time to squeeze the hell out of me. It's incredibly strong, and if it wasn't for the arrows I always carry in my hand, I would have been squashed by what I fear most. Thank you, Prot. I owe my life to your deadly poison.*

Protvor smiled, but he couldn't see it as he didn't have enough strength to lift his head. *I don't know what all that means, but you're welcome. I still feel the power of your song, but I can't figure out why the cat skedaddled. I scanned while Getik was jabbing you with that thin shiny thing, and the cat was still running when it moved out of my range.*

Maybe my rasping voice frightened it and it decided to get as far away from here as possible. I'm glad that we didn't have to kill it, though. Next time I'll try to frighten cats away with my raspy voice before we take more drastic action. Please come and help me up before Getik pokes another needle into my misused body. He smiled at Getik's make-believe scowl.

From behind, Protvor put her arms under his and around his chest and lifted him to his feet. *You must be as heavy and as strong as one of the big cats. I've never lifted anyone as heavy as you.* Although she grunted with the effort, she held him steady when he swayed and staggered.

He felt the painful throbbing of a few cracked ribs but resolved not to sag again because his strength was returning, albeit very slowly. He knew the ribs would mend quickly, and he now knew the healing ability was one of the gifts from the ancient alien woman. After a few dozen steps in a circle with his good arm over Protvor's shoulders to keep upright and take some of his weight, he could weakly stand on his own feet without too much pain.

"I don't sense danger close," he told her. "Would you please carry my bag, Prot? I haven't the strength for it yet. Getik, would you mind carrying my ax? I will take my bow and arrows as they don't weigh much. The boat's that way, Prot" —he limply lifted a hand in the direction she must take—"but go slowly until I get a little stronger."

She took his rucksack, shouldered it, and started walking, not looking back but using her senses to scan the area around her. She slowed down quickly when she sensed he couldn't keep up. Getik followed alertly in the rear and kept an anxious eye on Kryger, who seemed to be quite unsteady and short of breath. He sensed and marveled at the iron discipline that kept Kryger going and was grateful his "son" was still alive.

As Kryger began to recognize landmarks, he steered Protvor directly to the boat. Getik uncovered it and assisted her in situating Kryger, who immediately lay half on his back on the none-too-wide backbench. He reminded Getik to go slowly at first and to fly low between the trees for Prot's sake and then, hardly conscious, dropped off into an exhausted sleep.

Getik, very concerned about Kryger, realized what he'd been reminded of: that Protvor would naturally be nervous, maybe terrified, until she adapted to the sensation of being in the air. He asked her to sit close to him and explained every step to her and what to expect, trying to put her at ease. She at first clung to the seat because it felt to her as if the unfamiliar boat were going to fall over every time it dipped a little sideways to pass around a tree, but Getik's confident calmness and incessant explanations eventually brought her uneasiness under control as he guided the boat among the trees. She kept her eyes open, looking at the passing trees and the ground a few meters below.

When, after many minutes, he saw her relax, he told her he was going a little faster and higher up and that there was nothing to be afraid of.

"I'm not afraid, just a little nervous because this is something completely new for me," she told him. "You and Kryger are here with me, and I trust you both. I also know that you wouldn't do anything to harm me or make fun of me." She smiled for the first time. "I can hear Kryger snoring lightly, and if he trusts you *that* much, why should I be afraid? I now realize why Maksika told me not to try and fly the spacecraft on my own and just to make sure that it doesn't fall into the wrong hands. He knew that I would have panicked because I knew nothing about the sick-in-the-stomach sensation off the ground."

Getik replied, "It will pass very quickly once you accept the strangeness as not out of the ordinary."

Protvor exclaimed in wonderment as she looked down on the treetops passing a little below them and then relaxed completely as her attention was diverted away from herself. She turned around to look at Kryger and see if he was all right. After seeing his rhythmic breathing, she faced forward again, but her head kept turning from side to side and downward to the rapidly passing treetops. Getik, who sensed what she thought, asked her if she would like to see the trees from a little higher up. She enjoyed the sensation of seeing the jungle from above and not having to be on the alert for danger and eagerly said yes.

Getik told her she would be taught to fly an airboat like this and much more. She would have to learn a lot of new things and eventually be exposed to the outer surface of the planet and visit other planets across a vast black emptiness. Maksika had showed her a mind-picture of the darkness outside and the stars, but it hadn't struck home yet.

They eventually arrived at the city—another wonder to her—and Getik descended carefully and landed in front of the administrative building. He called out Kryger's name, who immediately woke and sat up slowly so as not to put strain on his aching ribs. He said he felt better and was able to get down unaided and carry his own weapons.

While Kryger showered, Getik introduced Protvor to Tirr and the new councilors. He arranged sessions for the girl to be taught to understand their language, to read and write, and to take various courses for skills he knew she would need to adapt to her new life. She was allocated a room close to Kryger, and Gorsmat was given the task of teaching the girl good manners and arranging for suitable garments for her.

While Protvor's education was in progress and Getik was recording his knew knowledge into computer storage so that interested others could be taught, Kryger, now fully recovered, asked for a boat because he wanted to see if he could activate and handle the alien craft.

He was welcomed back, and of course, the team of engineers first asked where he'd been. Kryger told them some of the truth in a few sentences: that he and Getik had gone to visit the Ancient One in the dead zone because he was told the spacecraft belonged to him, that they wouldn't have made it there and back but for their luck in meeting one of the inhabitants who guided them. He warned them that that area was extremely dangerous and should not be explored because of the big reptiles and numerous predators.

He concluded by saying, "There's nothing worth venturing in there for, not even the scenery. We went there because the Ancient One knew how to handle this ship. I'm going to open and deactivate the ship so that you can study it and start making some changes for me. Getik will be along later and will tell you a few things about this metal you are messing around with and a few other things you should know.

"There is a sort of bath somewhere in this hangar that you should fill with salt water. If you immerse a sheet of the metal in that, it will become pliable for a few hours, and you can bend it into any shape you like. But after that the metal will harden, and no amount of immersion will make it pliable again because it becomes super hard. Can you believe that's possible?

"The seats will be too uncomfortable for a human being, and that is the first thing that should be changed, if you would be so kind," he addressed Rampokka, the chief construction engineer. "Would you remove and alter the seats to fit my proportions?" he asked politely.

"Ever since we discovered this place, we prayed for a glimpse of the inside of this craft. Just open it for us; let us take a look around, and then we'll get to work."

Kryger laughed. "I've been longing to get my hands on that ship too, but you have to allow me time to figure the controls out and move it to where it's more convenient for you to work on. It may take some time because there are deadly weapons I don't want to activate by mistake since I need you around to make the thing operational."

They all laughed, but their faces remained serious. "Okay, you can move it close to the workshop, but first we'll have supper since it's near our rest period. Join us, please. We'll throw a few spare mattresses together for you. After our rest period, we'll contain our curiosity and stay out of the way until you tell us that it's safe to enter the hangar."

Kryger thanked them all and said he would appreciate a meal since he'd missed lunch because of his anxiety to inspect the ship from the inside.

During supper, Kryger had second thoughts. What if Maksika's memory wasn't that accurate after twenty thousand years? If he'd forgotten one small detail, Kryger would be locked in that semi-intelligent box until he died of hunger and thirst. Maybe he should make sure the ancient being was in contact with him before he entered the craft, and he also should take certain precautions. The access door was the sliding type, which he didn't like because it could easily jam.

Kryger didn't sleep much because he recalled and mulled over every scrap of information the old entity had transferred. He felt more at ease when he recalled there was a switch behind a small blue panel to manually immobilize the craft, but the panel must be unscrewed first, which he determined must be his first task since the craft might have to be deactivated if anything went wrong. There was a toolbox in a compartment behind the left back seat since it was a prototype and Maksika and his companion were thoroughly versed in repairs, should the craft run into trouble off-planet during test flights.

16

After breakfast he approached the craft with a large crowbar in one hand and a thick bar in the other. The others looked on from the safety of the open door to the workshop. He put the bar down below the door and requested in the Scrii language that the craft deactivate its shield and open its door. The shield disappeared, and Kryger was surprised by the speed at which the door slid open. He thought perhaps the inventors had planned for very quick entry and takeoff in emergencies.

"Door to remain open for repairs," he instructed the craft. He put the heavy bar lengthwise in the doorway and the crowbar across it with one-third of its length outside the door. Then he bent a knee; put his foot on the bar; and with a hand on each side of the doorway, pulled himself into the surprisingly fresh-smelling cockpit.

There is an obstruction in the door, the craft informed him.

"Ignore! Door must stay open for maintenance personnel. Do not take preventative action," he instructed the craft. *Whatever type of brain controls this craft has,* he thought, *is damn sensitive.* It would seem that twenty thousand years hadn't affected it much, if at all.

Understood, the ship replied unemotionally.

An intruder might take a long time to die from starvation, he thought as he located the toolbox, which was firmly held down with metal straps, and so were a number of other gadgets. Spares, he thought. He unfastened the box, closed the locker, and put the toolbox next to the pilot's seat, which was on the right-hand side. Then he unscrewed the small blue panel that protected the disable toggle switch but didn't remove it.

He sat to study the control panel, which he realized was exactly the same as in the picture Maksika had transferred to his memory. The seat was much too big and felt very uncomfortable because of the peculiar, sharp triangular contour of the back support to accommodate a lizard person's ridge, and the shape of the seat and hole against the backrest for the stumpy tail. The ship's controls were between the front seats for dual operation, which he would get used to. Although he preferred to use his left hand, he was used to having the joystick between his knees for faster responses in a dogfight. It worked more or less the same way as the joysticks he was accustomed to, but its location was awkward as he had to lean over slightly to his left.

He knew the undercarriage of the craft was slightly concave to keep it from rocking when it was grounded on a level surface, and he'd been told that the semi-intelligent ship could follow and execute simple instructions and fly unmanned when required. "We are moving next to a more convenient place where you must ground," he informed the ship.

He very slowly and gently moved the control stick forward just a fraction as he wanted to see how the ship would react. The ship performed a slow shift from the position it had maintained for ages, and he steered it to the appropriate place, and as he brought the control stick to neutral, the ship settled on the ground. Kryger slowly let out a pent-up breath; he was impressed—and relieved.

Kryger advised the ship that he was going to deactivate the controls until the repairs were complete, and it again replied with the unemotional *understood* response. He thought it best to communicate with it until he'd handled it more and knew what to expect through experience. He opened the panel and flipped the thumb-size switch up into the off position. The almost inaudible hum ceased.

He had been taught everything about the ship and could rebuild it if necessary, but all the scientific knowledge of the lizard people had also been transferred to Getik, and he should not be excluded from anything concerning the ship. Kryger thought he should remind Getik that they needed to open the engine compartment and check the fuel cores. One fuel core is supposed to last for a hundred years in full flight. The ship had been hovering for a long time, which shouldn't have used many of the cores, and the ship automatically replaced a core when it was depleted.

There was a vault full of spare fuel cores under the floor of this hangar, and he thought he should start looking for it while he waited for Getik. His thoughts were interrupted by loud cheers from just outside. When he reached the door, the others were there in a tight group.

"You did it, Kryger! This is a miracle come true." Rampokka was jumping up and down like a child. "Can we look inside?"

"The craft is deactivated and open." Kryger stepped out. "Just don't touch anything that looks like a button or a switch. When you're ready we can take out the seats and modify them if possible. Otherwise we'll have to build new ones. We'll wait for Getik to take charge of changes to the operational system."

After they had inspected the cockpit and sat on the awkward seats, Rampokka's team went to work. They removed the seats; assembled four new adjustable, more comfortable seats that could slide backward and forward, adjust up and down; and bolted them in place. Kryger was pleased as even the self-adjusting jerk-stop straps felt comfortable. It was a vast improvement on the Scrii seats.

Kryger was still testing the strength of the seats when Getik arrived. He made a detailed sketch and showed Getik where he preferred the joysticks to be located. Getik inspected the cockpit, pondered for a while, and then asked a somewhat crestfallen Rampokka to remove the front seats since the changes that had to be done were mostly under the floor.

After a number of rest periods, Getik, with Kryger's able assistance, completed all the preliminary changes, including the mounting of Big MAG in the nose of the craft. Further improvements and changes could be done by wizards of the Golden People on Nevus.

At last the ship was fully checked, provisioned, and ready for its first test flight. They both went back to the city to collect their equipment, and Getik arranged for them to be let out of the inner world. He had already had Kryger's space suit repaired and one made for himself. Kryger almost didn't recognize Protvor since she was dressed in pants, a blouse, and shoes, but he recognized the hunting knife in its sheath attached to a suitable belt. He smiled and greeted her.

She addressed them in the local language: "Hello, Getik, Kryger. Gorsmat insists that I wear these ridiculous clothes, supposedly to get used to being civilized, but I refused to go anywhere without my knife. They threw together a space suit for me as well, but I have to sit on my tail inside, which is a bit awkward. I'll get used to it, I guess. Is the ship ready?"

"Yes," Getik answered quickly, "we have to take it for a test flight to check it out and get used to it. We'll be back within a few rest periods if everything goes well, and then the three of us will depart for Kryger's home planet."

"I'm a bit frightened at the prospect," Protvor remarked, but she smiled eagerly. "I've been in the simulator a few times and know what to expect. I've been shown what a day and night is and have been scared out of my wits. I think I can now tolerate the darkness with nothing but stars over my head. I told myself that I just have to get used to it because I am too adventuresome and don't want to be left behind. I'd rather be back in the dead zone than spend my life doing the same things every waking period. The only thing I'll miss is Gorsmat's food."

Kryger smiled. *She seems really happy,* he thought. "I promise that we will not leave without you, but first we must make sure that the ship and its weapons are operational since we made quite a number of changes. The inside is now worlds apart from what Maksika showed you."

Suddenly a deep sorrow showed in her face. "Oh, I must tell you the sad news. Two sleeps ago, Maksika conveyed to me that he was dying. He seemed content about it and said he kept an eye on you modifying the ship and that both of you did excellent. The craft won't let you down, but you should add additional weapons as soon as possible."

Kryger stilled his mind and projected, *Maksika?* When he received no response, he intensely repeated the name and searched the ether for a faint trace of the alien's presence. He found none.

"He's gone, Getik," Kryger said with heartfelt sorrow as he accepted the fact that Maksika was at peace at last. *Today you're not where you were, but you will live in our memories forever, Maksika.*

They stood silently for a while, and then Kryger told Protvor that she needed to finish her outstanding tasks. "We'll see you in a few days, Prot. Give my regards to the council and Gorsmat, and please tell her that I also like the food she makes and I've missed it."

They took leave of Protvor and shouldered their bags. Kryger didn't want to leave the battle-ax, the bow, and the quiver behind because they were the best he'd ever had, and he wouldn't find better anywhere. There was enough storage in the ship so they wouldn't be in the way. He admitted to himself that he had grown quite fond of these gifts, and they had served him very well.

Getik sat in the left front seat, his back and neck supported by a clip-on hard cushion because the seats were too big for him. Kryger lifted the small blue panel—which now closed with a keylock—and flipped the switch that brought the craft back to life. The nullifying shield that protected the ship immediately flashed into existence, and the craft lifted a few centimeters off the ground. He allowed the ship enough time to check and integrate the new circuits into its memory bank.

The sliding door, which had been improved too, hissed close and locked after a few seconds when the ship was ready. Kryger gently eased the joystick forward and steered the craft toward the open hangar door. With the shield on, as Maksika had assured them, the craft could be detected only by direct sight.

He knew the ship would respond to the slightest movement of the joystick, and once they were outside, he was careful to take his time and ease the atmospheric power-control lever forward to increase speed and lift the ship above the trees. In theory he knew all about the ship, but he had to get used to handling it because it was nowhere near anything he had piloted.

They headed for the southern gate because Getik was told that Bug ships had been detected passing over close to the northern gate. Although they were told the ship couldn't be detected by any instruments known to the Scrii, they didn't want to take any chances. The technology in this galaxy was somewhat different from that of the lizard people, and instruments could exist that might detect the ship.

Kryger took his time, and even did a tight backward loop when he pulled the joystick right back. There wasn't any noticeable increase in gravity, and he was satisfied that passengers wouldn't suffer at all from his antics. He did every maneuver he knew and concluded that a normal fighter would feel like a heavy lump of metal compared to this nimble craft. But the question remained: How good was it in a real battle?

Getik watched the instruments to make sure they still functioned as they were supposed to, and both were impressed with the craft by the time they arrived at the gate.

He communicated with the guards in the observatories, and the massive gate slowly trundled open after they double-checked that no Bug ship was near.

Kryger took the ship through and waited in a huge man-made tunnel for the gate to close. Then they were told the second gate was open and were wished a pleasant trip.

Just remember to knock at least once when you come back, Engineer Getik, the guard-in-charge joked good-naturedly.

Getik grinned because he was notorious for his bad manners with the councilors. *Thanks, I'll try to mind my manners if I can contain myself. Please check if your gadgets are picking us up when we get out of here and let me know immediately.* He received an affirmative answer.

Kryger gently touched the speed control to get the ship moving. He had a plan ready if they were sighted by a Bug ship. As they exited the tunnel, he suddenly saw far-off stars and was overwhelmed by the feeling of freedom. He pushed the accelerator lever three notches forward, and the ship responded eagerly. Within minutes the planet was just a black disk silhouetted against the yellow sun. He pulled the lever two notches back and the ship slowed down drastically.

Nothing had ever happened at the gates since they were constructed, but the sensitive, far-reaching instruments were constantly on the alert and bleeped a warning when anything was detected. The guard told Getik, *There are only warning bleeps from one of the new very sensitive deep-space scanners, which is confusing because we don't see anything on the visual monitors and nothing about an approximate position of any object. My guess is that we're picking up the emission of your driving force and that the instruments can't pinpoint it. Maybe you're still too close.*

Getik smiled happily at Kryger while he thanked the guard. He knew that Kryger had received the communication as well.

"Wow!" Kryger exclaimed. "I've never been in anything this fast in normal space," he confessed. "I hardly touched the throttle, and it leaped more than two million kilometers without any feeling whatsoever of speeding up. Soon I'll be pampered to such an extent that the fastest Nevusian fighter will feel so slow, I'll want to get out and walk. I'd like to test the ray guns and my own MAG, but there's nothing out here. I'm also a bit reluctant to test the MAG with the deflection shield on. Will the bolt fired from a weapon inside the shield be let through, ship?" he asked in the Scrii language to ease the uneasy feeling.

"Affirmative," the ship's controlling intelligence answered in its reserved voice. "The driving force generated by the engine goes through as well, but anything from outside is deflected. A solid projectile will also be allowed to escape, but such have not been tested."

"There you have it," Getik interjected. "We can test your MAG on the moon of the fourth planet, and if we're lucky, perhaps a Bug ship will be departing when we—" He abruptly stopped talking when a ship popped out of subspace about twenty kilometers in front of them. It immediately began to decelerate. "Speak of the cat, and you step on his tail!" he exclaimed. "It's a damn Bug ship!"

Kryger had instinctively turned after the ship and was following it to one side because he wanted to double-check that the Scrii ship was invisible to instruments developed by the Bugs. They were rapidly overtaking the braking ship, and perhaps, if the Bugs were alert, their powerful minds would sense the nearness of another ship, albeit a much smaller one. Soon they were within firing range. The maximum range of the death rays was around three kilometers.

"The Bugs are not detecting us," Getik remarked. "I'll keep a tab on their thoughts."

They were in danger of passing the ship, and Kryger had to pull the acceleration lever back the last notch. He was within one kilometer when he turned toward the Bug ship and activated the guns. The ship stopped decelerating and went straight for the planet at the same pace. Getik exclaimed with awe in his voice, "Damn me, son, I've never experienced anything like this! Their thoughts just ceased abruptly as if cut off by a master switch. It was a really weird sensation."

"But the ship didn't explode as usual." Kryger thought for a moment. "Maybe the controller ceased to exist so suddenly and quietly that the ship didn't know about it and couldn't respond to the controlling Bug's death sensation. That could explain why a ship explodes when I put a hole in it. I might as well try the MAG and see what happens."

With the warning of the bolt ricocheting inside a shield foremost in his mind, he apprehensively sighted the MAG manually and pulled the trigger. The Bug ship drifted serenely on, but no bolt ricocheted through the cockpit.

Kryger sighed. "Maybe I missed, and maybe our shield absorbed the bolt or something, but how could I miss something so huge from this close."

"Maybe you didn't hit anything vital because it was from the side. Try it from the rear where you have a good chance of exploding the engine if it was running when the controller ceased to exist."

Kryger tried twice from a safe distance, but the ship still headed straight for the planet. He turned the ship away from the planet, for they must see how the craft performed in subspace.

"Oh well, next time—if there is a next time—I'll try the MAG first. You know, these rays are extremely dangerous, and in the wrong hands could cause large scale death and destruction. Of course, it will also take the questionable fun out of a dogfight."

"You must bear in mind that the guns were invented for something much more dangerous than your dogfights. They could also speedily remove the Bug menace if, by a million-to-one chance, their ships were bunched together and one could catch them unawares."

Suddenly another ship popped out of subspace some distance from them.

"Your fantasy gave me an idea. I can only hope it works." He moved alongside the Bug ship and sent a thought to the Bugs inside with the certain knowledge that it would instantly be transmitted to every Bug in the galaxy.

Hello, Hullenii Bugs. This is your lucky day, lucky because I am out of ammunition. I'm your old friend whom you so fondly call cat-face. I've just disabled one of your ships with my last missile, and I hope it crashes over your parked ships. I escaped your trap in a small ship that you were too dense to notice. You almost killed me, you miserable vultures. I'll be back soon to repay you in kind, right here on this gloomy, discarded planet.

What! You were reported to be dead. Where are you, cat-face?

Your instruments are antiquated. I'm here, right behind you Bug-mug, in a perfect position to blast you. It's a pity that I can't do so.

Kryger smiled happily at Getik when the ship immediately began to accelerate and take frantic evasive action. "When we come back," he said, "I hope to find a good number of Bug ships here protecting the planet because I can't imagine them abandoning their breeding ground so easily. A few passes and most of them will just be dust—if I can resist their combined mental power before they realize what's happening. The remainder we can track down afterward because they can't control or hide their destructive greediness, which is a dead giveaway at all times. That's how we find them, and that's how I was led into their trap."

"Ah…I believe that most of them will be here, but I think there'll be more than just their own ships. There might hardly be parking space in orbit because they are terrified of you. This planet might go down in galactic history as the most densely protected planet of all time. By the way, we managed to fire the reversion ray during daylight over the area where they lay their eggs—some of which might soon begin to hatch—but they won't know the difference immediately since their hatchlings are slow growing. They might be able to catch the little Buggies, though, and take them off-planet, but that won't make any difference. It will be a number of years before they realize that there's something wrong with their new generation."

Kryger grinned wolfishly. "If they bring their minions along for the fun, it will make for a lot of scrap metal, a graveyard of derelict spaceships, which perhaps will pose a danger for arriving and departing ships. But that can be taken care of one way or another. Anyway, have you any suggestions as to where we should head to test the engine and the speed it can achieve? Also, please make a note of our location so we can find our way back if for some reason the ship is unable to do so."

"It's not necessary, but I'll do it. Just remember that this is my first time in space, and I don't feel as relaxed as you seem to be. Maksika told me—I don't know if he told you too—that the ship homes in on a permanent subspace signal gadget that is buried under the floor of the hangar."

"He told me. I know it's your first time away from home, and that's why I'm teaching you to never trust a gadget until you've tested it personally. I don't like the idea of a homing signal because your enemy might have it too and can therefore home in on yours, and maybe that's how the Scrii's enemies found them. In any case, I'm going to ask my people to replace the navigation system with one of ours, which is easier to operate."

"You may be right, son. If their enemy is still out there, and if they come this way again, they may investigate just to make sure there aren't any survivors. If they find the signal device where it's located now, I shudder at what may happen because we're totally unprepared. Wait; I'll contact them and ask them to relocate it in the vicinity where I found you on the outer surface."

"That's a good idea because I have an uneasy feeling about the whole setup. In some ways the Scrii weren't as clever as they should have been." When he stopped speaking, Getik closed his eyes, went still, and contacted Rampokka.

17

"Let's give the craft a good shakedown. Maksika told me that, about a hundred thousand light-years in the direction they came from the next galaxy, they found a civilized biped nation who were still in the liquid-fueled-rocket stage of spaceflight. This ship is supposed to do close to a thousand light-years per hour. It'd be a good test for the ship, but do you think it's worth spending four to five days in subspace in the hope of finding them?"

"On many occasions I've spent more than eight days in subspace, cooped up in the cockpit of a small purportedly fast scout ship—the best we have. It was never much fun, just a necessary ordeal. Subspace is a sense-numbing, terrifying experience at the best of times, and you have to learn to suspend your imagination. We used to joke that one doesn't have to be mad to be a deep-space scout pilot, but it sure helps to keep you sane since you see nothing but an impenetrable grayness."

"Okay, why not? I'm game. I'll go anywhere under any condition as long as I'm with you," he said with a smile, "but the more you talk, the more I want to get off and walk home, so let's get going before I change my mind. I'll set the course because I've been thinking about the coordinates. I can't understand how Maksika remembered them for twenty thousand years, and he was fourth generation or something like that. On the other hand—he had enough brains to discard half and not even be aware of the loss." He punched a few of the weird symbols on the navigation board and then said in the Scrii tongue, "Ship, take us there."

The ship adjusted its course, and within seconds Kryger felt the brief sickening sensation when they entered subspace, but it was over even as he felt it, as he'd experienced it hundreds, if not thousands, of times. Getik turned gray in the face and made gulping motions for quite some time before he managed to say, "Hell! That was terrible! Does this happen every time you go FTL?"

"Yep, but you get used to it if you do it often enough, my friend. That was a brief sensation compared to what we experience in our slower ships. You get the same nauseous feeling on exit, and you just hope that you don't exit into the midst of an enemy fleet as happened to me a few times before the invention of subspace detector gadgets. Now *that's* a terrible, numbing sensation which can get you killed if your reaction is slow and your enemies are more prepared than you are. Unfortunately the Bugs were recently able to duplicate our subspace detectors, and I assume that they have passed the knowledge on to their minions because they are too empty-headed and lackadaisical to build anything themselves."

Getik looked at the uniform grayness outside the transparent cockpit and almost recoiled. He shuddered and commented, "You seem unconcerned. How can one get so accustomed to flying in this muck that one can ignore it? We won't see anything even if we hit it."

Kryger laughed. "That's an understatement, or wishful thinking at best. If we hit something at this speed, we won't know it until our souls wake up in the hereafter. But in theory subspace is empty. No ships were ever lost in it because when a ship starts to malfunction, it is slowed down and ejected into normal space. I had sensitive subspace detector equipment in my fighter, but the only objects it ever detected were Bug ships in determined pursuit."

"That sounds reassuring, but my stomach seems to be in revolt. Oh well, as the saying goes, what cannot be changed must be accepted. I'll just have to learn to look elsewhere and focus on something else. I'm beginning to regret my suggestion of a long trip. What do you usually do to pass the time?"

"Before I got used to it, I suspended my imagination and tried to sleep since I usually didn't get enough of it, but I propose we pass the time by talking—telling stories, jokes, and whatever comes to mind. It seems that the Scrii didn't believe in flight- or space suits, hence the convenient toilet…which I like for long trips because we don't have to exist on tablets and a mouthful of liquid as I always had to."

They passed the next couple of days by relating some of their experiences. It was the first time Kryger had told anyone some of his less hair-raising exploits.

On the fifth day, Kryger was woken up by deceleration he hardly felt, but the slight change was enough to alert his battle-trained sensitivity that something was happening. *This is another thing that needs to be changed,* he thought irritably when he realized the ship was decelerating to exit subspace. *There should be a warning.* He shook Getik awake and told him to quickly get his seat upright and strap in. They'd barely finished when the ship popped into normal space quite close to a planet bathed by a yellow sun.

He ignored the noise made by Getik's involuntary nausea and pushed the normal-space speed-control lever only one notch forward so as not to build up too much speed, while he employed his senses to check ahead for sentient life and if their arrival had been noticed.

"Oh damn!" Getik exclaimed. "There's a sort of desperate battle being fought on the other side of the planet! Do you sense what I sense?"

Yes, I do. His brilliant green cat eyes blazed furiously. *The damned red lizards have come to this galaxy again as Maksika had expected, and they are indulging in their favorite sport. Let's go see what this baby can really do.* He pushed the lever another notch forward and was once again amazed at the speed the craft attained almost immediately. In just about a minute, they saw a space station surrounded by ten black ships that had formed a rough, slowly moving circle around it at a distance of about two kilometers. At irregular intervals, one of the black ships fired an explosive missile into the station. Kryger got the impression that the weird hissing that accompanied the explosion of the missile inside the station was merry laughter at the thought of the desperation and panic of the creatures inside. The occasional missile from the beleaguered station was casually destroyed with a countermissile.

"There are only a couple of defenders left in the station," Getik remarked, "and they're running out of air. There's no way we can rescue them in time because they can't reach their space suits, so you might as well go close and use the rays."

Kryger activated the guns and sprayed the ships as he made a run in line with them just outside the circle. The impression of hissing laughter changed to one of alarm, and then a few missiles hit the ship's shield. They felt the ship shudder as each missile hit the shield and was deflected, but none penetrated. He completed the circle so fast that none of the ships' commanders had time to consider escaping.

"This craft is as deadly as Maksika said," Kryger remarked. "I don't sense a single one of those creatures, so all of them must have been vaporized. I don't think the rays touched the station, but I don't sense any life there either. What do you think?"

"They suffocated when you were about halfway through the circle. The lizards are all dust, son. Shall we go see what we can do to help on the planet?"

Kryger turned the ship toward the planet. "This isn't fighting; it's just plain annihilation!" he said vehemently. "But I know that the ship was built for a special purpose, and I now see why. My fighting skills are useless. All I have to do is sneak up close enough and turn the rays on. It feels like murder on a grand scale, but I suppose I have to do it. I don't have to like it, but perhaps this ship is what is needed to bring peace to this galaxy."

"Of course you don't have to like it, son. What's fair in what these lizards do anyhow? Did you perceive how they enjoyed destroying the helpless station as slowly as possible? I don't have hatred in my soul, son, but in those few minutes I got to hate them passionately. Maksika said they'd destroyed one galaxy, and they may have destroyed all sentient life in the second one by now as well, and now they're starting on this one. The Bugs are novices compared to this, but at least they consume their victims. We must eliminate the Bugs as quickly as possible and then come after these red destroyers. Ah…I almost forgot: they didn't detect our ship, but it's possible that they were just too preoccupied to check their instruments.

"My people will clone this ship without the death rays because I transferred Maksika's scientific knowledge into our computers, and I'll do the same for your people. We must build as many of these nearly indestructible ships as rapidly as possible, for there is no other way. Nor will we be given a second chance. We must ensure that the enemy can't capture one of these ships. I don't know if the red lizards have subspace communication, but if this group is not heard from within a reasonable time, you can be sure the incident will be investigated by a huge fleet."

Kryger was thinking along the same lines and with mind-search was trying to locate the rest of the fleet that must have landed somewhere on the planet. He detested the lack of physical locator instruments on this experimental ship, but it wasn't catastrophic. It made things a little more difficult, but at least he had the able Getik to assist him. "I don't sense any disturbance on this side of the planet, so the lizards must be on the dayside."

"They are! The whole lot of them have landed in a bunch in the suburbs of a city after destroying any military installations they thought they saw. Some of them are looting at their leisure, and they're killing anything that moves. And, of course, the big shots have rounded up citizens for their favorite sport. For them the real looting will start after the planet is devoid of intelligent life. There's a single ship in a tight circular orbit high above the parked ships that's supposed to look out for intruders, but since that possibility never occurred before, their attention is on screens that monitor the 'sporting' activities below. I'll point you to it, but try your toy gun again because we have to determine why the damn thing doesn't work when it's supposed to. I'm regretting the fact that we thought we wouldn't need handguns."

Kryger was once again amazed at the delicateness and accuracy of Getik's talents. When those trigger words were uttered, access to hidden knowledge and blocked talents had been opened for him, but he'd been too busy making the ship useable to examine what he'd gained. He already knew he was more sensitive than before, but he had to examine the newly opened pathways. He must make time, and soon.

He steered the ship where Getik indicated toward the dayside of the planet. It would be easier to see the black ship in the sunlight than on the nightside, where it could be detected only when it was silhouetted against a backdrop of stars. It was a difficult task without detection instruments, but he couldn't fault the exceptional scientific knowledge of the Scrii. They just concentrated on creating a ship that could wipe out all life in an armada because they weren't a warlike nation. They had much finer senses than Getik, and maybe they would have used their senses to locate the enemy.

Even though he was thinking of upgrades to the incomplete ship, he was alert and spotted the black ship an instant before Getik pointed and said, "There she is!"

Kryger scanned the ship and immediately sensed the enjoyment and envy the creatures experienced from scenes they were witnessing, but by then he was close enough behind the ship and aimed the gun. There was no explosion, but he sensed the utter panic and incomprehension as to why they were losing air so rapidly and so suddenly. They hadn't had any warning, and most didn't even think of the closeted space suits they'd never used before.

"Your toy gun works fine after all," Getik remarked without enthusiasm in his voice. "At least the scum experienced for a few seconds the helplessness that their countless victims must have felt. It's a pity they died so quickly, but it'll teach them. Let's go after the other riffraff, son."

Kryger pointed the ship's nose down and, after a few minutes, entered the atmosphere. He took it easy because it was the first time he had entered atmosphere in an alien ship, and he wasn't sure how the craft would behave if pushed. There was no hurry; a few extra minutes wouldn't make much difference since many native lives had been lost already, and they too might be hostile until they realized he was after only the invaders.

There was the usual buffeting, but the buildup of heat he always experienced was absent. He figuratively took his hat off to the Scrii people, for although the craft lacked rearview monitors, he knew there was no flame to advertise the craft's rapid entry. The ship behaved extraordinarily well, and soon they were down to about five kilometers above sea level. He guessed they were traveling close to the sound barrier. He leveled the craft out and pointed it toward the glimmer of the dayside.

He thought that maybe he could confiscate a usable gun from the enemy or obtain one from the inhabitants because the little MAG couldn't be used on an individual in a crowd, for the energy bolt wouldn't be stopped by anything except distance. He could use the bow if necessary, but it was chancy because it was too slow against guns, but he'd worry about it when the time came. First he must make a pass over the parked ships to eliminate any of the red lizards in and about them, but there would be thousands of them scattered all over the city. He'd do what he could, but the natives would have to deal with the remainder as best they could because they couldn't spend weeks here.

Getik, of course, had sensed Kryger's thoughts and concentrated on guiding him toward the city being plundered by the lizard people. The ship was absolutely silent except for the whistling of displaced air, which could even be heard inside the cockpit.

The sunlight was almost too brilliant, but their eyes adjusted quickly as they rapidly entered the dayside. He reduced speed so as to minimize the whistling sound when Getik told him they were getting close to the city. Then he slowed down even more and lowered to hug the ground and avoid visual sighting.

"I've been a bit slow in the mental compartment since you rescued me from the inimical attention of the Bugs, and I just remembered that Quarr's first priority is always information," Kryger remarked. "I know that you can, but would you mind finding the commander of these lizard people and seeing what information you can gather regarding their reason for being here?"

"Quarr has a top-class mind, as I already know. Keep on this course while I close my eyes to concentrate on what I do. The city's on the other side of those hills in front of us."

"Okay. I now can sense their thoughts too."

Kryger abruptly closed his mouth because Getik required absolute silence to focus. Kryger detested the jubilant eager-to-kill-torture-and-plunder thoughts he picked up, but he endured, for he required those nauseous thoughts to home in on. Then he saw the tops of the gigantic ships over the tops of the hills to his right and immediately changed course. He also reduced speed to what felt like a veritable crawl and switched the guns on, although their range was close to three kilometers.

Oh well, he thought and shrugged his shoulders. *I might turn some unfortunate citizens into dust in the process of cleaning up, but they eventually would have died anyway. I don't like it, but it can't be helped because these rays aren't selective.*

The hundreds of ships were not parked in orderly rows but in random clusters between and sometimes over smashed houses in the once orderly suburb. The many groups of lizard people busy loading loot didn't notice the approaching craft as Kryger began a zigzag pattern to ray as large an area as possible in one pass, and it was necessary to make a few tight turns to include out-of-the-way ships. When he was finished, he hovered to one side. Getik had just opened his eyes and was shaking his head as if shuddering.

18

"Good! You wiped all the ones up here out, but there are many thousands running amok in the city," Getik told him. "What I learned is that this is an expeditionary task force, and they're leisurely clearing the way for the rest of their kind to immigrate to chosen planets void of intelligent life. This is the second one along the route. They're more or less following the route the Scrii took all those years ago and will visit every solar system until they reach Faraway. And, yes, they've known about our homing signal for centuries, but their ancestors were quite sure that it was a buried signal they missed when they razed the planet. To them the beacon was always there, and now they're following the signal, but they want to check if any Scrii settled on other planets along the way. If they can't find the beacon, they'll destroy the planet because it's a source of irritation for them.

"Things are not going too well for them in the next galaxy because they finally had the misfortune to attack an old advanced race called the Hulleskrik, which is a yellow-brown, green-tinged type of humanoid lizard seemingly well versed in warfare. Apparently the Hulleskrik are a peaceful type, which the reds mistook for cowardliness, but they realized their blunder after the third attack on the ancient home planet of the Hulleskrik, who retaliated by taking the fight to them on their planets, which were wiped out one by one. From then on, whenever the reds decided to try their luck on another less advanced race, the Hulleskrik awaited them as if they'd been informed beforehand. Warfare is a way of life for the red lizards, and they fight among themselves if they are idle for too long.

"After we've developed a sizable fleet of ships like this one and we've cleared this galaxy of the Bugs, I think we should try to join up with the Hulleskrik in wiping out the red lizards because they, like the Bugs, will never change if they behave the same after what—forty or fifty thousand years? We have some time, about ten years as far as I can ascertain, before they are to return and report, so we may have time to hunt Bugs to near extinction. They can detect subspace signals like our beacon, but the commander didn't think about subspace communication or reporting to his leaders.

"That's the gist of it, son. Although a transgalactic journey takes about half of one of our years for them, we must make sure that not even one of their ships is able to make the return journey. You have more experience, so what do you recommend we do to stop them—put a hole in every ship?"

"Thanks for the info. We'll have to wait and see, dear friend," Kryger replied. "I'd prefer to keep them intact because the locals—since they've already entered space—can learn, with a little push, to use them to defend themselves. The only requisite will be that they'll have to paint them another color because I'll tell my people to destroy any black ship they meet without hesitation. The first priority for me is to find a usable gun or two, then go after them and maybe see if the locals can help. You'll have to stay with our ship to keep the red lizards from reaching theirs. Tilt the ship's nose to use the rays at a downward angle and limit their range."

"I have a better idea. I'm able to sense if anyone comes back to a ship because their brain pattern and thoughts are much different from that of the locals. It'll be much more expedient if you go see if you can get guns from a ship, since there should be more than enough around, then come back here and pot individuals we come across from the open door. The main reason is that I sense some thousands of the reds in an amphitheater in the middle of the city with a number of locals in the center they're using to have their sports with. We can hover low over the locals and rotate in a circle with the guns activated to eliminate those in the stands. The shield will protect us from retaliation in those few seconds."

"Okay, my friend, it's a good idea. Now drop me at the nearest ship. All their ramps are down, and the hatches are open too."

Getik handled the ship very carefully as it was his first attempt, but he'd watched Kryger and knew how to go about it. He hovered close to the ground, and Kryger told the ship to open the door and keep it open. Then he scanned the area, jumped down, and entered one of the black ships. There were small heaps of dust scattered around with guns and recharges in each one. He picked up the nearest one. It looked like a normal blaster, but the trigger grip was a bit awkward as it was meant for a three fingered hand. He ejected the magazine and put in another one, then aimed through the open hatch at another ship, fired, and saw the black paint smolder briefly, but the blast didn't even make a slight dent in the hard shell. He gathered two more guns and as much recharges as he could carry. Then he returned to the ship and, with a serious face, told Getik to proceed to the temporary sports arena.

Halfway there, Getik diverted and took care of a group returning with what looked like heavily loaded antigravity platforms. The platforms serenely kept on flying, and perhaps some would crash against ships. Getik was a bit more confident in his handling of the craft, and Kryger turned his attention to the buildings they passed. There were well-built multistoried buildings that told him the inhabitants were proud of their workmanship and quite advanced as evidenced by their space flight development. He briefly wondered if they were capable of producing and handling FTL spacecraft, but he doubted it because space stations were not needed for such ships.

They reached the amphitheater, and Getik made the ship hover a little short but above the high wall so that they could take stock of the situation as he activated the deadly rays. It seemed that the red lizard people were fond of strong drink because empty bottles were being hurled by boisterous, obviously intoxicated spectators at the few remaining prisoners in the center of the wide sport field. The field was just about covered with gore and mutilated bodies, but about twenty or so victims were still standing proudly in a bundle, although those on the outside were bleeding from multiple wounds inflicted by a dozen taunting red lizards who were dancing naked around the group and lashing out now and then with short swords and whips to inflict a painful wound, which was accompanied by a hissing kind of hooting and followed by a swig from a bottle in the other hand. They clearly enjoyed inflicting pain on helpless victims.

Kryger put the rifle down, asked Getik to hold for a moment, and retrieved his battle-ax. Then he told Getik to go ahead and drop low enough so that he could jump down to give the torturers a taste of their own medicine.

"Will do, son," Getik agreed, "but before you jump, let me dust off the rabble in the pavilions because they're armed to the teeth and maybe too drunk to shoot straight, but one never knows how lucky they might get. They're obviously used to this grisly kind of victory celebration, or whatever they call it."

The revelers didn't notice the invader until it dropped down and hovered to one side of the killing field. Few were sober enough to make it to their feet before being turned to dust as the ship made a quick complete circle. Getik deactivated the guns and then lowered the ship to about two meters above the surface, and while the lizard people in the arena stood stock-still in shocked incomprehension, Kryger told the ship to open the door and then jumped down.

Getik immediately shifted the ship away so that he would have a clear view of the arena, locked the controls, and jumped for the doorway, where he grabbed a blaster since

Kryger was exposed to danger and might need someone to watch out for him. He squatted close to the open door on one knee with the blaster ready against his right shoulder and a finger curled over the trigger.

When the lizards saw a lone warrior jump out of the craft armed only with a long-handled ax, they recovered from their shock, let out an ululating cry, knocked prisoners aside, and converged on him. Only one close to an exit decided to flee, perhaps to warn his compatriots. Getik shot him high between the shoulder blades and saw his headless victim tumble into the exit before he shifted his attention back to Kryger's adversaries. He relaxed a little when he realized that none were armed with handguns.

Kryger thrust the still poisoned spear tip into the stomach of the foremost attacker, pulled it out, and took a sideways swipe at the one next to him, who was ready to slash Kryger's face with a whip, which he fleetingly saw had small cutting blades at the tip.

The rest tried to form a circle around him, but Kryger would have none of it. He did a fast shift to his left, deflected a downward flashing sword blade, and followed up by amputating the arm. The victim started to howl and lost all interest in the fight as he bent over and tried to stem the flow of blood with his remaining hand. Getik permitted him to suffer for a while and then blew his head off when the ululation started to irritate him.

Kryger suffered the stinging cut of a lash on his face while he removed the head of another attacker. Instead of instinctively jumping away, he grabbed the lash and pulled the wielder into the ax's spearhead. He immediately let go of the whip and slashed the arm and upper torso off a sword wielder. In the same motion, he swung the ax in a quick circle to cleave the head of another. The stinging slash to his face seemed to enrage him, for he disposed of the remaining three in quick succession. The fight lasted less than one minute.

Blood was dripping down his forehead, and he quickly wiped it from his eyes with one hand. Then he looked around. The attackers were dead but still bleeding profusely. Only the whip wielder was still alive, on his knees, clutching his stomach with both hands, and moaning like a lost soul in hell.

It must be the first time in his life he feels the pain he inflicts on his victims, Kryger thought. *I don't think he enjoys being at the receiving end.*

"He's never met serious opposition before," Getik replied as he came up to where Kryger stood. "I won't put him out of his misery because he's dying anyway, unless he starts that irritating howl like the other one. Only two decided to flee, but they weren't sober enough to be fast."

"Thanks, old friend. That's good news. I sense the survivors coming this way. Let's hear what they say, although we won't be able to reply in their lingo. You'd better do the talking, and I'll only reply to direct questions."

They turned and faced a group of about fifteen locals, some who were not injured. Kryger lowered his ax, spearhead in the hard ground, and leaned his arms on the shaft. Getik did the same with the blaster but kept a ready hand around the barrel.

They studied the group. The women wore loose dresses, and the men were clad in baggy trousers and some sort of tunic. Their gray faces reminded him of pictures of gorillas he had once seen in history files, but their mouths were smaller and the lips fuller. Their exposed limbs and necks were hairy except for their faces. Their eyes were a sad brown, but they walked proudly upright with straight backs. The individual in front had a pale white face and very light-brown eyes. Something vaguely resembling a toga was draped around his shoulders. He looked a bit older than the others and was unhurt. They halted, and the toga carrier looked up at Kryger and addressed him in a strange language that sounded like barking coughs: "On behalf of myself and my people, I thank you, big warrior and little warrior. We're a peaceful people, but the invaders didn't want to trade or talk. They just destroyed what looked to them like military installations around the planet and what few shuttles we depended on to supply the people in our orbiting space station. There are many invaders loose in the city, killing and looting. We only have hunting guns and a few experimental missiles, but we were never attacked before and don't have experience in this sort of conflict. Where are you from? We've never seen anyone as powerful who can move as swiftly as you, big warrior."

Kryger smiled. The painful stinging on his forehead and scalp was almost gone. Something in the spokesman's tone didn't sit very well with him, but he couldn't sense what it was he didn't like. Perhaps it was the haughty I'm-in-charge inflection. He included everyone in his reply because they should hear it as well.

Our arrival here was pure chance. We are testing an experimental ship and inadvertently ended up here. The people in your space station are all dead. We were too late to save them, but there are some lifeless enemy ships circumnavigating the space station and more than a hundred ships here you can learn to use. Be sure to paint them another color because I will destroy any black ship I encounter without first inquiring who's in it. Actually, my companion is the one you should talk to because he is my commander. He shifted attention away from himself to Getik. *I only do the personal hand-to-hand fighting.*

"I can understand what you say in my head, and apparently you understand what I say." The spokesman turned to his companions and told them to attend to one another's wounds as they knew where to find the first aid room in the stadium. Then he completely ignored Kryger and addressed Getik: "You have strange weapons. Will you help us drive off the rest of the invaders?"

We'll try, but our time here is limited. Come into the ship with us, and we can talk and introduce ourselves. He switched to his own language. "I sense another convoy heading for the ships. Let's attend to them first, son. There's something about this guy I dislike, but I can't pinpoint what it is yet." He told the ship to open the door and keep it open. He jumped and climbed in since he had left the craft to hover about a meter above the arena.

"I can't sense it either, but paleface seems to be a big noise used to ordering everyone around because he told the others to attend to their own wounds without giving a single thought to their well-being."

Kryger helped the older citizen into the ship and then jumped in. The citizen sank into the seat closest to the door without invitation while Getik took the ship back the way they had come at a blistering pace. They were just in time to see a large convoy arrive at the black ships. He immediately activated the rays, and the group ceased to exist.

The spokesman was impressed. "I didn't believe what I saw at the stadium, but now I must. Can you sell us some of these weapons?"

Getik decided to follow Kryger's lead. *No, unfortunately not. A dying enemy of these red lizard people gave us this experimental ship, and we are on a test run to see what it can do. As far as we know, these guns are the only ones in existence, and we dare not dismantle them to see how they work. The science is way beyond our capabilities, so we are trying to understand what this ship is capable of doing. By the way, my name is Getik, and my companion is Kryger.*

"My name is Bolmakisi, and I'm the chief of this city. Most of my council members were killed outright when they captured us. It seems that they were the fortunate ones."

Kryger had an unkind thought: *I wouldn't be surprised if you were hiding behind them underneath a desk or something.* But he recalled that he hadn't seen the chief or anyone else cringe in the arena.

Getik turned the ship around and headed for the inner city. He decided not to let the chief feel excluded and useless. *Can you point us to where the enemy is looting the city? Kryger will go after them one by one since I cannot use these guns because I might kill a lot of innocents. We took a couple of their guns because we didn't expect to become involved in a fight and didn't bring any of our own, but we'll try to destroy as many of them as we can. Those that escape you'll have to hunt down on your own. We have another enemy to combat at home more deadly than this one, an enemy that can blow a planet apart if they get annoyed enough.*

"That's a terrible thought. Most of my people will be in the jungle by now. Those that aren't may either be dead or prisoners of the invaders and will be tortured to death. They should deem it a blessing if they are killed instantly by your weapons, believe me, but they will not give the invaders any satisfaction by showing fear."

Okay, Bolmakisi, we'll see what we can do when we get there. He switched to his own language: "Son, you heard what this dignified moron thinks. I just can't understand this alien mentality, and I don't think it's wise to expose yourself to danger needlessly for the likes of them. I'll scan a building, and if there is a chance to save locals, you may go in; otherwise I'll ray the building and move on to the next one. Okay with you?"

"Yes, we'll probably never visit this planet again, so we might as well clean it up as best we can in the shortest time we can manage. The rest is up to them. They must realize that it's foolish to just wait in a bundle to be murdered and do nothing in retaliation."

Bolmakisi pointed his finger. "That way is the center of the city, which is also the main business district. You can see the multistoried buildings from here if you go a bit higher. I saw that the invaders are concentrating on the business district because they captured me and others right there in the administration building at the start of the main street."

Getik speeded the ship there. The main street teemed with thousands of boisterous lizard people loading goods and valuables onto parked platforms. He cleared the whole street in a second. *What a murderous weapon Maksika's people invented,* he thought, but without revulsion. *We'd better make very sure that it never falls into the wrong hands.*

Kryger now brought his recently enhanced abilities into play. To his astonishment, he found that his scanning ability now gave him a clear mental picture of the insides of buildings he scanned to ascertain whether there were any natives present worth rescuing. He told Getik what he was trying to do, and the older man approved since he too was sorting out impressions.

Kryger asked him to rise above the buildings and use the rays at a downward angle since they weren't stopped by a few walls. Thus, they went from building to building and rayed whatever lizard people they sensed inside. When the lizards became scarcer to find, they came across a sort of supermarket where cornered locals in the upper story were fighting back. There were five antigravity transport platforms partly loaded with loot parked in front of the wide entrance. He asked Getik to let him jump off at the corner and to check whether there were any convoys on their way to the ships while he went inside to lend a hand because a resisting group was worth rescuing.

Kryger removed his flight suit and was clad only in his shorts. He retrieved his rucksack and donned a pair of soft shoes. At Getik's question as to why he had removed his flight suit, he said, "The boots are much too noisy, and the suit might get ruined by a blaster bolt, which would leave too big a hole to self-seal. I might need it on the trip back, so I can't chance damage since we didn't bring any spares."

"Okay, son. Good luck. You're a fast healer, but try not to get wounded."

Kryger filled his pockets with recharge magazines before he grabbed a blaster and jumped out. He scanned the ground floor for occupants before he dashed through the entrance. The floor was strewn with overturned shelves, discarded goods, and a number of bodies. All were mutilated in some inhumane manner, and it was clear they all had died painfully. Some were disemboweled, and others were cleaved open from one shoulder through half the chest. He had never seen such barbaric slaughter, and it nauseated him.

But there were two naked lizard bodies. One was shot through the head and the other through the chest. He took time to study them. At first glance they appeared to be more or less the same species as Maksika, but they were bigger, and their color, even in death, was a dull pinkish red.

He made his way to the wide stairs and started up but kept close to the wall and scanned for any presences ahead. He encountered more bodies of the lizard people and thought the locals trapped on the top floor weren't related to Bolmakisi and those in the arena because they hadn't waited around to be slaughtered like sheep. He heard a few sharp cracks and decided the locals were using the ancient, at least to him, percussion type of rifles or handguns. A ricocheting bullet passing close to his right ear, or so he imagined, confirmed this.

At last, on the next floor, he heard what sounded like imprecations in the red lizards' clicking language, which wasn't even related to Maksika's language.

19

Kryger stooped and slowly ascended the last flight of stairs. A wound would heal quickly enough, but a ricochet or a bolt through his head might be fatal. He kept close to the wall when he sat on a stair and peeped around the corner; at the same time, he opened his mind to receive impressions from the invaders and the locals.

There was an expansive reception area with a tall ceiling before the only door to a hall, but the door and part of its frame had for all intents and purposes been destroyed by blaster bolts. Someone had pushed a concave, polished, reflective shield of stainless steel in front of the door when blaster fire began to wreak havoc and perhaps discovered that it deflected the bolts. From different positions in the hall, a sharpshooter fired a gun at irregular intervals at a lizard's exposed leg, head, or arm.

More than a dozen lizard people were barricaded behind overturned wooden tables and chairs that generally brought a halt to the solid bullets, but occasionally a bullet penetrated and killed or wounded one of the lizards, and none dared to make a run for it, dissuaded by the number of bodies lying with their faces pointed toward the stairs. He grinned when he thought the sharpshooter seemed to prefer to take them on the run.

Judging by the continuous chattering, the lizards were upset because things weren't going as well as they'd expected. Apart from the dead, a number had broken limbs and various other wounds. It was a situation they were unprepared for.

Kryger counted eighteen alive. If the blaster ran out of bolts, there was always the possibility that the sharpshooter inside the hall would take a hand when a lizard exposed himself, but he had to make sure the sharpshooter didn't mistake him for an invader. Therefore, he sent a thought to the cornered locals: *Don't shoot the stranger on the stairs because he's here to help,* and hoped they understood.

He put a spare magazine next to him on the stair and aimed the blaster around the corner. Hoping the sharpshooter would see he was firing at their enemies, he shot the farthest lizard in the side of the head. He quickly shifted aim to the next and killed five before they became aware of the enemy on the stairs. A piercing scream of rage, or perhaps a warning, went up.

Most dove to the other side of the barricades and became targets for the sharpshooter. Having no other choice, they jumped up and charged Kryger but were mowed down by his and the sharpshooter's rapid firing. Only one reached Kryger when the blaster's magazine was depleted. Without thought, Kryger threw the empty blaster at him, and when he ducked, Kryger leaped across the reception area to meet his adversary on level footing. The lizard man slashed him with a short sword, but instead of shying away, Kryger shifted inside the arc and clutched the sword arm as it swung sideways. He heaved upward, put a foot in the lizard's stomach, and fell backward, pulling the lizard toward him and hurling him down the stairwell. He heard a prolonged screech, and then there was a loud thud, and the terrified screeching stopped. Kryger stood up facing the door but ready to shift sideways rapidly if he sensed hostile intention. In this weaker gravity, he could move fast and, if necessary, would reach the door within seconds and be inside before they knew what kind of whirlwind was hitting them.

But the shiny barricade was pushed aside, and a brown-faced, gorgeous-looking woman clad only in shorts stepped out with a hunting rifle in one hand.

"Relax, big man. I had a thought that you couldn't be one of them, and I saw what you did. I want to thank you for rescuing us because our ammunition was nearly depleted. Where are you from?"

You put up a good fight, and the reflective shield was a brilliant idea. You should arm yourself with their guns as I did. Ah, yes, I don't know your language, but I can pick up your thoughts when you speak, and you seem to understand my projected thoughts. He picked the gun up and slammed a recharge into the slot after he'd ejected the spent magazine.

To answer your question, we're testing a small experimental ship and came this way by pure chance. The plausible fib was close to the truth and wouldn't do any harm. *We found black ships destroying a space station and decided to test our ship's guns. There are now a number of lifeless black ships circling your derelict station, for all aboard the station were killed by the invaders. We decided to come and see if we could lend a hand as we have information that these red lizardlike people intend to conquer our galaxy.*

I didn't count, but there are about a hundred undamaged ships parked a short distance away. They are intergalactic, and your people could learn to use them to guard this planet. I have to run since we still have to check other buildings for invaders.

The woman told the others still inside the hall to come out and arm themselves with the weapons lying around. Then she joined Kryger, who was on his way downstairs after grabbing a new-looking blaster to add to his collection of off-world weapons. He noted that she walked alertly, lithely, and silently like a huntress, and he immediately liked her. She had certain qualities lacking in the chief and others he had met briefly in the arena.

They were halfway down when her companions started the descent. He sensed that they had armed themselves and were determined to use the strange guns at the first opportunity.

"I'm a huntress and also a pilot," the woman told him. "I was buying supplies and ammunition when the invaders rushed into the building and began slashing and killing people indiscriminately. They paused to enjoy the screams when they inflicted pain on unarmed shoppers. There were too many to get past, so I told my colleagues to run upstairs to the conference hall. I grabbed what ammunition there was on the counter and had to kill two of them before I could escape. The invaders immediately followed and blasted the door while they uttered sounds which we interpreted as weird laughter. My name is Vethol, by the way."

I'm glad that I decided to come to your aid. I'm Kryger. Bolmakisi and his fellow prisoners in the stadium showed a remarkable indifference to defend themselves against the invaders. They seemed to rely on pride and a show of indifference to dissuade the lizard people from continuing their torture, but they started screaming the moment they felt a blade or a whiplash. We arrived just in time to rescue about a dozen of them, including the chief.

Vethol snorted through her nose. "Pfah! It's a pity that those inept gray-faced politicians survived. I don't know why we tolerate them. They set themselves up as our hereditary rulers and can't control their greediness. They always found some implausible reason to delay our space project or the development of some sort of defense force because *they* decided that there would never be an enemy and dismissed the legend that we were visited by friendly aliens thousands of years ago who gave our technology a boost as pure fiction. No wonder we were caught unprepared. We should kick them out because of this fiasco.

"This city is called Kokfit, and we call this planet Bawyaan. The saying is that we're all Bawyane and we all must work together, but we don't. Ah, yes, I should explain that we're all the same species throughout the planet, but some are born with gray or pale faces, and ancient tradition led us to believe that that was a sign of superior mentality. I suppose it was accepted after a time, but first-rate intelligence and leadership abilities are absent in the traditional rulers. It's time to get rid of this inane tradition."

It's quite clear that you urgently need to put all effort into developing a space-defense force. You have less than ten years to prepare to defend your planet against the next wave of red lizard invaders. They intend to gain a foothold in this galaxy, and you're directly in line from the next galaxy. You have a ready-made fleet, as I said. You will need to study the ships very carefully before you try to use them because they are alien and different, much more advanced than what you were trying to develop. Remember that the invaders have crossed the darkness between galaxies in them.

They had arrived on the ground floor, and Kryger walked toward the entrance.

"I have enough influence to take charge of the project, and if a politician tries to interfere, he won't live to rue his meddling. We brown-faces are fed up with their avariciousness and incompetence. This invasion was the catalyst we needed to replace them with knowledgeable people. It's high time that the gray faces learn to do honest and useful work." Kryger knew she was uttering the truth as felt by the majority. He quietly and honestly wished her every success.

They arrived outside just in time to see a body tumble from above and land with a squashy crunch on the road a few meters in front of them, followed by a blaster and magazines that made a clattering noise. The ship was right behind the body, and an angry Getik told Kryger even before he put the ship down, *That damn Bolmakisi fool tried to take possession of the ship! He thought that he could fly the ship, seeing how easily I controlled it. The damn idiot moved to the door, grabbed the gun lying there, and pointed it at me, ordered me to lower the ship and get off, saying that he was commandeering the ship for himself to safeguard his planet! The ingrate moron didn't even know one end of a gun from the other!*

I noticed that his finger wasn't even on the trigger. I got mad, so I told him that the gun wasn't even loaded. He took his eyes off me to look uncomprehendingly at the gun, and I tipped the ship on its side. The clumsy clunker plummeted out the door and even forgot to yell. Getik was sputtering in rage as he landed the ship and came to the door.

Vethol laughed because Getik, in his dismay, had broadcasted, and she was sensitive enough to pick it up.

"He did himself a favor because I would have shot him in the belly to make him suffer as he did others," she told an astounded Getik. "Anyway, it wasn't the fall that killed him; he forgot to order the pavement to move aside, which was a suitable ending since we wanted to put a stop to his insufferable haughtiness and disdain for people who dared question his ill-thought actions for quite some time."

Getik looked at Kryger. "Did you rescue this girl?"

Oh, sorry. This is Getik. Kryger held his hand toward Getik and looked at the girl before turning back to Getik. *This is Vethol, and she was the one decimating the reds upstairs. Maybe you can spare a few hours to take her to a lizard ship and explain the basics of what the instruments are for and how to operate the craft. It could save her life and that of countless others.*

Getik looked at her and liked what he sensed and saw. *Okay, come aboard while we expunge what's left of the invaders. There's one group left on their way to their ships and a few scattered here and there, which the locals can take care of. Let's go get them before they reach the ships.*

Kryger gestured for Vethol to enter before him, which she did with a lithe jump. He told her to sit in his seat, and Getik immediately sped toward the black ships. The convoy had just reached their ships and demonstrated confusion when they found no one there. Getik didn't waste time and rayed them all. Vethol was impressed.

"How do your guns work?" she asked.

We don't know. Getik gave the same answer as was given to Bolmakisi since it was the easiest way out. *The experimental ship was given to Kryger by the last survivor of an enemy of the red lizards, and we're still figuring out how everything works in the hope of duplicating it. I don't think the guns can be duplicated since we might render them useless by disassembling them. The ship is half-sentient and answers only to one who can speak its language, which is very difficult to learn.* The girl didn't harbor any intentions of hijacking the ship, but he might as well warn her beforehand. He landed close to the nearest ship.

"Kryger, you might as well stay with your ship and see if you can locate lizards we have missed. I don't think it's necessary to keep watch, but it won't do any harm. I learned a lot from Maksika, so I'll study the instruments and then transfer their functions to Vethol hypnotically as we go along."

They had the usual rations with the usual comments uttered by an appreciative Vethol. When she and Getik left to inspect the selected black ship, Kryger closed the door, reclined his seat, and relaxed while he fixed his senses on scanning as far as they could reach, which was an astonishing distance now that he'd started to use his unblocked abilities. He knew that even if he fell asleep, his roaming senses would nudge him awake as they were trained to do if anything inimical came into range.

He recalled the image of the ancient but still beautiful alien woman as she floated naked in the life-suspension unit and wondered how she had kept her sanity for the long millennia of solitude waiting for him and Quarr. He knew that neither she nor her long-departed race could have known about Maksika and this revolutionary craft because he was a chance factor. Still, he was grateful and owed her a debt he could only repay by doing what she had said he was born for. He fell asleep with the images still fluttering around in his memory.

Kryger woke up a few hours later when the ship's door opened. Getik and Vethol carried a heavy instrument each, and he assisted Getik in getting his gadget through the door since the smaller man was grunting heavily as he lifted it up to door level. He put it down and then took the one from Vethol, which she lifted effortlessly up to him. Getik explained, "If I interpreted the hieroglyphs correctly, the one I carried could be a subspace communicator, and the other one picks up the beacon on Faraway. I want to study both these gadgets to determine whether they can be used to warn us of invasion fleets. We just want to go get some service diagrams of the ship and some recordings of their language. It might be worth our while to study both because their written language is close enough to Maksika's. Oh, and I've showed Vethol how to change the frequency on the communicators so that the reds won't catch on when her people use them."

While they were away, Kryger moved the gadgets to the back and secured them. There were enough compartments for Getik to store the rest of his loot if the items weren't too large.

Then his eyes fell on a grounded transporter, and he went over to inspect it. It was similar to the sleds at home and Getik's boatlike flyers. He studied the controls. There were engraved symbols on them that he could vaguely discern. Getik was right; the written language was close to the one they had been taught. He flipped the only switch, and the platform came to life. *It uses antigravity too,* he thought, *so the red lizards must have quite advanced technology.*

He pushed what was obviously the lever to control the platform to the side, and the transport moved sideways but stayed level. Just then the other two exited the black ship with arms full of what looked like colored plastic pages. He amusedly offered them a lift to the ship, which was only a few steps away. Both smiled and continued to walk.

Dump your load and let me show you how this thing works, Vethol. It would save you a lot of walking exercise. There are plenty of them parked here and in the city, and there are even a number floating toward that far mountain. He pointed to a hazy mountain range.

She came back, and he explained the principle and the simple controls. She tried it and was delighted. "The enemy's technology is a million years in advance of ours. It's no wonder we were a walkover for them, but Getik implanted a load of knowledge into my mind to help us along. As soon as I've come to grips with it, I'll study a ship again, train a few pilots, and then I'll very carefully try to get a ship up into space. After that we can find out how to use their weapons out there where it's safe." Her voice and thoughts were grimly determined.

At that moment, Kryger's searching senses picked up an approaching force of a few aircraft focused on attacking the grounded alien spaceships. He realized that they would be killed out in the open. His ship was fortunately very close, so he quickly flipped the switch to off and, when the craft grounded, told Vethol to sprint for his ship because they were going to be attacked.

Vethol was mystified but nevertheless did so, for she instinctively trusted the big hairless stranger. Getik, who was included in Kryger's warning, was already at the controls and, the moment they were in, ordered the ship to close the door and expand the shield. He took the ship up to one side just above the height of the black ships and handed control to Kryger.

Are you going to fight or run? Getik asked.

They're Vethol's people in a few aircraft, Kryger answered. *Of course, they dismissed my warning that the invaders were dead and that they needn't attack. We'll see how this ship takes whatever they throw at us, and we either sit still or buzz off until they're finished. It seems that the reds overlooked a few stored aircraft when they attacked, and it may have taken a few hours to fuel and arm them.*

"Thank you, my friends." Vethol's voice was emotional. "Can you take me to our radio station on the other side of the city so that I can bring them up to date?"

No problem, girl, but it's too late to stop these brave but misguided pilots.

The planes arrived, and to Kryger's surprise, they were propeller craft. There were only five of them, and he wished he could fly one of them just for the experience and the thrill of being slow. But they were hopelessly inadequate against anything the invaders had. On the other hand, he thought, if one had only rocks to throw at an enemy, one did so. He thought they must be a brave or foolish lot to believe they could do anything against so many advanced ships and figuratively took his hat off to them but refrained from trying to influence their intentions.

"We had jets and rocket planes, as well as rocket spaceships, but they were destroyed by the invaders before they could take off," Vethol said as if she was apologizing.

We understand, Kryger assured her. *These invaders don't want opposition and prefer a helpless planet where they can loot and torture at leisure to satisfy their cruel appetites and warlike nature until they've wiped out every intelligent being.*

One airplane veered and dove at them when the pilot saw them, but the others stayed on course toward the black ships. The pilot opened fire with what could be only an old-fashioned percussion type of machine gun. He was quite an expert, and the solid bullets made bright splashes in front of the shield over the cockpit. Vethol, who had her head between the seats to watch the performance of her fellow pilots, instinctively ducked. The pilot made a tight turn behind them and fired two missiles that were deflected by the shield.

Meanwhile, the other four had disposed of their bombs against four ships. Kryger flew closer and saw that the ships had hardly a mark on them, and he drew Vethol's attention to it.

As you can see, conventional weapons have no impact on these ships. I suggest you give your scientists one ship to study its construction and the invaders' weapons to see if they can duplicate and improve on them. You have enough ships around your space station and one in orbit up there above the ships to practice on with their weaponry. Take one for your personal use, and go talk to your nation and get them organized to hunt down any escaped red lizard people. I don't envy you because it's a daunting task.

While he was talking, their attacker sprayed them with bullets from behind, which just bounced off the shield and the hull of one of the black ships, not even making scratch marks on its unshielded frame Then they felt an impact, although not severe, and the next moment the ramming aircraft careened off the shields and crashed against a black ship, where it exploded. The bomb it was still carrying exploded brilliantly, and the cockpit darkened instantly to protect their eyes. The remaining four broke off, circled once, and wondered why the invulnerable small ship didn't fire on them. Then the engines revved and the aircraft turned away.

I detest the needless sacrifice when a brave man dies for nothing. Kryger's tone was disapproving. *Okay, let's take the girl to the stadium as it's time that we return to give our own enemies some attention before they miss us. We have a few years to think about getting into another argument with the reds.* He couldn't have dreamed that it would be sooner than he or Getik suspected.

At the stadium they said goodbye to Vethol and promised they would return in a year or two if at all possible.

20

Kryger reluctantly became airborne, and when they passed the space station, he told the ship to home in on its beacon. "Unable to comply," the ship told them. "The signal became inoperative shortly before we arrived here."

"I wonder what went wrong," Getik said. "These reds were convinced that they were the only fleet here and they were going to destroy the irksome signal."

"Provide the craft with our coordinates." This was a test for Getik.

"I didn't make a note of them, but I think I still remember." Getik wasn't apologetic but sounded none too sure as he coughed up the numbers.

Kryger repeated the long numbers with a smile. Getik was really surprised and blurted, "That's quite correct, but I only told you once when you asked me what they were. How do you do it?"

"A good memory is part of the survival game, my friend. One learns to leave nothing to chance, even though it may seem a sure thing. I have to take a chance now and then, but even then it's based on a related experience or forced by dire necessity."

"That seems to add up with what you did on Bawyaan," Getik retorted while the course was set. The ship shifted to line up, and when Kryger pushed the accelerator lever, it leaped away and almost immediately entered subspace.

Thirty-one hours later, the ship popped out of subspace at the point where they had tested the Scrii weapon on the Bug ship—and they were in for an unexpected shock. The planet below them was enclosed in a seemingly solid blanket of ships of all kinds.

"Phew!" Kryger exclaimed. "It looks as if the Bugs gathered all their minions from a thousand planets to safeguard their eggs or something. Oh damn, I didn't think they'd take me so seriously! I hope they didn't discover the inner world, for it's obvious what happened to our beacon. I bet the Bug ships, if any, are on the inside closest to the planet because they value their armored carapaces above everyone else's hide, and they still think I kill them by mind power, which is a blessing."

"Give me a minute or two to find out. Faraway still seems intact, but...who knows?" Getik concentrated his formidable mind power.

Kryger slowed the ship to a veritable crawl, for all visual and detection instruments might be trained on space in all directions, but the sun was behind him, which might confuse eyes until the ship was close. He waited for Getik to complete whatever he was doing.

Getik opened his eyes after some minutes. "You're right, son. The Bug ships are bunched together on the inside of the blanket, and only a handful are parked at their hatching place. It appears that they are taking no chances. As far as I can ascertain, all the Bugs are here for a determined effort to get rid of you. More than seven hundred of them are bunched together on about a hundred of their ships, and they're all ready to link the moment they detect you. I don't think anyone can survive the focus of *that* much mind power.

"The planet inside is still undiscovered because the Bugs are concentrating on getting ready for you when you show up, as you were quite convincing at the time. One person died when he was trapped on the surface while burying the beacon and a Bug ship arrived and bombed the place—a thoughtless gesture of immature spite, I would guess—where your fighter crashed.

"I'm so scared that I am about to puke, son, but I suggest that we protect our minds with the toughest shields we can manage and then sneak in as quickly as possible and get to the Bugs and eliminate as many as we can before they link and fry our brains. Fortunately they're bunched together in two parallel rows, and we may get most of them before they even realize what's hitting them. I'll transfer the image of where they are to you."

Kryger received the representation and determined that there were three layers of ships with a gap of more or less four kilometers between them, and then the Bugs below the layers all by themselves and fairly close together about halfway around the planet from where they were. They were drifting the other way, and he'd have a chance to shoot them from behind, but he must go closer and then flash very fast through the three layers to reach the Bugs.

"We'll never get another chance to destroy a great many Bugs at one go, and we have to go in even though I am so shaken that I'd be wobbling back and forth if I was standing up right now. If we survive the linked power of the Bugs, this could become the biggest graveyard of ships in the galaxy," Kryger expressed his thoughts.

"We'll shoot the first row in the back, and then if we can, we'll turn around for the second row. Of course, the Bugs will know by then that we're here and link to sizzle our brains. I'll go in fast and hope to catch them dreaming of my demise, but I must focus on them alone at first. Fortunately the ship will keep us from smashing head-on into other ships. I can't predict what will happen, but at least we'll get most of the Bugs. I suppose I should be grateful that I won't have to go and sniff them out one by one on eight hundred planets. Are you ready?"

Getik swallowed and nodded wordlessly since the next few minutes might be their last in this lifetime, but he thought at Kryger, *Uh…the Bug ship rows are just about a kilometer apart, and I remember that Maksika said the two guns are pointing slightly to the sides because there is no point in having two ray guns aimed straight ahead and shooting at the same target. Although they start overlapping at a distance of about two kilometers, the beams spread out too. So as their range is at least three kilometers at any speed, they may spread wide enough at maximum range. I suggest you slow down a bit when we reach them and go through in about the middle since we might get both sides in one go.*

Kryger felt the butterflies in his stomach flutter a little less and the beginning of hope. *As usual, you're quite right, old friend. Because it's the kind I'm used to, I always think about guns shooting straight ahead where you aim, and I forgot what Maksika told me. Okay, get your shield into place. We must get going before I develop second thoughts.*

"Ship, shield to maximum," he ordered, made sure his own mind shield was tightly in place, closed his mind to all thoughts except of the goal they must accomplish, and pushed the speed control slowly forward. The gaps between ships wouldn't be difficult to get through to reach their target, but speed would be the deciding factor because the Bugs must not have time to link, but even if they did, the craft would flash through their ranks fast enough once he was in position. First, he must get very close before he started the dive through the layers to get behind the Bug ships because there was a very good chance the small ship would be seen the moment it passed in sight of a ship not touched by the death rays.

Before he started the powered dive, he activated the guns to silence ships he would pass on the way down. His nerves were at breaking point because the chances were practically zero that they would survive against this overwhelming force of fighting ships, but this craft wasn't ordinary in any way. As always under severe stress, he unconsciously began humming the power chant the moment the ship's nose dipped. His sense of freedom took over as he accepted death and once again embraced combat. Nothing could be so hard yet so easy…

As they darted through the supposedly protective three layers in a sharp slanting dive, ships were deprived of sentient life, but the ride was bumpy and erratic as their craft dodged ships directly in their way.

Getik's senses sharpened as he again was affected by the power of the chant. He calmed enough to cautiously check the location of the Bug ships and waved his hand to show that Kryger must move a little to the right—as if Kryger required directions. He gave the thumbs-up sign when their course was more or less straight toward the Bugs.

Kryger felt the brush of a Bug's alarmed mental probe, but by then he was close enough and felt the utter panic as they briefly realized something out of the ordinary was happening. He grimly kept on course while he sensed the fleeting alarm of Bugs as they uncomprehendingly died ship by ship when the craft flashed through their ranks. He also felt the alarmed, puzzled thoughts of a number of Bugs on the planet below.

But the alarm must have gone out because missiles were raining on them. The craft couldn't dodge them all, and it shuddered as missiles exploded against the shield. *Hell! They're quite accurate at this speed,* he thought. *The Bugs must have brought the very best of their slaves along for protection because none of the missiles go even near a Bug ship. I wonder how long the shield can withstand this bombardment.* But he just had to ignore it and put the anxiety aside.

At last they passed the last pair of Bug ships, and Kryger put on a burst of speed and went closer to the planet to get out of sight and range of the too-accurate marksmen. The power song ceased when he exclaimed, "Phew! I'm glad that run won't have to be repeated. Did we miss any?"

"Not up here. I too am glad that they were stupidly bunched. Damn, I forgot to close my eyes and almost soiled my pants! Yes, I wouldn't want to experience another run like that—ever."

Kryger forced a laugh. "One never gets used to it. Let's quickly go clean up on the surface before they recover their wits and skedaddle out of there. I just wonder what their minions will do when they find out that they're free to decide their own futures."

So saying, he reduced speed, put the ship's nose down steeply into the atmosphere, and slowed just enough not to become a flaming meteor, for even this unique ship had limits, although the ship was intelligent enough to slow down on its own to the limit of its capabilities. Still high up in the atmosphere, he leveled the ship and pointed it straight to where he sensed the remaining Bugs and their utter confusion because they couldn't get any response from those in the orbiting ships.

I just hope that we reach those Bugs before they decide to take off. Hunting them down would be difficult because they may scatter all over the galaxy.

I agree wholeheartedly, son. This is a one-time opportunity of their own making, and we must wipe them out as best as we can along with their eggs and youngsters. They're at their chosen breeding place, burning up the ether with their panicky mind-search and getting nowhere.

Would you please check if there are any observers in the area? They may be able to escape if they're beyond the penetrative distance of these rays.

Getik went silent for a moment to check. *As luck would have it, there aren't any. They've been withdrawn because of the massed Bugs' presence. The few animals we might destroy would have been killed in time by the voracious little Bugs anyway. Steer left by two degrees and slow down to a crawl because they're only about twenty kilometers away.*

Kryger knew but said nothing. He pulled the speed control back all the way, and he'd scarcely taken his next breath when the ship sped over the fissure. Out of the corner of his left eye, he saw four parked Bug ships about two hundred meters away. Bugs started to run toward them, and he made a tight right loop-roll into the fissure and activated the rays as he leveled out. He deactivated the guns when they reached the waterhole, for the fissure would be devoid of life up to the first sharp bend, or for about three kilometers. Then he pulled the speed control all the way back to let the ship hover next to the waterhole.

"I don't sense any Bug life, son, but I feel uneasy. Maybe it's because this was way too easy and over too quickly to feel real. I'll ask my people to come and check the eggs. Be silent a moment while I do so, and I might as well tell those ships upstairs that their masters are dead and that they're free to go home and try to live peaceful lives or be destroyed by war. If they take my advice seriously, it will save us the necessity of going up again and finishing the job. We'll give them an hour or two to make up their dull minds."

"Let me put the ship down before you do so. I feel the need to stretch my legs a little to stop the shaking."

While Getik did his self-appointed tasks, Kryger quickly took his flight suit off and told the ship to open the door. He stepped out barefoot into the hot sand and sun, and the door closed behind him. Although his feet quickly started to ache, the heat and the hot sand felt good after the long flight and confinement of the ship. He walked into the rather large waterhole to cool his feet and then looked around to see if he could spot Bug eggs since he was curious how big they were. As usual, he continued to scan the area as far as his senses could reach.

There were plenty of Bug and game tracks around the waterhole situated against the southwest wall of the fissure, which flattened out to the east, and he wondered what the country had looked like before the red lizard people unleashed the hellfire bombs on the planet. The sand was still fused in places and burning hot in the midday sun. He noticed a hollow filled with sand close by, and a cracked egg, as if it was starting to hatch, projected out of the sand.

He went over and picked it up, but it crumbled in his hands. He cautiously dug around with his hands and felt another one. He gingerly removed the sand around it until it was fully exposed. The egg was grayish and nearly as big as his helmet. He grinned. No wonder they had trouble laying the eggs, he thought. It too crumbled when he tried to pick it up. So the rays destroyed the eggs as well, he thought with gratitude and suddenly felt redundant with no prospect of hunting more Bugs. The rays were deadly weapons, invented to annihilate an enemy more destructive than the Bugs, and it did the job perhaps too well.

Without questioning or repressing the sudden impulse, he sprinted for the ship, and while he ran, he realized that his senses had picked up a fast-approaching ship and that the occupants radiated hate and an fervent desire to take revenge for the inexplicable demise of their masters.

21

Before he could form a mental yell for Getik to let him in, the door was opening, as Getik too had sensed the hatred of the commander in the rapidly approaching ship and was about to call Kryger to warn him of the danger when he saw him a few steps away, running like a deng. He stood aside just in time and told the ship to shut the door and maximize the shield just as Kryger dove inside. Getik dashed for the controls, but the ship was flung violently into the air when a bomb exploded almost underneath it. He grunted and swore when he hit the doorframe with his shoulder as the ship turned on its side and then steadied itself.

Kryger saved himself from a bashing by grabbing the armrests of a seat. "Follow that ship," he said in the lizard tongue, and the ship responded immediately. Fortunately, because of the ship's gravity-neutralizing ability, the violent acceleration from a standstill didn't affect them at all.

Are you okay, Getik? he asked as he moved into his seat. His eyes scanned the instruments in front of him as the craft accelerated to catch up with the fleeing ship.

"Apart from damaged dignity, a bruised shoulder, and a sore arm, yes. This beauty of a ship saved us just in time. In another ship we would have been blasted, and only a few pieces of scorched mincemeat might have been left. I'm grateful that you sensed the approaching ship. I think it was already on its way to the breeding grounds to investigate the absence of communication when I broadcasted the news that their masters were dead, and it was closer and faster than I realized.

"What I gathered in those few moments was that the commander of the ship was under the impression that he was an adviser to a Bug named Hinkstol, and when the fool received my message, his dream of a promised planet for his exclusive rule evaporated. Revenge was uppermost in his mind because the deluded idiot really believed that a Bug would keep its promise."

They were closing in fast on the ship, which was accelerating furiously to attain orbit speed. Kryger was beginning to love the Scrii ship, for it had unusual attributes that were very, very useful. He realized he was still shaken by the narrow escape. He pushed the speed control a notch forward for more velocity since he wished to disable the Bug-lover's ship while it was still in the planet's attraction field, for he'd decided that such fools didn't deserve a clean, instant death.

"Strap down, Getik," he told his friend in a somewhat unsteady voice. "We may have to perform some acrobatic tricks. I'm not going to ray that ship as I want to wipe the self-satisfied expression off that stupid moron's grinning mug. He must know that his foolish, vengeful action is going to cost him his life. There seems to be a battle going on up there between the Bug minions, for I saw a few flaming ships enter the atmosphere some distance off. Would you please check it out while I concentrate on our attacker?"

Getik strapped himself in and closed his eyes. He'd never seen a real space battle, and he'd dearly love to see one, but only from a safe distance. *First things first,* he reminded himself and went to work.

High above the stratosphere, they caught up with their attackers. From that close but moving a little lower, Kryger saw the entire ship clearly. It was huge, almost cruiser-size, and the shape looked like a copy of a Bug ship. He carefully aimed Big MAG at the ship's rear and then stabbed the trigger button once. He waited, finger ready to push the button again.

The ship seemed to hesitate a moment before it stopped and then started the long fall to the planet's surface; its nose dipped, and air started to blow out as a thin contrail. He knew panic would reign when the ship inexplicably lost power. He followed closely to blast any escape craft because the commander would be in the first—if he could reach one—but saw no craft emerge from the hull during the ship's death-plunge. *They obviously expected to escape unscathed and were caught unprepared because they can't detect this magnificent ship,* he thought. He was used to war and didn't feel any remorse or satisfaction when the ship exploded in the barren desert.

He lifted the craft's nose and was about to put on speed to go see what was happening "up there" when Getik opened his eyes and said, "It's a bit jumbled, but it seems that all of them up there are at a loss about what to do without the orders of their self-appointed deities and whether they really are dead. Many of them are old enemies, and I gathered that some of them boarded a few of the ships we emptied of life to investigate their continued silence. They couldn't explain the empty ships and started to accuse one another of underhanded deeds. They didn't see us at all when we went through them because all eyes were glued to instruments they relied on to detect any ships approaching from space.

"The ship you holed was full of humans, although a little different from us. The commander's name was Gwai, and his 'friend' Hinkstol was at the breeding grounds. He was complacent, but when his ship inexplicably lost power and started to plunge, he was paralyzed and screaming with fear. He didn't know what was happening to his ship since they didn't detect us. I don't think that anyone was paying attention to instruments anyway."

"While I followed that ship down to make sure that no one escaped, I thought of another guy with the grand delusion that he could dictate to a Bug and get away with it," Kryger remarked. "He was a brilliant scientist by the name of Pupaul, but Quarr killed him in a fair fight when he challenged her because he thought that she'd be a walkover. He was toadying up to a Bug named Gorrel.

"That was my first encounter with a Bug. My brain was still undeveloped, and if it wasn't for Quarr's courage and the intervention of a lovely alien woman who waited for an eternity for me to arrive, I would not be here right now." Kryger briefly described the circumstances and the confrontation while they sought an opening in the confused melee to flash through. Ships were milling around just about everywhere.

Kryger took the first large-enough opening he saw, but they were spotted by a battleship that immediately came after them. He made a tight U-turn and, sidestepping the missiles fired after them, activated the rays and then made another U-turn out of the ship's path. The pursuit ship kept on accelerating, but he didn't think about what eventually would happen. Then he went into orbit.

"I've been thinking, Getik—and don't make fun of it! These rays are the most devastating weapons ever invented, and I shudder to think what would happen if it ever falls into unscrupulous hands. I'll discuss it with my dad, but I think he will agree with my way of thinking. I can imagine whole planets being denuded of life to make way for immigrants.

"This ship is safe as long as we don't change its language. I will talk to Mike, our organic computer, and teach him the lizard tongue in case anything happens to us or we get too old to fight when required. He—we think of him as a person since he has acquired a personality—will never divulge such information when asked to, and he will only teach someone about something when circumstances require it and the person is absolutely trustworthy. Like Maksika, he can sense the innermost thoughts of anyone through any shield, and if he can't get through a shield, he will not pass on any skills or divulge information."

"That is a more advanced type of computer than anything we've developed." Getik paused to gather his thoughts for a moment, and Kryger told him the story.

"We didn't invent Mike. My father found it, but it's a long story. Mike was developed by a long-gone civilization of people whose build resembled those reptiles we encountered in the dead zone, but they were warm-blooded and had downy hair like Prot and her ilk. They respected all life-forms and never killed except in self-defense.

"It may be a good idea if you're willing to supervise the changes I'd want done on this ship back home. That way our scientific wizards won't examine the ray guns if you can keep their inquisitiveness at bay."

"Okay, I gladly will because I've had my own misgivings about the ray gun technology being available to scientists or anyone else. I therefore didn't mention the existence of such a development in my transfer of information to our computer. At the time I was thinking of small ray guns being developed and used by losers to settle grudges, thereby wiping out evidence of such misdeeds. It can very well happen, you know, even in a peaceful, advanced civilization.

"But watching this battle is pretty boring. All one sees is a brief flash when a ship blows up; otherwise one doesn't hear or even see the flash of guns or anything else except the crazy, slow motion-like maneuvering of ships. The space around Faraway is quickly being turned into an orbital scrapyard, and there's nothing we can do to prevent it. I saw a few ships disengaging and making a getaway, and maybe others will soon follow that sensible example."

"I agree, my good friend, but when one has to participate in a battle, there's never any time to get bored. We, Quarr and I, because trouble seemed to follow us wherever we went, developed a few tricks to stay alive and get out of the action when our fighting craft was damaged.

Those tricks and inventions saved thousands of lives, and those so saved became even better fighters.

"Okay, I'll try to get planet-side again without being seen. They're not our worst enemies and may become allies against the red lizards."

"Fine, we can only try. We might as well pick up Prot, a few tools, and fill up the ship's feeder with enough fuel bars for the next twenty centuries, and also a few sheets of the metal if they have some available—just in case your engineers may need it to make some of the changes."

Kryger checked where the heaviest fighting was taking place and, hoping everyone's eyes and attention were fixed on their instruments and not on idle sightseeing, made a fast dive through the melee. His senses were wide-open, but he didn't pick up any interest in the fleeting ship. The ship automatically slowed sharply to a safe speed when they hit the atmosphere, and Kryger headed toward the fissure.

The fissure was quite shallow in places, but they deemed it prudent to continue to take it slowly rather than risking things out in the open desert, and of course, Getik was scanning the ether to check whether anyone had become interested in where they were going. They flew over small unknown waterholes, animals, and sometimes luxuriant vegetation.

After two hours, Getik told him the entrance to the inner world was quite close—that he couldn't sense anyone interested in them and that they might as well get inside. Kryger followed directions, and they soon came to the concealed entrance.

The same gate commander who had let them out a few days ago was on duty. He feigned nonchalant surprise. "Back so soon? You must not have enjoyed the outing, Getik. Is the fight out there worth watching?"

"Nah, believe me, and there will only be losers. If you want to set up a scrapyard selling bits and pieces of spaceships, now's your chance to make a killing. There are a number of intact Bug ships up there, and a few at their breeding grounds may be dented a little and perhaps could be used for collecting scrap in orbit, but you'll have to get someone to change the controls first.

"I need a bath. Now please open the gate, or I'll get out, remove my space suit, and treat you to a real manly smell."

"Goodness no!" the guard gasped in mock alarm and, with an exaggerated show of fumbling haste, pushed the button that opened the gate.

They tolerated an impatient Protvor for six days while Getik was busy making a comprehensive report to the council and, in between, collected what he thought they might require for the relatively short journey. Kryger prudently made sure there was enough to eat (specially prepared for him by a sad but proud Gorsmat) for a month, if need be, and that the water tank and even their canteens were full. Then he said goodbye to everyone he knew, and they departed. The gate commander wished them a safe journey and said he didn't envy them the darkness of space and preferred his feet safely on solid ground with perpetual daylight readily available to see by.

Kryger told him he had admirable good sense. Before they left the tunnel, they made sure it was safe to go and then followed the fissure for some distance just on the off chance of being observed. Space was remarkably devoid of ships with crews, but only after making sure no one who could detect them was around did Kryger send the craft upward. He set the course and, after entering subspace, taught Protvor the functions of the new controls while Getik reclined in a back seat.

Thereafter, there wasn't anything to do except wait for the time to pass. Kryger still didn't really believe the fact that the journey, which previously had lasted for about sixteen hours at top speed in his old fighter, would now take less than three.

As expected, Mike abruptly greeted him after an hour.

I didn't expect you to move out of range, Kryger, but it seems that I'm not as far-reaching as I believed I was. Is there anything new to report?

Kryger knew that Getik had sensed the abrupt communication, so he included him in his reply.

Hello, Mike. I didn't realize that I was getting out of your range until I tried to contact you. The report is too sensitive to transmit, so wait until I get to you. Meet my friend; his name is Getik. He will accompany me because he has additional information. In the meantime, will you please tell Quarr and my father that I'll be there in about three hours? Before you tell me that I'm still too far away, check my speed, will you? It will be part of our information for you to store.

*I've already checked your speed, and it's astounding, if that is the correct word to use. I will tell your family, but your father is at...*Mike gave him the relevant coordinates. *He's trying to defend one of our allied planets, which is under attack by a very big fleet with sophisticated weapons. Maybe you should go and help him if you are able to do so because our fleet is taking a beating. Getik, your mind is quite powerful, but I sense a third, undeveloped mind with you, which I'd like to meet and check out. It has potential that can be developed.*

Mike, as was his wont, abruptly cut the connection as soon as he had said what he deemed necessary and sensed what he usually wanted to know.

"What an astounding creation, son, and those *are* the correct words! I know it's an insensitive machine, but it's more powerful and perceiving than any Sensitive I've ever known. I assume that we go to assist your dad."

Kryger directed his words toward Protvor in Getik's language: "You heard the exchange, didn't you?" When she nodded, he continued, "Do you mind if we go lend a hand? It will take about another five hours. The fight won't be very exciting or long because of this ship's incredible weapons. The loss of many ships with their crews should set back my people's enemies for quite a few months, hopefully even years."

"I've never been outside our planet's perpetual sunshine, and of course, seeing a fleet of ships in battle never even occurred to me," she replied. "Yes, let's go. I'd like to see and learn at the same time."

"Thank you." A thought occurred to Kryger, and he switched to the Scrii language: "Ship, can you change direction in full flight to another destination without exiting into normal space?" He'd never before thought of asking because he was used to the fact that ships and fighting craft always had to exit subspace at their intended destinations before that could be done, but this was an advanced alien ship, and perhaps it was able to.

"Affirmative. Enter the new destination, and the course will be adjusted without a change in speed."

Marvelous, Kryger thought, punched in the new destination, and told the ship to go there. He felt a slight, momentary change in gravity, but that was the only indication that something had happened.

"The destination is about five thousand light-years from my home planet and maybe a little more from here, so we might as well get some sleep." He reclined his seat, and his breathing slowed within a few seconds.

Protvor was nonplussed. She whispered, "How can he do that so easily as if there's nothing to worry about, fighting in about five hours' time? He just dropped off into sleep like that." She made a silent snapping motion with her fingers so as not to disturb Kryger.

Getik smiled sadly. *To him it's the sensible thing to do. He was fighting these kinds of battles since he was barely able to run, Prot, and he thinks that it's just a job that needs to be done; that's all. Maybe you and I will get used to it in time, but I very much doubt it. Because of this ship's unique construction and killing ability, we will never be involved in real furious battles as Kryger has been, just in complete extermination of enemies. You'll see what I mean.*

I don't comprehend what you are telling me, but, then, I'm new to all this. I guess I'll find out as we go along.

They lapsed into silence but found it difficult to relax; their imaginations were not yet trained and under control.

22

Kryger was sensitive to any change that affected the smooth running of the ship and abruptly woke up when he felt the slight deceleration. *Maybe I'll get used to it,* he thought, *but there should at least be some kind of warning as there's no feeling of the violent deceleration that has always been part of my life.*

He took hold of the controls the moment they popped into normal space. There were no signs of a battle being fought, and he wondered if Mike had given him the wrong coordinates.

No, Kryger, Mike interrupted his thoughts. *They shifted half a light-year away a while ago to regroup because they were in danger of being decimated. The enemy fleet detected them a few moments ago and began transiting there. The coordinates are…*and Kryger punched them in as he received them.

Tell Dad to immediately shift again at least two million kilometers away from where he is now, please, Mike. I have a new dangerous weapon and don't want our fleet anywhere near where the enemy is when I arrive there since I cannot distinguish friend from foe when they are mixed up in dogfights.

Okay, I will tell him. Mike seemed to be as cheerless and unconcerned as ever, but Kryger knew he cared because he needed honest and sincere people to look after. It was a compulsion built into its organic brain by its creators. He told the ship to shift to the new destination, and it did so. When they popped out into normal space, he quickly asked his dad if they had shifted.

Yes, son, we did so a moment ago because Mike said that you urgently don't want us anywhere near you when you arrive. Why?

Just then ships began popping into normal space all around. Kryger's craft automatically began dodging those ships that almost collided with them while he replied, *It's because of a deadly weapon, Dad, which I'll explain in private. The enemy is arriving in droves, and I have to get busy before they have time to think.*

Ships that had sighted the lone little fighter started to fire missiles at it, and as he stopped talking, he activated the ray guns, increased speed, and began to weave in and out among the already-arrived ships. He felt satisfied when he quickly glanced at Protvor and noticed she was tense but calm. She'd do, he thought and then focused on the job of making sure every ship that emanated human thought received a lethal ray bath.

It was a big fleet, second only to that of the Bug minions around Faraway, and he thought they'd never stop popping out of subspace. They seemed to be very determined to fight, perhaps because they thought they had the Nevus fleet on the run, but they were confused by the absence of the ships they had expected would greet them on arrival. Those he recognized as Bikan ships were as suicidal as ever, and they set the example of changing course to ram the little fighter when their missiles just glanced off its shield, but the crews ceased to exist when they got into range and the ships continued on crewless. Thirty minutes later there were only a few dozen ships floating around.

"Do you know if any got away, Getik?" Kryger asked.

"The last ship to arrive, son, veered to one side and broadcasted a message to ask what was happening. When the ships didn't reply, the fleet commander or whatever he was took fright and wisely decided not to stay and find out what caused the silence. There are dozens of ships of various sizes just floating around and hundreds that just continued on into the great void because they sped up to get clobbered sooner. What do we do now?"

"I'd like to go home right away, but I must talk to my father first." On rare occasions Kryger had intuitive flashes of second sight, but he wasn't alone and was distracted by

Getik's talk and question. He felt something, but it quickly faded, and he didn't intuit that he wouldn't see his family or home planet for at least another year.

He deactivated the weapons while he flashed a tight-beam thought to his dad: *Hi, Dad. Only one ship, which seemed to be the flagship, escaped. You can come back if you want to board a few ships devoid of life and examine their weaponry or take some of them back for the wizards to study. They're still intact because the alien weapon given to me along with the fighting ship only destroys anything that's alive. Do you mind if I go home straightaway? I've been away for far too long.*

After receiving an affirmative answer, he asked, *Will you please let our defense posts know not to fire on a strange little fighter-size ship they cannot detect with instruments but may see, since it has no radio with which to identify itself? I'll discuss the sensitive information I have with you in private. Okay?*

Okay, son. I know you well enough to realize that you want to keep vital information from becoming general speculation. How fast is that ship, really?

About ten times faster than anything we have at the moment, and it can change course in subspace. He suddenly had an urge to tell him about the Bugs. *Some good news to amuse you in the meantime, Dad: I unwittingly lured the Bugs into a trap and believe that most, if not all, are dead, but I don't want to pass other sensitive information this way, not even to Mike. You'll realize why when I tell you about it. If anyone asks what happened to this fleet, just tell them that I'm very persuasive and that you don't know how I did it. That's as good as any explanation I can think of right now, but I know that you'll improve on it. See you at home, Dad.*

He punched the coordinates for Nevus and told the ship to go there. He was looking forward to seeing his beloved Quarr and son within a few hours.

"Is that all there is to a battle in space, Kryger? I thought it would at least be hectic," Protvor said as she unbuckled her seatbelt.

"No, let's keep our seatbelts on. I've had an uneasy feeling on and off since we eliminated those lizards at Bawyaan, almost the same feeling I had after I was shot down on Faraway. I don't think it's my imagination. Can you feel anything out of the ordinary?"

"Give me a minute or two to check if I can sense anything, but keep talking."

"To answer your question, Prot," Kryger continued, "in this ship, yes, but if you qualify to be a fighter pilot, you'll be taught real combat in ordinary fighting craft, which is rigorous and calls for your undivided concentration. It's sometimes very hectic, and you have to keep your wits about you. In this ship you don't feel the effect of heavy gravity when you take a tight turn, but in a normal fighter, you will experience the effects, and I assure you that you won't like it, but you'll have to endure it. Our ships are not as advanced as this one, and our weapons are designed to destroy ships, not just the life within the them. You must promise me that you'll never tell anyone about the guns in this ship. If anyone asks, just tell them that you don't know how they work or what they do. Okay?"

"I don't know why, but I know you have a good reason to ask this of me. Yes, okay, I'll pretend ignorance and never talk about them."

"The reason is that there are evil people on every planet in the galaxy, and they don't hesitate to abduct and torture a person they think has a secret that may give them power over other people. This ship is very advanced in some ways and has secrets that make it virtually invincible, as you've witnessed, and even to hint at it may cost you your life and unnecessary, excruciating pain. That is one reason why Maksika's people made the ship so difficult to enter, and you know that they made sure that if someone managed to enter, that someone would be unable to operate the ship or leave unless they knew what to tell the ship in the correct language.

The three of us are the only people who know how to handle the ship and speak to it. There are only two other people I know that I would trust with this ship, but I also know that they'd rather not."

Protvor sensed the utter conflict behind the words, but she didn't understand why anyone would kill or torture someone to gain knowledge of the ship and its guns. Intrigue was foreign to her and her people's direct nature.

Getik interrupted, "Son, there was a vague something, but it gradually faded just after I began a full scan of the ether. It felt like some kind of radiation, but I can't be sure because it was gone too soon. You have a surprisingly sensitive mind, son, because I was never aware of anything unusual."

"Thank you, Getik. Maybe it was nothing, but anything I can't explain bothers me. I'll tell you when I feel it again.

"Prot, I'll ask Quarr to teach you as much as she can, but first you'll be taught our language and whatever else you may need to know by Mike. You'll grow fond of Mike because it behaves like a considerate human being, and we think of it as a person because it has acquired a humanlike personality. I'll take you and Getik to him after I've said hello to my wife and child and reported what I know to my dad. Mike will assess your aptitude while you're being taught, and afterward we'll make arrangements to train you as a pilot or whatever you decide to do after Mike is finished with you."

"I have no idea what you're talking about, Kryger. I've learned a lot from Getik's people, but that's quite different from what you're telling me."

"You're a brave girl, Prot, and that's why I asked if you'd come along. I have no doubts about your potential, but some things one can only learn the hard way by making mistakes. Just have faith in yourself because you're exceptionally gifted, as Maksika perceived, and he didn't make a mistake."

"Thank you for the kind words, Kryger. I'll keep them in mind when things get difficult."

"One thing I forgot to mention: when Mike is finished evaluating you and while he's teaching you the finer points of telepathy as he understands it, he will manufacture a bracelet for you similar to the one I'm wearing. It also has a compass and keeps Nevus time. When you think through it—which is quite simple and easy—it amplifies your mind-to-mind communication, and it enables Mike to locate you if you get lost or are stranded anywhere within his range. You'll get one too, Getik, since you might need it to amplify your thoughts if you need information or want to pass vital info to Mike in an emergency. The only way to get it off your wrist is to think it off, and that is one test you must pass before he lets you go because no one else can use or influence your bracelet.

"Mike used to think that he could track a bracelet-bearer anywhere in the universe, but I found out that his limit is about eight hundred light-years when I tried to flee from the Bugs toward Faraway. That range was good enough until Maksika told us of the new danger we must prepare for. Now it means that we'll go out of his range many times when we battle the red lizards. Perhaps Mike can increase that range by expanding his brain capacity, which is vast, and for all I know, he may already be working on it."

Kryger felt a sort of gratitude that the Bugs were no more. At least he didn't have to pit himself against them anymore, but just then he felt the disturbance again, as if someone was watching them.

"There it is again, Getik!" he said. He had a sudden premonition that disaster was in the making and that he wasn't going to reach Nevus. The ship suddenly veered off at an angle. Its engine stopped, but the power in the cockpit stayed on, and the instruments seemed to be functioning normally. Although he knew there was nothing he could do in subspace, he tried the controls, but none responded to his hasty efforts to take the ship into normal space. The gravity increased alarmingly as if they were accelerating at a horrendous pace.

"Ship, what went wrong with you?"

The ship, as always, replied impersonally: "Outside influence shut the engine off. All functions are suppressed except cabin control."

"Ship, can you exit subspace?"

"Negative. I have no control except partially over gravity."

Kryger felt the gravity build up as the ship's velocity kept increasing. He was inured to such gravities since he had been born on a heavy planet, but he saw Protvor black out and then sensed that Getik had succumbed too. He concentrated on his bracelet and felt it getting quite hot. *Mike! Warning! Something happened to my ship, and I don't know what it is. Do you receive me?* He put all his power behind the thought.

You are speedily moving out of range again. I sense a force field around you, and it seems to be some sort of traction field. Mike's thoughts faded fast even as he transmitted his findings.

Kryger kept a mental watch on his companions because he wanted to know when they returned to consciousness. After a considerable time, the velocity evened out, and the awful pressure also receded gradually. When he sensed that the other two were with him again, he shifted to speech so he could continue to think while he was talking. "It seems that an outside agency is capturing us with some sort of traction machine right here in subspace, where I know it's not possible with any technology I'm aware of," he told them. "I know that there's no natural phenomenon that can do this. So it means that there's a very advanced civilization somewhere out there that spied on us and then decided that they wanted this craft. The force-traction field leaves us enough power to stay alive but nothing more.

"Logic tells me that they are after the weapon, and the ship may be a bonus. I suspect that it doesn't matter to them whether we stay alive or not, but we'll surprise the hell out of them. Getik, do you notice that the heat did not increase as happened on our test trip to Bawyaan? To me it means that the traction beam is a type of force field that acts as an isolating shield."

"Son, I was so scared that I didn't observe anything before I lost consciousness. I admire your fortitude and calm thinking for so young a man under such terrifying circumstances. They really make them tough where you came from. Don't you ever panic?"

23

"Thank you…I think. What will be, will be, so let us dispense with panic and calmly anticipate possible scenarios. For instance, are they telepathic? Presumably. Otherwise, why did I sense them? The bigger question is, What are their intentions? If they wanted to kill us, they could have done so by cutting power to the cockpit, but maybe they couldn't because it's not a function of the traction force. We would have been frozen within minutes if that happened. Mind you, I'm just thinking aloud, so I could be wrong.

"Okay, it's a given fact that their science is far superior to ours. We can't prepare for that, but we can be ready if they are telepathic and if they're hostile. First and foremost, I must show Prot how to generate and maintain a tight shield all the time. We don't know how much time we have, so let's start with that. Prot, will you allow me to enter your mind to show you how to do it? Getik can shield us while I do so, and afterward he will test the effectiveness of your shield."

"Can you do something like that, son? I question the effectiveness of your kind of shield since I've been reading your thoughts since we met, except once for about ten minutes from when we attacked the Bugs until we wiped out the last bunch in the fissure. So how do you think that kind of shield, which seems to work only under extreme stress, will keep out a really determined Sensitive? Why teach Prot to create a block that only works sometimes?"

Kryger smiled because Getik sounded genuinely concerned. He closed his shield and dared the older man to try anything to read his thoughts. Getik tried, then tried to force his way through. After a while, he shook his head. "How do you do it, son? I've never come across anything like that. Your mind is closed tighter than a fish's rear orifice, and that's watertight, airtight, pressure tight…anything tight."

Protvor laughed and Kryger smiled. "My shield is on all the time because I have sensitive secrets to protect at all costs, even with my life if necessary, but I usually create a tiny hole in the shield in friendly territory so as not to be totally isolated. You have a very powerful mind, old friend, and you've been peeping through that hole at my outer thoughts, but you've never tried to enter my mind, which I really appreciate."

"To be truthful, I was so sure of my superior brain that I never even realized that there was only a hole to get through. You should have told me." Getik's voice told Kryger that he was laughing at himself.

"There was no reason to, but now you know the reason why I'm conditioned to flash-fry anyone's brain who tries unauthorized entry. But enough; time may be short, so let's start. Can you create what we call a cocoon around us?"

"Sorry, son, I can read what you mean, but I don't know how."

Kryger almost sighed aloud. "Okay, you have the power, so I'll show you how to do it. You'll have to change seats with Prot for a minute or two because I don't want to leave the controls, as I want to be ready if the ship's power is restored."

Getik and Protvor changed seats. "I don't want to do this unprotected, Getik, even if I don't sense any intrusion. You must drop your shield completely, and I'll expand mine to protect you. It makes it more difficult, but I've done it before. Lean over so that our helmets touch."

Both leaned over until their faceplates touched. Getik's shield vanished, and Kryger's shield immediately enveloped them both. He showed Getik how his shield worked and how to expand it to form a cocoon around the cockpit, how to contract or expand the cocoon while still being aware of influences or thoughts from outside. When he was finished, he told Getik that he was going to withdraw and did so. He looked at his bracelet and saw that two minutes had elapsed.

Getik hesitated a moment before he tried the new shield and experimented for a minute or so. "Son," he said quietly, "I have never been so embarrassed. I thought *I* would teach *you*, but you're teaching me things I never even knew existed."

"What you must bear in mind, my friend, is that you come from a peaceful environment and that not one of your people ever had occasion to think or prepare for survival against overwhelming forces. I learned the hard way, but with a lot of expert assistance, I must add; otherwise I would not have survived. Now you can change seats with Prot again, make yourself comfortable, and tell me when you are ready."

Getik made himself comfortable, created the cocoon, made sure it was secure, and then announced himself ready. He found it surprisingly easy to maintain the shield.

Protvor didn't know anything about creating a shield, and Kryger, as he had surmised, had to start with the very basics. He stimulated various centers in her brain and then imprinted the principles of creating a shield. He showed her how it worked and quietly told her that the shield would be permanently in place when he withdrew his probe—until it was time to teach her how to manipulate it. He also implanted three passwords: one to close the tiny peephole, one to open it, and one to drop the shield. By this time Protvor's face was gray with fatigue, and he implanted the suggestion that she go to sleep to let her subconscious assimilate the principles. She did, and he withdrew. It required a lot of energy and utter concentration to do a precision job of linking certain centers and altering thinking patterns. He didn't feel happy about the forced development, but under the circumstances, there wasn't any other option.

He gently tested her shield and found it solid, except for the peephole, as he preferred to call it. "Thank you. You can drop the cocoon," he told Getik in a whisper. "We must let her sleep until she wakes up naturally. It took nearly eight minutes, but the structures of certain centers were too underdeveloped to allow her to shield her thoughts, although as you know, she didn't broadcast them. I found a clever filter-block, and I think Maksika put it there to stop her from broadcasting. I must complete a few other changes later on if there's time.

"I'm famished after spending all that energy, so let's eat a decent, substantial meal—if you don't mind rummaging in those food containers at the back. Afterward we'll have to ration food and water as a precaution."

"Oh, I don't mind—I'm hungry too. Keeping up the unfamiliar cocoon shield required a surprising amount of energy. I suppose it's because it's new to me and I must practice a bit to lock it into place." He returned with enough food to satisfy any hungry man and handed Kryger his share. "There's enough food for a month. Did you have a foreboding of disaster?"

"No, I just thought that I'd like to taste some of Gorsmat's cooking for a while longer and maybe treat Quarr to delicious alien food—which I can now forget. It's normal procedure to stock up, usually with ration tablets. We have to use the water very sparingly because the ship's tank wasn't designed for long periods away from home. I filled it out of habit, even though I thought that we'd be home in a few hours."

After he'd finished his meal, Kryger told Getik he was going to sleep for a while.

"Would you like me to take your seat until you wake up?" Getik offered dutifully.

"Thanks for the offer, but I'll wake up immediately if anything happens. Since we don't know how long it will be before we arrive at our destination, we have no choice but to wait patiently for as long as is necessary. Our abductors will regret their arrogant, thoughtless act unless they have an urgent and very good reason; that I promise!"

He didn't recline his seat to be comfortable since he was used to sleeping in an upright position when there was a possibility that instant reaction might be necessary. He still missed his old fighting craft because he was not used to this pampering with gravity neutralizing, but it had its positive sides. He was tired and promptly went to sleep, as was his wont.

Kryger awoke when Protvor stirred restlessly in the copilot's seat. A quick glance told him that Getik was asleep and that Protvor was only half-awake. He decided to leave her to wake up properly while he made use of the convenience. He would be back in a flash if he felt any change in the ship's smooth condition. Quietly he loosened his straps and moved to the back of the cockpit, where he finished his business as quickly as he could.

When he returned, Protvor was still in her seat but stretching her whole body to get her blood circulating properly. He used mind-speech so as not to disturb Getik's rest.

How do you feel?

Strange, but strong in mind, she replied immediately. *Only one thing bothers me, and that is that I feel sort of pressed down in my seat, as if I have fallen from the top of a big tree on my back, which makes it difficult to get up and move about, and it feels as if I can't breathe.*

Kryger wondered what could cause such a feeling since he was sure he had done a proper job in the correct brain centers. He was caught unawares when Getik suddenly spoke: "Prot, you've just described exactly how I feel. I thought that some internal damage was caused by that tremendous gravity buildup we endured, but I didn't want to worry our friend because he seemed okay."

Kryger, who had taken his space helmet off when he went to the back, hit his forehead hard with the palm of his right hand. "Damn! It's what Quarr and I call overlooking the obvious. I come from a planet with about three times the gravity of Faraway. That's why I didn't notice our increased gravity, which is much less than that of Nevus. I ask your forgiveness for my oversight, but as a reason for my forgetfulness, I can only say that I've never taken anyone to Nevus who came from a low-gravity planet. We have a method to make you adapt to our gravity within a couple of weeks. In the meantime, to conserve energy, all I can do is advise you to move only when necessary since your bodies will adjust if you have to endure it long enough."

"It's okay, son. We can't move about for long distances anyway, and we can manage our breathing."

24

According to Kryger's mental calendar, their confinement lasted for eleven days, and he appreciated the fact that it gave him time enough to complete Protvor's tuition. On the tenth day, he felt the start of a rapid deceleration, and so did his companions. None of them expressed the obvious opinion that they seemed to be close to their destination. The deceleration lasted for about fourteen hours before the ship popped out into normal space. Unfamiliar stars greeted them, but Kryger did not waste time by admiring them.

"Ship, is your power restored?" It was something he kept in mind all the time since he usually had only Big MAG to depend on for defense. He still had to aim it manually and pull the trigger by depressing a button. It was inconvenient, but now he was thankful that Getik's engineers hadn't had the know-how to aim it automatically.

"Negative," the ship replied. "We still have that force field around us and are being drawn to the planet behind us. I still only have power for the shield and other vital functions."

Kryger was surprised at the ship's detailed reply. *Perhaps it is developing real intelligence,* he thought amusedly. Then he looked at the display of stars that were visible through the cockpit canopy. Protvor was silent because seeing so many stars still overwhelmed her, but Getik exclaimed with awe in his voice, "We must be in another galaxy! But gravity is back to normal—at least for a while until we land, if we land."

Being drawn backward into a planet's atmosphere was a weird experience, but being shielded by a force field made the descent smooth. Kryger's companions were calmed by his seemingly unconcerned demeanor, but inside, behind a tight shield, he was worried as he didn't know with how much force they would land. He was quite sure the abductors weren't too concerned about the welfare of the craft's occupants since normally the crew of a fighting craft would have run out of sustenance or oxygen during eleven Nevus days.

He made sure the speed lever was pulled back all the way because he didn't want the craft to take off at speed when the force field and whatever inhibited the craft's engine were removed, as they might end up against something very solid. The ship might be intact, but they—the crew—would have to be scraped off the cockpit canopy and the instrument panel. He thought about other possibilities.

"Ship, switch the cockpit lights off, and inform me if there is interference or attempts to switch the shield off from outside."

"There are attempts to switch the stand-alone power off, but the shield is blocking the frequencies. I have strengthened the shield."

"Thank you, ship," he couldn't help saying. Again he was surprised at the ship's unexpected intelligence.

"I know what that means. I've been learning from one of you who leaked thoughts on a frequency I could understand, but the leakage stopped a while ago."

Kryger was floored. The ship had been learning from Protvor because she had been the only one without the habitual shield. Mike's creations were the very best, much better than the fastest mechanical computer, but they did their job and never talked in any way or transmitted thoughts like Mike did. Then he laughed out loud.

"You two heard that! Well, I never would have thought it possible. Maksika's people were brilliant in some ways. Wait till I've had Mike have a look at this one! When things have been normalized and it's safe to drop your shield, Prot, you must continue with specific tutoring, and we must try to do the same, Getik. I'd love to see what we end up with.

"We're entering a huge hangar or something. We'll see what our kidnappers look like and have in mind, but we sit still and do nothing until they've tried every method they have to enter the craft. We close our shields and keep mum if they try to communicate. Let them sweat for a few days if necessary. If they have good shields, they may become unguarded after a few hours of finding no response, and then we can intercept their thoughts. I'll get the red lizard blaster I've kept as a souvenir since it may come in handy."

"Good idea," Getik commented.

"I'll follow your lead," Protvor answered.

After a couple of hours, the ship unemotionally announced, "The traction field is switched off. Engine interference is still present, and a complete power shutdown is still being attempted in various ways."

"We haven't seen anyone yet. I suppose they're hiding behind a protective shield to see if we're alive and ready for conflict. I wonder if the air is breathable, but since we don't have the instruments, there's only one way to find out." Kryger got up, fetched the blaster, and then sat in his seat again. They could see out, but no one would see them unless a strong light was brought to bear directly into the cockpit.

After another hour, the ship reported that the shutdown attempts had ceased. Another half hour passed, and then they saw a bald head, about the same contours as Maksika's, quickly take a peek from behind an opaque screen and then promptly withdraw. When nothing happened, the head appeared again and peeked longer. It was gray with fear, and then the naked body followed in a tumble as the humanoid creature was pushed hard from behind.

An expendable, Kryger thought. He saw that it was a humanoid lizard the same shape as Maksika, but with a green-tinged, yellow-brown body and a pale gray stomach. It tried to scramble back into the shelter, but the door was closed. Fearfully and very reluctantly, it approached the ship, and Kryger listened to the unshielded, fearful thoughts: *I don't care if Bupens can read my thoughts and punish me. He thinks that everyone should jump to do his bidding without question but doesn't care to risk his enormous body. Without regard for my life, I was just told to go and enter the stolen craft and shut it down. What will be done to me if the pilots are still alive, and why didn't Bupens order the scientists to check?*

The frightened thoughts, sometimes incoherent, continued steadily while the lizard timidly approached the craft, ready to bolt at the slightest movement or sound. Kryger learned much, and he almost felt sorry for the fearful, hapless creature that was ready to sprint anywhere. It reached the ship at last, checked where the door was, and then quickly thrust out a three-fingered hand with an opposing thumb to reach for the door.

It squealed in a high, terrified pitch when its fingers almost broke against an impenetrable surface, and while clutching its injured fingers in the other hand, it bolted back to the shelter while it kept screaming that the shield was a solid force field. The poor creature bounced off the still closed door and fell on its back. Then, while banging its fist in a futile attempt to gain entry, it received harsh orders to complete its assigned job.

While it fearfully sidled back, the door opened again, and an older-looking humanoid lizard came out. It was naked too, but its scarcely existing waist was encircled by a belt with what appeared to be empty pouches. Kryger intuited that this was a voluntary exit because it felt sorry for the terrified youngster. It spoke in a quiet, reassuring way when it passed the reluctant youngster, who recovered somewhat and followed close behind the older one.

The older one's thoughts were calm. He didn't care much what the leader might do to him since he was tired of being forced to do things against his will. He was a prominent scientist, and Bupens would think twice before punishing him for defying an order. He would inspect the craft and then check whether the pilots were still alive after their unwarranted abduction. He carefully put the flat of a four-fingered hand on the shield and patted it. Then he moved around the nose to the other side while patting the solid-seeming shield.

Kryger admired courage and decided to talk to the older lizard that still walked proudly and unafraid. He told Getik to take his seat because he had handled the ship before and knew what to do if a serious situation developed or if engine power was restored. He put the blaster down next to the door and told the ship to open up because the shield would allow him to stand or sit in the door. The ship hovered a little more than a meter above the floor, the height Kryger had originally found it at.

He sat with his feet hanging over the edge and waited for the scientist to complete his inspection. The blaster was within easy reach just to the side of the opening. After a while, the scientist came around the rear with what looked like a thoughtful expression on his face. His face brightened when he saw Kryger, and he quickened his pace. The other one let out a high squeal and fled to the back of the hangar, which seemed able to accommodate a cruiser.

I'm sorry this happened to you, but I'm glad to see that at least one of you is still alive. You are weak if you have to sit down. What can I do to help? I kept the acceleration down to the absolute minimum because I cared about your lives, but our leader wasn't concerned about your well-being when he coerced me to grab your ship. He didn't even dream that no one would be able to enter this ship. Are you able to pick up my thoughts?

Yes, Kryger answered, *but what's wrong with the youngster?*

Cuckbung was a pilot and got caught alive by the cold-blooded Roffs—the red race you destroyed in your galaxy, where we first saw your ship while watching to see where they were going and what they were up to. Anyway, he was taken to one of their spaceports and gleefully tortured until he was out of his mind. Then they ostensibly forgot about him, and he thought that he'd steal a small craft and flee directly home. The ship was deliberately left for him to take and was equipped with a subspace tracer, and so they found our planet. His body healed, but his mind will never be the same, but enough of an explanation. What can I do to help you regain your strength and those of the others, if they're still alive? My name is Bot, he added as an afterthought.

Kryger was already astounded that a ship could be grabbed in subspace a galaxy away. It logically followed that they had to see that far to do so, and he decided that he must have the technology one way or the other since it was invaluable. He listened to the explanation, but his senses and most of his attention were concentrated in and around the shelter, where he suddenly sensed imminent treachery.

"Ship, shield down!" he shouted while he slid down. Then he jumped forward, grabbed the humanoid, and pulled the surprised being to the door while uttering a loud call for the shield to be restored.

You sure can move fast for one who seemed so weak. What was that for? Bot was still calm, as if he didn't care what happened to him.

As an answer, Kryger turned him around and pointed to the opaque screen. He said one word: *Treachery!*

The next moment, a mobile gun sped through the door, stopped, and spewed a stream of bolts directly to where Bot and Kryger were standing. Both instinctively closed their eyes since there wasn't time for any other response.

By that one-in-a-trillion chance, the angle was exactly so that the bolts deflected straight back toward the gun, which melted instantly along with the lone operator.

Serves you right, you deceitful bastards, Kryger thought as he sensed consternation and cast surprise from an entity behind the protective screen.

He picked up its thoughts: *See! I was right to take the ship. It has the lost self-defense system of the Scrii, and we can't take the chance again that we might damage it by brute force or get killed in our efforts to breach the shield. Instead, let's do it by stealth because it seems that at least one of the pilots survived, and our chief scientist is very chummy with it.*

He also picked up a murmur from Bot: *So the old legend of a self-defense shield is true.*

Your thinking is faulty, and I don't have the faintest idea of what you and your people are dreaming about. The angle of fire was right for a perfect ricochet, and the chance of that being repeated is about one in a billion trillion. This is just a shield that deflects whatever is thrown at it to any trajectory the object is subject to.

Bot twittered, which Kryger interpreted as laughter, and said, *Yes, I read the truth in your thoughts. I'm also reading the thoughts of the astronomical Bupens, and he plans further treachery, the overbearing u-gwaiyi.*

Kryger briefly wondered what an u-gwaiyi was but, since his attention was more on the unshielded thoughts he could so clearly follow behind the screened shelter and elsewhere, quickly abandoned the thought. Did those humanoids think—without even a single attempt to communicate—that their victims were non-Sensitive, dumb, or what?

Finally he found what he was looking for in an underground bunker. The operator or attendant of the power inhibitor wasn't really required, and it was "listening" to what its loathed leader was planning to do to take the pirated craft over. It was therefore easy for Kryger to induce a command to shut the machine off, which it promptly did without being aware of what it was doing.

He could have influenced the attendant to sabotage the machine, but he was picking up thoughts that it might be needed for something more menacing than keeping a small craft immobilized. The ship, as previously instructed, announced that engine power was restored, and Kryger, having accomplished what he wanted, gave full attention to his "guest," who said, *Aha! I think I just heard a mechanical voice speaking in a lost language of a race of my people that vanished centuries ago, but it's of no interest to me except in a pure academic way. Our great leader, who forced us to steal your ship—I want to add that for the record—against our better judgment, may now realize that he caught a marimackgwari by the tail* (Kryger received a picture of a raging tigerlike reptile with a long muscular tail), *and he wants to know if he can come out and talk to you. You just saved my life, and I must warn you that he has some sort of deception in mind. We detest him, but he is too powerful to take on. Beware of his tremendous mind power. Physically he's a throwback, but mentally he's a mutant.*

I want to meet the immoral thief face-to-face, but please warn him that he'll die immediately if he tries any tricks. I've had enough of his nonsense, and I won't take any more. Tell him that, but stay with me no matter what he orders you to do so that I can shield you too if necessary.

Kryger already knew what Bupens had in mind, but he had to give him a chance to reconsider, and he also knew the well-upholstered leader wouldn't stand a chance against the powerful mind of a single Bug.

He found a sharpshooter inside the shelter behind a low partition with orders to shoot him at a given signal, and he promptly put that individual to sleep. He was angry enough to teach the self-conceited Bupens a serious lesson or two if he could control himself.

The shield around the hideout flickered out, revealing a double door, which opened to let out four quite hefty individuals.

Bupens's so-called councilors, Bot remarked sarcastically. *The u-gwaiyi is too much of a coward to risk his precious hide and sent his sidekicks out to test the reception.*

So I see, Kryger replied. *I can talk to them, but I don't want to waste time. I need to get out of this space suit and wash myself after being cooped up in it for twelve days, and so do my companions. Please tell them that I'll only talk to Bupens and that I promise not to bite him unless he misbehaves.*

Bot shouted something in a language Kryger almost understood since he picked up Bot's thoughts as well.

After about a minute and many explanations, a ponderous entity shuffled out from an alcove behind the double door where it had taken refuge in the belief that it would be safe if bolts began to fly. Bupens's upper body was nearly twice as long as that of Bot and the others, which made his arms and legs look short. He walked with a slow, measured step that, to Kryger's trained eye for details, signified enormous strength under that excessive blubber. The enormous belly was yellow tinged.

Bupens came to a halt behind his cronies, looked down on Kryger, and asked suspiciously, "Where did you learn our language?"

I don't know your language, but I can sense your thoughts when you talk to me, and I can project mine. It's the only way I can talk to and understand other sentient beings. It was an old story meant to put another species at ease and was close to the truth. *Why did you steal my ship without caring about the lives of its occupants?*

He felt like using stronger language but controlled his emotions; the enormous humanoid would have been only puzzled by the unfamiliar expletives. He was forcing the issue since he knew what was coming and wanted to get it over and done with so he could talk to decent beings and see if they could help him get home again without starving to death on the long journey.

"I want your ship for the advanced technology it displayed in disposing of the Roffs so easily. What's one ship and a couple of lives compared to the needs of a planet? I always take what I want, and you'll give me your ship so that I can have the technology examined and copied. If you behave, I might consider giving you another ship to get back to your galaxy."

Kryger blew derisively through his mouth and saw Bupens straighten in anger. *Well, come in and take it, then. This ship was personalized to me by the Scrii and won't let anybody in or out without my personal assistance. Even then it will destroy half this planet if anyone tinkers with it.* It was so close to the truth that no Sensitive would detect the improvised untruth. *So I invite you to try, but remember that you will die if you try any tricks to force me. The choice is all yours.*

There was a collective gasp from everybody, and Kryger caught a thought from Bot: *The legendary Scrii went to their island galaxy when they disappeared some centuries ago. Now we know!*

But Bupens did what Kryger knew he had in mind. He told his cronies to link up with him, and then Kryger felt a crushing force close around his shielded brain. Bupens tried to compel him to switch the shield off and hand the craft over. The force of the coercion would have crushed a normal being's resistance, but to Kryger it was just an irritation. A Bug would have laughed the attempt off and reached out to tear the creature slowly to pieces.

He'd realized a while ago that he and his companions would be in constant danger as long as Bupens and his cronies were alive, so he contemptuously sent a bolt into the linked brains. He felt surprised that the effort didn't leave him weak, but then he realized he hadn't put much power into the bolt. It wasn't a Bug trying to control him.

Bupens, unprepared for retaliation, recoiled so violently that he fell over onto his back with his legs held off the floor by his rounded torso, and the other four fell against one another before they dropped to the floor. Kryger looked at an openmouthed Bot and shrugged.

They asked for it. They might just be stunned, but I sincerely hope not. Can you get a legitimate council or something elected to make decisions? I sense that there is imminent danger to this planet, and I will help you, on the condition that when the Roffs are defeated, you help me get back to where my ship was when you grabbed it. Right now we need water. My companions and I are dehydrated. He formed a picture of what was required.

I understand, but I need a small sample to test whether our water is compatible with your constitutions since you are from a different galaxy, and I also need a sample of your DNA to test whether our food will poison you. If so, we'll have to manufacture everything you need. It won't take long because this huge building is a small city, a command center as well as a tuition center, and just about everything else. While you're getting me the samples, I'll get people to remove these bodies. I can see that they've voided themselves, so they're dead.

Kryger noticed again that these people seemed to prefer oral speech and realized it would be useful to add their language to his vocabulary.

I'll have the power inhibitor switched off so that you can move your craft to a more convenient place than the middle of the hangar. I also have to check whether our type of refresher will affect you since we don't use water to cleanse.

Bot twittered when Kryger told him he already had the inhibitor switched off and that he would move the craft to the corner just behind the shelter that seemed so popular with Bupens, which seemed to be the entrance to whatever else.

Kryger told the ship to switch the shield off. *The journey of my life has had so many twists and turns,* he thought, *but it is just as it should be.* It was his turn to laugh somewhat embarrassedly when Bot told him that, for the record, she was a female just past childbearing age as she turned to go get the ball rolling.